ALSO FROM MIA HEINTZELMAN

THE ALL MIXED UP SERIES

(Each book can be read as a standalone)

Mixed Signals

Mixed Match

Mixed Emotions

All mixed up series boxset

STANDALONES

It's Got A Ring To It - Releasing Fall 2020

Wrapped up in beau

DARK ROMANCE

Devastated: Wastelands academy book 1

The Stack w/a Emmaline Zanthi

PRAISE FOR MIXED SIGNALS

Mixed Signals is funny, snarky, and heart warming romance that I couldn't put down. I can't wait for the next book in the series.

— AUTHOR D.W. MARSHALL

I also liked the humor in the book, and the author's writing style was enjoyable.

— AMAZON REVIEWER, CRZYJEEVES

There's no mixed feelings on this one, I'm glad I read it.

— AMAZON REVIEWER, KATHERINE C.

Cute. Cute. Cute. This sent me into a tailspin. Think zombie but instead of brains, I wanted more books like this one. Cute with a bit of spice, and all things naughty and nice.

— GOODREADS REVIEWER, NICOLE

Mixed Signals was an unexpected surprise for me.

— GOODREADS REVIEWER, DESPINA

Enemies to lovers is my favorite troupe and this one just rocks it! If you like hate at first site books with convincing plot, great characters, hilarious banter, an uptight heroine, a swoon worthy hero, then please go for it. It was an enjoyable read and I like it a lot!

ACKNOWLEDGMENTS

This was a fun one! Thank you so much for going along for the ride with me. That you chose my book in which to spend your time is my honor.

More than anything this book is about new dreams, reimagining, and daring to journey down new paths. I'm so fortunate to be able to venture down the path of writing for a living, thanks to my husband, Daniel Heintzelman, who has allowed me to leap because he's my net, supporting me.

I have a ton of shout-outs to give because it took a lot of amazing people to help me get this fun story to market. Thank you to my Las Vegas Romance Writers family and especially my Thursday Night Therves. You are my fellow introverts uniting in dark corners and cozy nooks. You help me breathe life into my books and characters. Thanks for your invaluable, crazy, fun, and hashtaggable critique sessions.

To my editor, Faith Freewoman, I'm indebted to your polishing skills. You make my work shine. Thank you for your clear eyes and encouraging feedback.

A huge thank you to the librarians, bloggers, bookstagrammers, and reviewers. You are the unspoken heroes who spread the word like wildfire about stories, which feed the mind and nourish the soul.

Big hugs and smoochie kisses to my family and friends. You are the petals on my flowering tree and the frame holding up my house. You understand and support me even though I'm always with my nose stuck in a book or with my fingers glued to a keyboard spinning tales.

Mommy and Daddy I love that I'm equally both parts of your (semi-) social butterfly (okay, sometimes, anti-) and bookworm because you've given me a hungry mind and wings to soar.

My sister, Melissa DeGrazia, we're basically the same person in two bodies fighting with our reflections, but who better to have in my corner to support and uplift me? Thank you. Cheers to leaping in faith!

Finally, to my two daughters and my nieces and nephews, I hope my daring pursuit of greatness is inspiration and wind beneath your wings.

MIXED MATCH

MIA HEINTZELMAN

LeviLynn

First Levi Lynn Books edition November 2019.

Levi Lynn Books can bring authors to your live event. For more information or to book an event, visit our website at www.miaheintzelman.com.

Editing by Faith Freewoman

Cover design and Formatting by Tangled Covers

Manufactured in the United States of America

Cataloguing-in-Publication Data

ISBN 9780999049341 (trade pbk.) | ISBN 9780999049358 (ebook)

Name: Heintzelman, Mia, author.

Title: Mixed Match / Mia Heintzelman

Description: Mia Heintzelman | Las Vegas: Mia Heintzelman, 2019.

Subjects: Romance | Humorous fiction.

For my crazy mixed up family.
Thank you for believing in my dream.

Mixed Match

CHAPTER 1

Sophia Kent dug her fingers under the sides of the box, and for a split second this move to Portland didn't feel as daunting as she made it out to be.

But then she steadied her legs, squatted for leverage, and strained to heft the box, determined to pry it off the floor...and the dang thing wouldn't budge.

"Come. On." She heaved and struggled some more. Not even an inch. She gritted her teeth, wiggled her butt to resettle, and dug her heels into the thick, cloudy gray carpet, pulling up with all her might. Still didn't budge.

"Ugh." She groaned, finally releasing her hold. She was about two seconds from pouting and stamping her feet. *Let go and let God.* She breathed. In and out. Again.

But it still frosted her cookies something awful. She could do this. She needed to do this. With both hands on her hips, she kicked the box with her sneaker-clad foot, stubbing her toe in the process. "Ow!!!. Sugar-Honey-Iced-Tea."

"Oh come on, you can do better than that. Give me a good, pissed-off 'fuck,' or an angry-ass 'dammit.'"

Sophia almost jumped out of her skin at the voice, but quickly recognized it and rolled her eyes instead. "Must you be so crass all the time?"

"And say it like you mean it, too. I don't want to hear anything about h-e-double hockey sticks, either."

Sophia finally turned to see her flawless, perky cousin Julie standing behind her.

Even for as labor-intensive an occasion as moving, Julie was fierce in fluorescent pink athleisure wear with her bale of glossy curls bound by an equally neon yellow bandana. A far cry from the high school volleyball shorts and dingy black T-shirt Sophia dug out of the box designated for donations because everything else was packed.

Behind Julie stood her shiny new Italian wet dream of a fiancé, Nico, who was biting back a grin. Apparently they'd been there just long enough to witness Sophia's little tantrum.

"Peachy. Just doggone peachy." Sophia plopped down on the gigantic box of books. "If y'all love me, don't say anything. Just...shut up." She waved them off.

"I see you're still holding on to your little facade. What'd you do, look up a list of Southern euphemisms and decide to insert one every other sentence?" Her cousin was definitely one of those high-anxiety, blunt people you either loved or hated.

Sometimes it took even Sophia a good long minute to remember Julie was a worrier *because* her love was so fierce. She was a good person she just lacked...tact.

Julie picked up a roll of tape and started over to a group of boxes in the corner. But not before Sophia noticed the telling look she gave Nico.

"What was that about?" She watched a mischievous grin toy

at the corners of Julie's mouth, then she turned to Nico. "Well? The look, what did it mean?"

"This is between you guys." He stepped back, holding up his hands. A surefire sign Sophia hadn't misread the look.

She eyed him over the top of her nose. "Don't even try to sneak out. Tell me what's going on, because I know she won't."

A screech of tape jerked Sophia's attention back to Julie, who'd already sealed one box and moved on to another. "It means your mom is about to get hooked up, so now we've got to find someone new for you too. Whether it's here in Vegas or in Portland makes no difference. But hopefully it'll happen before you go falling into your mopey horror-movies-and-ice-cream phase."

"I do not have a horror-movies-and-ice-cream phase."

"You do. The first step to healing is acceptance. Now, accept you're not even from the South and please start acting like you again. I miss my crazy, sassy, foulmouthed cousin."

For a second Julie turned off the always-on, aggressive-boss-babe schtick. She was serious. "No more hold 'your horses,' or 'peachy,' or 'doggone peachy.' Just be you. You probably don't realize it, but you started this nonsense when you became a Harman.

"Since you're not anymore, I want you go to Portland tomorrow, live in your Barbie Dreamhouse there, and make it your own. I don't want it to be anything like this fucking life-less, lonely showpiece with its cold grays and modern lines. It's an outdated, two-story museum without the benefit of pictures hanging on the wall, or any signs that love ever lived here. Don't look back at this place, or Assface (yet another lovely term of endearment for Sophia's ex-husband, Austin Harman, whose name Julie refused to say aloud). You don't need him *or* his money."

Of course her cousin was right. A ton of money had been thrown at the house but it never felt like Sophia's home.

Julie looked down at the box she was working on and scrawled on the side with permanent marker. With a long inhale she seemed to reset herself to playful mode. "And for fuck's sake, curse like you're a badass, knife-wielding chef with your big girl panties on, not an elementary school teacher." She winked.

Nico, who just so happened to educate a couple of dozen second-graders every day, gave her a wounded look before he narrowed his eyes.

"No offense, babe." Julie flicked an apologetic pucker at him.

He winked in the totally smitten way people do only during the honeymoon phase. "None taken."

A roar of laughter from downstairs pinballed off the walls. Of course Sophia recognized the loudest, most high-pitched laugh was her mom. As expected, she'd proven to be as useless as ever—what with her ratio of two glasses of Pinot Grigio to one item of bubble-wrapped flatware.

But then a deep bass chortle joined the laughter.

Sophia bent her ear toward the hall. "Wait. Who all's downstairs?"

"My mom, Stan, and Aunt Helen. You know Aunt Helen sent us up here to help you see the 'merits' of staying." She laughed. "Oh, and your mom's boo is supposed to be on his way, and you know how that's going to go. It is going to be a straight-up shitshow. They've already been arguing about it." She was undoubtedly talking about their bickering mothers, who could come up with a bone of contention with anything and anyone.

"Already?"

"You know Aunt Helen is never going to let Mom live this

down." Julie cocked her head. The knowing grin she gave Sophia said *you know you want to go watch this train wreck with me.*

She did.

Sophia sighed, let her head fall forward and her arms slump at her sides, still annoyed about her inability to move the box by herself.

Acceptance is key. Weakness is only temporary.

"Fine. Let's go downstairs." She popped up off the box and walked over to hug Julie and Nico.

"You all right?" Nico asked before releasing her. His big, kind brown eyes gleamed with empathy and concern. "You do realize we're here to help. It doesn't have to be a one-woman show." He flitted a glance toward the world's heaviest box.

Nico really was a good guy. Sophia couldn't be happier that her cousin was marrying him. And while she appreciated the thought behind his offer, she couldn't pretend a one-woman show wasn't exactly the new city circus her life was headed toward. "Actually, it does. I kind of need to get used to doing things for myself." *By myself.*

It's funny how things don't work out.

She wrung her hands, wishing she could rewind the conversation to just before she took that serious tone.

"But...no sense in sweating the small stuff, right?" She shrugged, going for nonchalant while she swallowed over the catch in her throat. *Lord, I'm speaking inspirational Instagram now. Maybe I do need someone new.*

The second the three of them reached the bottom of the marble stairs, Sophia's mom jumped up from the oversized leather sectional where she'd been completely in her element with a full wineglass in her bedazzling, bejeweled hand. As always, she was show-ready with expertly highlighted chestnut hair, a shiny sequined blouse, and glossy red lips, *just* in case someone happened to have a readily available mic. "We've got it covered down here. Don't worry about a *thing*." Completely ignoring that she was still sitting next to the same two boxes she supposedly taped up an hour ago.

She set her glass down on the table, which clearly meant she was transitioning into business mode. Then she got up, walked over, and squared herself to Sophia, hands on each of her shoulders, her expression hopeful.

"Have you reconsidered yet? Given any thought to staying here in Las Vegas?" Her mom lowered her chin and deepened her gaze, as if she could somehow see inside Sophia's heart.

"No, Mom," Sophia's reply sounded strained since she couldn't believe she still needed to justify her actions to her mother at all. Somehow, some way, she knew her mom would turn everything around and make it about her instead of Sophia, but this was bigger than a move—bigger than running away from home. For Sophia this was about chasing a new life.

Lord, she needed a clean slate in the worst way.

Her mom's attention flicked to Julie and Nico. All the emotion and hope drained from her no-nonsense expression, the pained sigh and pursed lips directed at them a dead give-away. Their inability to talk some sense into Sophia was clearly unacceptable in her eyes.

Look how cute Julie and Nico are.

By September they would be married in a crazy, fairy-tale wedding. And Aunt Marian and Stan? Adorable. It didn't get better than two sweet people holding hands after finding each other so late in life. Even their romance was a result of her mom's meddlesome matchmaking.

And then there was her mom. A stubborn mule with Sophia's shared fate. Mom made it clear she'd given love the old college try with Dad and it didn't work out, and that was that for her attempt at love. No three strikes rule, just a one-and-done.

Stubborn ass, more like.

"When is the guy getting here, Mom?"

"Don't try to change the subject. Besides, like I told Marian. I'm simply going meet the man and be cordial long enough to send him on his way. All this mushy foo-foo stuff? It simply isn't in the cards for me anymore."

"Oh cards, schmards. So get some new cards—a new dream —and move on. I am."

Sophia knew all about new dreams. Two years ago it seemed like she'd figured out the answers to all the age-old questions about love and life. She was married to a man who could give her the world, and blissfully on the verge of her motherhood and a picket fence dream—a royal flush in terms of possible hands to be dealt, considering her own upbringing.

But then everything was taken away. Again. She was meant to be alone. And finally she was okay with it.

The second she truly accepted it, she could breathe. All the walls came down, and she was free—to go and be wherever and whoever she wanted, without expectations and repeating cycles. The fact that the divorce was finalized and the Patton Place house was now hers confirmed she was right. It was time to get a new dream.

But those were Sophia's cards, not her mother's. Down to the very marrow of her bones, Sophia hoped her mom would find the courage to open up again, try again.

No matter how much it hurts, or how much you just want to curl up in a ball and rewind time to do it all over again in some alternate reality where things work out. Where you end up in a perfect marriage with a beautiful, healthy baby girl in your arms instead of only in your heart.

This move to Portland was as much to prove the benefits of new dreams to Mom as it was for Sophia. She had to try. If Sophia could relocate to another state and start all over again, her mom could go on a few dates.

A smile tugged at her mouth when she thought about the cute little old man from church Aunt Marian was setting her mom up with. But then she met her mom's unblinking look as she raised a brow.

"What?"

"You're running."

"I'm not running. I'm daring to imagine a new life. What about you? Have you considered giving this guy, this Otis, a *real* chance?"

For all of two minutes they stood there. The question charged the air. A dang face-off/stare-down brewed, complete with squinted eyes and a nonverbal bluff call before Mom shifted her weight and stuck out her hip. Sophia couldn't take the silence a second longer.

"Mom, what are you thinking about?" A sputter of laughter erupted from deep in her belly. She knew good and well her mom had a flare for dramatics. No matter what harebrained idea floated around beneath the tumbleweed atop her head, it couldn't be a good one.

She watched as Mom rubbed her forefinger over her top lip while she continued biting down on the bottom one.

"Uh-oh. That's the same look she gave me before fixing me up with Stanley," Aunt Marian snickered...because it's obvious that she's warning Sophia.

"The woman is ruthless in her pursuits." Stanley added. "Watch out, now."

Everyone laughed, including Sophia. She could feel the tension in the room evaporate. If anyone knew her mother was a ballbuster of a woman, it was Sophia. They were connected down to their DNA, inseparable and insufferable together when they were teamed up. But it was time they stopped leaning on each other.

"Okay, Mom. I know this face. Out with it." She snapped her fingers bringing her mom back to earth.

Mom's brows knitted together, as if she was struggling to find the right words. "This is what I'm talking about. I mentioned to Marian *one* time that this guy had a nice smile, and now she's setting me up. I mean, he's nice enough, but I don't *know* the guy. Still, you want me to find someone, or rather, give this guy a real chance, right?"

"Right," Sophia said, still not following where her mom was going with this line of reasoning.

"All I really want is for my only daughter to remain living in Las Vegas with me. So...how about we come to a little understanding?" She used her most velvety voice for this part. And sure enough, Mom was preparing for a total bomb drop. "So we both get what we want."

Sophia gaped. Then closed her mouth again. "Umm. I don't get it. I'm moving to Portland tomorrow, so..."

"So let's make a pact. Let's give it six months."

"Give what six months?"

"If you don't love it and you find there's nothing and no one there for you, come back to Vegas." The velvety voice again. As if this was a completely logical conclusion. "Meanwhile, I'll give this Otis a shot, or keep dating for the same amount of time. *But...*"

Uh-oh.

"If there's no one meaningful, fine. I don't have to continue searching for someone I know isn't out there for me." And there it was. This was classic Mom. Her special brand of putting a time limit on happiness. Her warped idea of compromise. But Sophia's plans did not include letting her mom get off easy.

Sophia was just about to let her know what she thought of her little plan when Aunt Marian weighed in with her two cents. "Six months? Why not three or nine? Helen, now you know that's just so damn random. Hell, why not a year?"

Not to be outdone by her mother, Julie couldn't resist having her say too—since this was apparently going to turn into a full-on extended family discussion. "No, three is definitely better. If it doesn't work out, she'll be back for the wedding." Because naturally everyone's lives revolved around her cousin's nuptials.

Precisely why I'm moving. To be left alone.

"Oh, I get it. This isn't my life or anything. Why don't you all take a number and everyone can line up to tell me what to do since I'm so pathetic? Since obviously I'm incapable of making good decisions." Sophia laughed. By now, her irritation had morphed into hysteria. This was insane. "I'm not smart enough. Not good enough for people to stick around. Right, Mom?"

She threw her hands up and whirled on the guys, who both flinched back. "Nico, Stan? Don't you guys have anything to add while we're at it?"

Neither of them looked at her, and both were dead silent as they shook their heads. If she wasn't mistaken, Sophia would have sworn she could see the indentation of Nico's teeth biting the inside of his cheek. Or maybe his tongue.

Mom held out her hand and let it hang in the air between them. "Deal, or not?"

Sophia searched every one of the few wrinkles on her mother's ageless face, but there wasn't a laugh line among them. She was dead serious.

And Sophia was dead serious about her mother getting a second chance.

Shit. Here goes nothing.

She narrowed her eyes at her mom again, gauging her intentions. Then she looked at Aunt Marian, took two fingers and pointed them at her own eyes first before turning them on her aunt. "Watch her when I leave to make sure she's holding up her end of the bargain."

With her aunt in place as her insurance policy, Sophia sighed and shook her mother's hand. "Fine. Six months. Deal."

OLD PATTON PLACE still looked and felt like home.

Everett Monroe sighed, taking a few steps back from the portico onto the weathered, brick-paved walkway. Shading his eyes from the afternoon sun, he took a good long look at his grandmother's home—his family's home for generations.

As much as he hated the Harmans, he had to admit they did maintain most of its original colonial elements. The four forward-facing dormers were tucked between twin chimneys, accented by the matching black front door and shutters flanked at each window. The contrast with the crisp white paint and lush green landscape made it a dream house, but it was the flaws he remembered that made it a home. The cracks he used to watch settle in the walls and the hardwood floors scuffed from years of childhood games.

He rang the old, familiar doorbell.

After a few minutes he leaned in and placed his ear on the door to see if he could hear someone walking around. When he heard muffled music or television, he knew someone was home.

He rang again.

Still no one answered.

"Hello!" He searched the windows for signs of life. "Sophia Harman?"

All his instincts urged him to grab the door handle and walk on in, but he couldn't just march in anymore.

Instead he held down the doorbell this time, dragging the pad of his finger over the button and letting it linger for a moment. It was both strange and almost haunting to stand on the steps of his childhood home and not be able to let himself in the way he'd done a million times.

He rested his forehead on the door and squeezed his eyes shut. Balling and un-balling his fist, he flattened his hand against the sun-warmed black wood. A soft breeze passed under his nose, teasing him as it swapped the robust scent of pine and wet grass with the rich, savory perfume of home cooking.

"Sophia Harman." His voice was just above a whisper.

He checked his watch once more. Dammit. Already one thirty. Mike would want a detailed account before he headed back to the courthouse for the filing. Everett took one more glance at the house. For good measure, he rang the bell one more time...then shrugged, prepared to walk away, until he heard a woman's voice.

"Who is it?"

He couldn't deny the way his shoulders lifted and relief flooded him as he replied to the closed door. "I'm looking for Sophia Harman."

"What do you want?" The woman asked.

"I have a package for her."

Come on. Let's just get this over with. I want to see the look on your face.

From behind the door, Everett heard the footsteps growing muffled and then looked over toward the rustle of blinds in the window to his left.

"Can you hold the package up, please?" the voice requested from the cracks between the blinds.

He jerked the hand holding the summons up to face the window. He opened his mouth to protest. Then closed it again.

The next thing he heard was the deadbolt being unlocked. A slim woman with a body for days appeared in the doorway with a phone glued to her ear. He gasped as a carnal urge shot to his groin, tightening every muscle.

This is Sophia Harman?

CHAPTER 2

Off the cuff, she looked like every other mixed Black woman with a wavy mass of hair piled in a bun on top of her head. She wasn't quite petite, but she had a tight little body with endless curves. Then she stepped into the doorjamb and the sun highlighted her every feature.

Warm brown skin hugged her high, dusky pink cheekbones. Then there were those deep-set almond-shaped eyes and lips that seemed to plump up with every word she said into the phone.

Everett wanted to drag his teeth over her bottom lip. He felt his own lips part, and he prayed he wasn't staring, although he felt himself doing it.

"Um, Mom, let me call you back." Her voice oozed a soft familiarity. She sounded like a long-lost friend. He felt instantly comforted by it. And was there a hint of a Southern accent?

"Yes," she said into the phone. "We'll finish talking about Otis then. Now go on. Someone's at my door and I'm being rude."

The woman on the other end of the line was still talking when Sophia ended the call and slipped the phone into the back pocket of a pair of skin-tight jeans that hugged every inch of her toned thighs. He watched her shift in place, wringing her hands. At the moment, all his senses had fallen by the wayside except for his sight, which was riveted on the ruching effect of the slight breeze on the braless woman before him.

With every move of her feet, her breasts bounced, aiming her pointed nipples right at him. He could only thank his lucky stars he'd worn boxer briefs today since all the blood had been sucked out of his brain and limbs and hardened at his groin.

Look her in the eyes. Her eyes, dolt!

Averting his eyes was pointless. She couldn't have been more than five and a half feet tall. His almost a foot height advantage made it impossible for him not to see the generous cleavage from an aerial viewpoint. Plus, just knowing that she was wearing a practically see-through white tank top with those thin straps set off a surge of shivers down his back.

He gripped the letter tight and swallowed hard past the lump in his throat. Heat crawled up his neck and he could feel his cheeks burn. He was almost drunk with delight. For his own safety, he took a step back, but Sophia seemed oblivious to Everett's growing problem. She laughed a little too long to be normal.

"Mothers." She feigned exasperation, and bit down on her full bottom lip, which Everett couldn't deny was dangerously sexy.

"Yeah." He croaked, because he couldn't seem to put a coherent sentence together.

What are you doing? Quit stalling.

Once more he opened his mouth—and closed it just as fast.

As he cleared his throat, Everett tried to remember what

he'd imagined this meeting would be like. He'd been building up to this moment in his mind for so long, reveling in the sure-fire adrenaline rush he'd get, the satisfaction he'd feel when he was crowned victor over the money-grubbing family who thought nothing of cheating to get what they wanted.

Even better, he'd savor the moment when he and Austin Harman's wife—the next best thing to Austin himself—looked at each other and knew a Monroe beat the Harmans at their own game.

This woman? She didn't look like she belonged in the same lineup.

What he didn't expect was the tightening of his abdomen. The erratic way his heartbeat drummed in his ears. How hot it was suddenly. Or, how every nerve ending in his body stirred at the fruity sweet scent radiating from her nearly naked skin.

Focus on her eyes, asshole. Those endlessly deep eyes. Ocean eyes. "Uh..."

Sophia gazed up at him. "Um...hi."

Her voice rasped with a husky undertone, and it did not help his current attempt to deflect the growing hard-on in his jeans.

She yawned, and within seconds, though he tried to stifle it, he yawned too.

Am I boring you? Everett cursed himself for staring at her lips and set his jaw.

With chin high and his neck exposed, unsure where else to focus his attention—given her minefield of a body—he straightened.

He was determined to do what he came here to do.

"Sophia Harman?"

"Actually, I'm Sophia Kent now. I took my maiden name back after the divorce." Her brows bounced as she shrugged, and those delicious lips parted with a slow smile. She slipped her hands into her back pockets and teetered on her heels, emphasizing those mouthwateringly pointy breasts even more.

She didn't keep Harman's name.

Everett knew about the divorce. He'd seen the filed decree, but in his mind he assumed Sophia would keep the last name— keep herself connected to the money. His hesitation was enough to make him pay attention, but it didn't change anything. She was still one of *them*. He was just about to do it, but then, as she lifted herself up onto her toes and leaned the slightest bit forward, he made the mistake of looking down.

He was drooling, salivating over the fucking enemy, imagining in 3-D and living color what the two of them could get up to if they took a few steps back into the house, not even closing the door. Which was bad enough, until she noticed where he was looking.

"Oh." She breathed, her eyes wide. A pink flush flooded her cheeks and she crossed her arms over her chest. "Oh, my goodness. Shit. I'm so sorry. I—"

"No, *I'm* sorry. It's just—"

"Don't. Really, it's not your fault. I just got up and threw anything on so I could get some unpacking done." Sophia threw her face into her hands and squealed, "I'm so embarrassed. I can't believe I've been standing here just about flashing you the whole time. You must think I'm some kind of—"

"I don't think anything." Everett lied.

He was thinking how horrible his luck really was. How kissable her lips looked. How easily he could remove the rest of her flimsy top and let her breasts fall free.

Clearly, both of them were humiliated. She'd given him a peepshow and he just stood there gawking like a fool. Like he hadn't arrived on business, with a plan. The plan was basically shot to hell now, since he couldn't tear his eyes away.

He teetered for a moment. Half of him was horny as fuck, and the other half of him was still slightly irritated with himself. She was a siren who knocked him off his game. Where were the fangs and the greedy claws? Where were the markings of the Harmans? Not this self-deprecating, sexy, lip-biting vixen.

To hell with it.

Lifting the letter, he safely focused on the lines between the bricks on the porch. "I'm just here for a delivery. Remember?"

*Just do it. She's one of **them**.*

Everett held out the envelope, just within reach, so she wouldn't have to be uncovered—for both their sakes.

As she accepted it from him, the heat of her skin brushed against his, forcing him to meet her gaze. Sophia looked back at him with a mischievous, almost lecherous look in her eyes.

He sucked in a stark breath, electricity coursing through his veins as he let go of the envelope.

"You've been served."

"HEY." Cousin Julie's chipper voice sang out of the phone. "What's up?"

"I'm freaking out right now." Sophia marched away from the formal living room window. She stood on the porch for at least twenty minutes after the bad news baron left, just in case someone was trying to prank her.

When he didn't return and no one jumped out of her bushes to scream "gotcha," she went back in, hitched up her Big Girl panties again, and pressed play on the movie she'd been watching while she unpacked. But before the twist could really get under way, she paused it again and paced back and forth along the length of the first floor. There was no way she could focus enough for an M. Night Shyamalan brainteaser right now.

"I don't know what to do. I still don't even understand what just happened." She sounded winded.

This cannot be happening.

"What happened? Talk to me." The panic in Julie's voice mirrored how Sophia felt.

She mumbled something, cursing under her breath as she shook her head. How could she make sense at a time like this? Nothing made any sense. She ran her fingers through her hair, still trying to catch her breath as heat crawled up her neck. The sound of her heart pounding in her ears would not quiet down long enough for her to get a grip.

"Come on, Soph. You're scaring me."

"I just— I don't—. I'm so..." She paced away from the kitchen bar, then turned on her heel back toward the massive granite island to pick up the summons again. Just looking at the document boiled her blood. What right did he have to stomp all over her dream? She just got here.

"What? You better tell me right now, or I'm calling Aunt Helen."

Despite the tattle-tale whining, she could tell Julie was serious. Sophia chewed the inside of her cheek, took in a deep breath and let her frustrations all whoosh out. "I don't know what the hell is going on in this whacky, crazy town. You want to know what just happened to me? I'll tell you," she said before her cousin could respond. "I just got served, that's what."

Always the one to crack jokes at the absolute worst of times, Julie was quick to jump in with a witty response. "As in you just got served...on the dance floor? Or what? I don't get it." Confusion bled into her giggle.

"Try to follow along here, will you? I was Just. Served. Papers. You know, legal papers. Lawyer stuff? Albeit, by a really cute messenger, who sort of undressed me with his eyes, but still. I just got served. The asshole is trying to destroy me."

"The hot messenger?" Julie's voice rose to a piercing shriek.

Sophia pinched the bridge of her nose and blew out a chest full of steam. "No, fool. Austin. You know, the asshole ex? Pay attention, cuz."

"Wait, what? I thought the divorce was final."

With an extra-dramatic inhale, which Sophia intended to be cleansing, she leveled her shaky tone enough to explain. "Austin is behind this. I know it and you know it. This is just another one of his antics, like with the car." Now she knew why he insisted on keeping the car title in his name only. It's always great to have your car reported stolen and repossessed the day before you move to a new state.

She grabbed a tumbler out of a kitchen cupboard and filled it with water straight from the tap while her heart raced and she could feel anger prickling her all over again.

"Behind what? I don't know what the hell you're talking about. Slow down and try to make some sense."

"Jules, I just got served. In thirty days there's going to be a hearing. Some guy named John E. Monroe thinks he's the rightful owner of this property." As soon as she said it, Sophia thought she might explode with frustration. She threw her head back and drank till the glass was empty, making a mental note to find the bottle of cabernet hiding in one of the boxes in the garage.

Through the receiver she could hear her cousin whispering, likely to Nico. Which was all fine and good and everything, considering that a little over a year ago Sophia watched the two of them fall head over heels for one another, so he already knew what an asshat Austin was. Especially now, she was fine with Nico knowing her private business, but she was smack dab in the middle of a dang crisis. And there was no way she was going to resort to calling Mom.

And risk giving her yet another reason to vie for her return to Vegas?

Not an option.

"You know I can hear you two, right? Can't you tell Nico about this *after* I get off the phone? I need you right now. I don't know what to doooooo." she whined as she padded back to the front window and peeked out again.

"Calm down. Breathe for a second. I need to think."

Sophia stared unseeing at the front porch, where she'd stood only inches away from the courier. Like a traitor, her heart did a little flip. How was it possible she was seething with anger right now and still she couldn't get the image of the courier out of her mind? It wasn't his fault. *Duh. Don't shoot the messenger.*

Memories of the tall, dark-skinned, chiseled man sent a new wave of heat washing over her. Just imagining him did things to her a courier had no business doing. He was all gleaming white teeth and brooding smolder.

Sophia shook off the thought.

Portland was not about men. She was supposed to be standing on her own two feet. Finding a comfortable fit.

But he was really hot.

She closed her eyes and shook her head again, wishing she could rewind this whole day and start all over again, excluding her probable eviction.

"I'm listening." Julie's voice blared through the receiver with renewed interest. "So, it was Numbnuts who did this, or this guy John Monroe? 'Cause I'm confused."

"Ugh. That's what I'm trying to tell you. The letter gave the guy Monroe's name, but it doesn't make sense. Think about the timing. It's not a coincidence the property was granted to me in the divorce and out of the blue someone else is claiming they're the rightful owner." No way. Something shady was going on here, and deep in her bones Sophia could feel Austin trying, once again, to destroy her.

"But how? Why?" Julie sounded so confused, but Sophia couldn't for the life of her understand why. Her cousin, more than anyone else, hated Austin—otherwise known as Numbnuts—as much as Sophia did now. Julie loathed anything and everything remotely related to the Harman family.

"He agreed to the divorce." Julie continued. "And why in the hell did you accept the summons? I would have jerked my hand back as soon as the words came out of the guy's mouth."

Sophia slid down against the wall and tucked her legs in, criss-cross applesauce. "Well, I would have if—"

"If what? What happened?"

Shit. "I was kind of...sort of...preoccupied." The words squeaked out, dying from lack of conviction.

"Go on." It wasn't like her bloodhound cousin was going to let Sophia sweep this conversation back under the rug where it belonged.

Sophia covered her eyes and said it quickly: "I was unpacking and I might have forgotten to put a bra on when I answered the door, so the messenger was kind of drooling over my nipples while I was drooling over him." She gritted her teeth, squeezed her eyes shut, and braced for the backlash.

If Julie saw him, she would not blame her. He was tall, flawless dark brown skin, with a casual effortlessness to him, and that was just his muscular frame in business casual duds. The face was all adorable cleft chin, full brows, bitable full lips, and deep dimples peeking through. What woman wouldn't lose a little drool when faced with him?

For the tiniest of moments she thought maybe Julie didn't hear her.

"Mmm, mmm, mmm. You slore." Julie laughed through her teasing.

"I suspect I should be offended, but I have no clue what you just said."

"Slutty whore." Julie was in stitches now. "Don't try to act all innocent. You know exactly what you were doing, going out there with your big old juicy melons in the man's face." Julie could barely finish her sentence she was laughing so hard. "I'm surprised he was able to hang onto the paper. I cannot believe you."

Sophia released a humiliated cackle. "I swear. I totally forgot. Mom called to tell me about the latest with Otis, so I just got out of bed and started unpacking. When the doorbell rang, I just...forgot."

"Sure you did. Exactly what did you think he was giving you?"

"It could have been mail. Filed copies of the deed. Who knows? Packages have been coming all week. It could have been anything." It could have. But lord knows fire had not bloomed low and tight in her belly in a long time. The courier's face flickered across her mind again, and again, just like that! She was turned on.

Thank God she just bought new batteries.

Julie sighed into the receiver. "Well...maybe this is good."

Um. Come again? "Exactly how is this a *good* thing?"

"First of all, don't worry about the house. Liz's boyfriend

Derrick has a friend who's a licensed attorney in Oregon. I'll have Derrick get ahold of him today. Second of all, besides this whole loner phase you're going through where you insist on doing everything yourself, you need to get over what's-his-face. As unbelievable as it might seem, someone new has caught your eye." At Sophia's exhale, Julie continued. "And third of all, if you're really doing this little pact with Aunt Helen, it might be nice to get out and have someone to hang with."

Ugh, the pact. "Don't remind me."

"You're the one who took the deal."

"I've got six months—less than six months, now. Five months and two weeks left, and already someone is trying to steal my house. You still don't think this is a sign? Mom might be off the hook in less than thirty days. And did I tell you she's been sending me Return to Vegas countdown emails? Ugh."

Julie put Sophia on hold for a second while she checked her work calendar and airline miles. She decided, despite Sophia's insistence that she could find a lawyer herself, Julie needed to be in Portland the following morning, come rain or shine.

Likely rain.

And bingo, there was the perfect flight. She got back on the line and gave Soph the deets so she could pick her up.

"I love you, Jules. Thank you so, so much." Sophia took a deep breath and closed her eyes, thankful to have chosen the right person to help her take down Goliath.

"Now, before I drag my ass all the way to Portland for four days, I want to know exactly how much wine you have, and how cute this messenger was."

CHAPTER 3

E verett bit the bullet.

The second the words were out of his mouth, Everett turned and walked away. He made it to within a few feet of his truck before he turned back for another look.

Just one more look at Sophia Kent couldn't hurt.

Who was he kidding? It hurt like hell. Which was why he quickly got behind the wheel and put as much distance between them as he could.

A half hour later Everett let the glass door crawl to a loud close behind him, announcing his arrival. His best friend-turned-attorney, Mike Kennedy was sitting behind his desk, per usual, eating God knows what.

Everett scrunched his nose and tried to wave away the briny, ammonia smell lingering in the air, procrastinating as long as he could before he met Mike's searching gaze. Of course Mike would want an update on their latest recon.

Mike heaved a loud sigh before clearing his throat. "Well?"

Everett glanced over at him now. Sure enough, his raised

eyebrows nearly reached the expertly edged hairline of his fade.

"I saw her." Everett shrugged. His tone was low and matter-of-fact, like he'd confessed something shameful.

"Okay, and?" Mike wound his hands in circles, urging Everett to spit it out already, but Everett just sort of stared through him.

"Dude, chill." Everett ran his hand over his close-shaven hair. "I told you. She was there. She accepted the letter."

Professionally they partnered up seven years ago, but their friendship had continued unbroken since elementary school. After high school, Everett started flipping houses alongside his grandmother, Babs while Mike hopped a plane to Berkeley in the Bay Area to study law at Boalt, now known as the UC Berkeley School of Law. By the time Mike passed the bar, Everett had a few dozen flipped properties under his belt, and Babs had handed over the reins to him and his sister Zora. When eventually they needed legal counsel to make sure all their i's were dotted and t's were crossed, it only made sense for Mike to be the missing piece to their puzzle, since the trust factor was already built in.

Plus, there was no one Everett would rather have guarding his six when the battle for Patton Place came to a head. Mike hated the Harmans on principle almost as much as Everett did, not even including having Everett's back. Babs might as well have been Mike's grandmother too, for all the years he spent playing, eating, and spending the night at her house.

He and Mike shared a brotherhood, which required thick skin for days with thin patience. Together they'd seen each other through the company's highest highs and lowest lows, and still their work ethic was closely akin to fuel in an engine. Countless workdays spent finalizing land purchases and orchestrating building projects turned into late nights at bars, hoisting beer mugs to toast the action high points of whichever hoop game was on the big screen.

In between those nights, Mike played the field with a revolving roster of women, who all ended up getting permanently benched. Everett mostly played it safe when it came to matters of the heart. He never figured out exactly how to play the game without getting hurt, so he mostly sat out.

Which was why Everett hesitated now to tell Mike any more about Sophia Kent.

Today was one of those days he hoped Mike wore his thickest skin, because Everett was feeling his own patience thinning, or Mike's.

Still without saying a word, Everett headed straight for the floor to ceiling window facing the east side of the building.

"Do I even want to know what happened?" Mike asked.

His question was met with silence while Everett stared over the horizon at the peak of Old Mount Hood in the distance. His burgeoning green city of parks and bridges and bike paths —as beautiful in the day as it was under the neon lights of the thriving nights.

On most days, watching the city come to life would calm him, but today Sophia Kent had crawled in under his skin and settled there. He wasn't sure what bothered him about her, but he didn't like it.

He was looking out the window, but she was all he'd been able to see since he left her on the porch. How her hard nipples poked out her shirt. Those full lips. And those hungry eyes.

Just thinking about her, he could feel himself harden, and he adjusted himself before he rolled his head back to crack his neck. Sweat beaded on his forehead and scalp, triggered by more than just the sun streaming through the glass. Suddenly suffocating, he yanked open his top shirt button, shaking his head.

"Is it hot in here, or is it just me?" He asked, turning to face his friend.

Mike's head popped up mid-bite into a forkful of salmon.

Everett grimaced and wrinkled his nose. "Tell me you didn't microwave fish at work, you Neanderthal. It smells like shit in here."

Unfazed, Mike chewed at a glacial pace before he responded. "So glad you're back, what with the winning attitude and all. It went extremely well, I take it?" He set his fork down into the Tupperware container.

The ice broken, Everett sat in the chair and tossed the papers onto his partner's desk. He twisted his neck to crack it again and sucked in a deep, cleansing breath, but they didn't soothe him. He was still antsy and unhinged. Unable to sit still, he got back to his feet and finally answered Mike.

"It's done," he stated.

Mike examined him for moment, as if determining his next words carefully, then shrugged it off. "Don't sound so enthusiastic. We've only been working on this...oh, let's see...for like the last two years. It's what you said you wanted, and I'm handing it to you." He leaned back in the chair and tilted his head.

"I'm fine," Everett muttered. He flashed a quick smile and hauled out his phone for a welcome distraction.

"Fine, as in, you're functioning on all cylinders? No. Fucked up, insecure, neurotic, and emotional? Yes. You're clearly not fine, Ev. Might as well let me in on it now. I'll end up suffering the brunt of it later anyway."

Everett replaced the phone in his back pocket.

This was why he went to Mike. He never bullshitted or beat

around the bush when it came to important things. Today, it was what he needed—the truth, straight up, no chaser. Mike had more than earned the right to be Everett's trusted counsel in business. Because that's what this was—business. *Isn't it?*

"I know. It's just..."

"It's just what?" Mike pressed, but there was a hint of annoyance in his tone Everett couldn't dismiss.

Heaviness washed over him, head to toe, and his chest tightened as he weighed the pros and cons of letting his friend in on this one. Why was he so conflicted about it, anyway? She accepted the letter. Nothing happened.

In his mind he played "what-if," figuring out how many ways things could go wrong. But, overwhelmingly, every step of what happened pointed to the fact that he just needed to just say it, if for no other reason than to get it off his chest.

The pressure of Mike's patience weighed on him. As a friend, he would wait for Everett's answer. As his in-house counsel, he would make a case for the benefit of the company. Either way, the silence was stifling and he needed to just...breathe.

Breathe.

Everett exhaled, coughed, and sucked air back in. He smiled and shook his head. "It wasn't him," he finally muttered in a near-whisper.

Mike jolted up and clasped his hands on the desk. "I don't get it. You knew Austin must have given up the property. Otherwise why would he have sent you a copy of the filed divorce decree? He's basically proving you were right all along. He's removed himself from the equation."

"Everything about this still feels wrong, though." Everett began to pace, unable to put his finger on the most bothersome part.

"No. *He* was wrong." Mike clarified. "His whole fucking family was wrong," he said, now stabbing his finger on the desk. "It's why we've put in all these hours to get Babs's house back."

As if it dawned on him, Everett stalked right up to the desk and lowered his weight onto his knuckles. "You're goddamned right. *His* family. Not Sophia's. She had nothing to do with it. You didn't see her. She's nothing like him." It all boiled down to her again. Whoever Sophia Kent was, she didn't deserve to pay for the wrongs her ex-husband's family committed a generation ago.

Everett let his chin drop to his chest for a moment, but when he lifted his chin again, he didn't feel any less conflicted. The knots in his stomach tightened.

"Sophia, huh?" His even tone judgmental, Mike leaned back in his chair again and crossed his arms over his chest clicking his pen incessantly. "Enlighten me."

When Everett failed to respond fast enough, Mike filled the silence. "No really. I want you to enlighten me about what kind of woman it takes for a man to give up a piece of real estate that's been in the family for generations, for a piece of ass. She must have really been something." He capped it off with a scowl.

"It wasn't like that, man. You know me. I don't have a problem claiming what's ours, and whether I like to admit it or not, I'm loyal to a fault," he reasoned, standing ramrod straight, his look unwavering, unblinking. "You have to believe me. I wouldn't let it give me pause if I didn't feel in my gut that something's wrong, you know?"

Mike advanced to rocking in his chair. "And you got all this from the few seconds it took to serve her with the petition? No really, how long has it been since you got laid?"

He should have known Mike would take it there, but he wasn't any less annoyed. Despite his fucked-up logic, Everett still, for some insanely inexplicable reason, felt compelled to explain his viewpoint. "She gave up the last name. She was getting settled in the place. From what I could see through the windows and down to the blue and green welcome mat on the front porch, she isn't anything like Austin Harman. She doesn't need to wear the money."

Mike rolled his eyes.

"Please. You know if she was anything even remotely like him there would have been private collection paintings or priceless vases. Some crazy expensive interior decorator would have been running around barking orders about where things should go. This woman isn't trying to prove she belongs anywhere near Bridlemile and Goose Hollow. I'm guessing she could not care less about what it means to live in the southwest hills of Portland."

To his layman, lopsided logic, Mike gave a noncommittal nod. But for Everett, it meant Mike could at least empathize with his hang-ups about the situation.

"So what are you saying?" Mike conceded.

"I'm saying...she's different. There's more to her than money, which means, when it comes down to it, she isn't a true Harman."

"And it changes things how, exactly?" Mike defaulted to lawyer mode, clearly failing to see how Everett's revelations about Sophia Kent were relevant when it came to legal ramifications.

But Everett was intent on getting his point across—and maybe once he spit it out, he'd be able to figure out what the point actually *was*.

"Because I went there. I went there personally to see the

look on her face, thinking if she was anything like the Harmans, it would feel just as good to win. And yes—" Mike didn't say a word, but he didn't have to—"she's pretty, and she does have curves for days." His back was turned to Mike, but if Everett knew anything about his friend, he knew his mind tended to hang in the gutter.

"But she's also young—probably in her mid to late twenties. And though she gave her best impression of someone who's carefree and happy, I recognize the sadness behind her eyes. She's a fucking pawn."

Everett pinched the bridge of his nose. "I don't know why, or what Harman is up to, but whatever it is, he wants her to go down for it."

Everett backed into the chair behind him and let the tension drain from his limbs into the smooth leather cushion.

Absentmindedly, Mike picked up a paper Everett unknowingly crumpled between his fists and the cluttered surface when he took his fists-on-the-desk looming stand. He placed it on top of a pile at the front corner of the desk. More than anything, Mike's astute attention still followed Everett's moves, watching, judging.

"Okay, humor me. What do you want to do about it? Withdraw the petition?" Mike asked. "I want you to think carefully, and before you answer the question, answer me this: even if she is this sexy pawn who came out of nowhere, what kind of person do you think it takes to marry an insidious, manipulative vulture like Harman?"

It was a good point. A point Everett had failed to consider.

He rubbed the back of his neck with both hands and clasped them behind his head, willing the tension away. "I don't know yet. All I'm saying is, let's just do a little more digging before the hearing."

Mike nodded and dumped the remains of his progressively smellier lunch into the trashcan beside the desk.

For a minute Everett lingered in the chair facing Mike, thinking about Sophia Kent's intentions.

He wasn't sure if Mike was right about her, or if Austin had stooped to a new all-time low, but before the hearing, Everett planned to find out.

THE THURSDAY JULIE arrived in Portland it was like the stars aligned. The rain mostly let up so there was only a light drizzle, and, by luck of the draw, on the way to the airport, Sophia's Uber driver, Kara, turned out to be a total foodie godsend. She shared a list of restaurants considered to be the best-kept secrets in town, *and* she also happened to have a pen and paper to go with her brilliant sense of humor.

Sophia waited in baggage claim by the carousel listed for the Vegas flight. As soon as she caught sight of Julie, she held up the sign she made. It read: *Can't wait to kiss my family Jules.* Kara's idea, which Sophia thought was hilarious, and just raunchy enough to embarrass her cousin.

But Julie didn't even blink. She let out an ear-piercing squeal and flew into Sophia's arms, wrapping her whole body around her. "I missed you, crazy girl."

Sophia let out a strained laugh, wheezing to catch her breath after Julia knocked the wind out of her. "It's so good to see a familiar face."

"Is it rude if I tell you I kind of hope you don't put down the sticky roots so you can come back home?"

"Yes." She pouted, setting Julie down.

"Okay, I won't say it, then." Julie giggled.

The lights above the baggage carousel flashed and suitcases

and duffels began spilling out. "Yes. There's mine." Julie yanked a large, shiny black suitcase by the handle and onto its wheels.

Sophia was pretty happy Julie's bag was one of the first ones to come out. Since Kara didn't have any other fares, she opted to wait curbside while Sophia hunted Julie down. Sophia ushered her over to Kara's blue Prius, practically bouncing off the pavement to introduce Jules to Kara and Kara to Jules. Sophia could hardly wait for the three of them to talk weddings and food. And hopefully find out some more well-kept secrets about her new home city. At the very least, she might have made her first friend in Portland.

No matter how many times she did it, stepping out on faith was still kind of lonely at first.

As Kara navigated through traffic, their conversation was wild and high-pitched—and any talk of the house or lawyers was strictly banned. As soon as the word wedding floated into the confines of the car, Julie talked nonstop about her Italian wedding. Her colors were ivory and blush pink. "Think elegant and romantic meets classically traditional," Julie exclaimed with fingers spread and hands raised so Sophia and Kara could see her vision. She went on to include lots of silk, low, shimmery lights, and flowers galore.

Everything and the kitchen sink in just the first ten minutes of the ride.

By the time they reached Bridlemile, they'd discussed her entire wedding, starting with the bridal getup (tiara, veil, Cinderella ball gown) in exhaustive detail, the Alfa Romeo waiting outside the church, the music playlist (an eclectic range from the Cha Cha Slide to La Tarantella), and Nico's cute cousin, Gianni, who'd apparently seen a picture of Sophia and was already smitten.

All of which left only about ten minutes for Sophia to

exchange numbers with Kara, and for Kara to recommend a great Mediterranean restaurant downtown off Vista.

Half an hour later, Sophia whipped up a quick bite for her and Julie to eat. They were supposed to be talking about her appointment later in the afternoon with the attorney before Sophia gave Julia the grand tour of Patton Place. When they were armed with their food and their respective glasses of rosé and cabernet, the two women sat on the plush sofa facing the slate fireplace. Though hours would pass before the sun set over Portland, Sophia turned the fire on. It made the room feel cozy and warm. But even with it crackling in the background, she decided to snuggle up with her favorite throw for the rundown on the lawyer.

"So, he's friends with Liz's boyfriend?" Sophia took a sip of her cabernet.

"Yes. His name is Jacob Bornstein, and they were in the same fraternity in college, so it's no big deal." She forked a ginger turkey ball. "They help each other out all the time."

Julie held up her index finger while she finished chewing, savoring the citrusy, tangy-sweet flavor before she began. "Oh, my fucking god. Soph, what are you even doing?" She closed her eyes and swallowed, then licked her lips. "This food is amazing. My taste buds are shooting off fireworks. The flavor," she moaned.

She moved the plate around under her nose, inhaling deeply. "Hmmm. My nose is in sensory overload. What did you even put in this?" She shoveled in another mouthful. "I can't believe you were in the kitchen for like, fifteen minutes, and you came up with this shit like it was nothing."

"It's just some ground turkey with chopped ginger and lemon zest. I promise you, it's really not a big deal." Sophia blushed, pushing a thinly sliced cucumber roll around her plate.

"To you, maybe. To me, I want to stuff my face with it. I want to sleep with it. Bathe in it. Marry it, it's so good. Why in the hell aren't you packaging this shit and selling it? Better yet, take it on Shark Tank so we can both be bazillionaires."

"I don't know." Sophia looked away and cleared her throat, stabbing a turkey ball with her fork and putting it in her mouth. "It didn't work out before." Her argument sounded weak even to her own ears.

Which Julie confirmed when she rolled her eyes. "Please. You have an actual ginger root in your refrigerator. A *root*. Normal people don't have roots in their refrigerator. Plus, you and I both know Fuckhead was the one holding you back." She took one more bite and wiped her mouth before continuing. "Restaurants were practically begging you to come cook for them."

Glancing around uneasily, Sophia took a deep breath and exhaled. "They didn't want me. They wanted Austin Harman's wife. They wanted headlines." She took a long swig from her wine glass, leaving it only a quarter full.

"Yeah. Okay, sure. Keep lying to yourself," Julie scoffed. "No restaurateur is going to risk having someone unskilled cook for them just for some publicity."

The words hung in the air for the slightest moment and Sophia let the idea marinate while she watched the neon flames in the fireplace. More to herself than for her cousin's benefit, she shed some light on the seed she'd been nurturing.

"The other day I was walking around downtown, checking out the sights."

"Uh-huh." Julie nodded encouragement as she dragged her last meatball through the dab of lemon sauce left on her plate.

38

"I wanted to visit Powell's books and taste the Voodoo Doughnuts. But while I was walking near the southwest end of Broadway I spotted an empty building. It wasn't much to look at, but there was definite potential. Kind of small, and it would need a lot of work, but all I could see was a quaint restaurant with good food and weird decor. My concept is simple: bite-sized meals for people who want extra flavor without feeling stuffed. People can order as much or as little as they want."

"I'd be there. With your food and your impeccable taste, I would be there, no matter what size the portions. Probably the first person in line." Julie reached for Sophia's hand. "So, do it already. What are you waiting for?"

"I don't know." Her heart pounded like crazy. They were only talking about her starting a restaurant and already her nerves were going haywire.

"After your appointment with Jacob you're going to take me to this place. It's time for you to have something of your own. What else do you have to lose?"

Sophia thought about it. She didn't have much to lose when it came to the restaurant, but it wasn't everything to her anymore. "Uh, this house? Can we take a minute and remember why you're here? Some shady guy sent a hot messenger to my front doorstep to tell me my days in this house are numbered. I might not even be here long enough to think about putting down roots, let alone starting a restaurant."

"Okay, first of all, you have a divorce decree and a filed quit claim deed naming you the rightful owner. So, let's just slow your roll there, punchy. Before you go repack your boxes, let's see what Jacob has to say. And also can we talk about how you've totally been holding out. This place is a freaking monstrosity. It's huge. Might as well be a mansion. What the hell are you going to do in this big old place all by yourself, anyway?"

Sophia cut her a serious side-eye.

The size of the house and what it's worth never factored into the decision for her. It was always about the memories she made there and what the house meant to her now. It was physical proof that she could stand on her own two feet. After all she'd been through in the past two years, it meant she wasn't breakable.

"You know what I'm saying. If it works out, great—live your fairy tale in this castle. If it doesn't, so what? That doesn't mean you have to come crawling back home to Vegas, all wounded and feeling sorry for yourself. It's time you dreamed a new dream and made it a reality."

"This place *is* my new dream, my new start," Sophia reasoned. "I've been making this house my own, changing things around, painting, buying new decorations. I'm daring to imagine a life without a husband, or Ainsley, or my mother within a five-mile radius. This is it. All my cards are on the table."

Julie threw up her hands. "Well all right then." Sophia looked on as Julie checked her watch. "Takes care of one thing. We've got just enough time before the appointment for you to take me on the dime tour of the house and spill your guts about this messenger you've not-so-discreetly mentioned twice."

Sophia climbed the stairs with the sound of Julie's light footfalls behind her.

"I've already seen the great lawn, the kitchen, the office, the wine cellar, and the flipping French doors. Now, spill."

"All right. Okay. Fine. Just let me show you my room real

quick," she huffed, even though she was dying to talk about him.

"Wait. What's in here?"

Sophia stilled as Julie stopped in front of the door just at the top of the stairs. Her heart stopped and her feet felt like they were stuck in cement. "Do you mind if we skip this one?"

Julie seemed to notice Sophia's panic and released the brass knob. She knew exactly what was on the other side of the door. Sophia had called her a million and one times and sent a gazillion photos to show her the progress as she was decorating it, making room in her life. Even with the door shut, the pink and yellow colors and the large "A" monogram framed and mounted above the crib painted across Sophia's mind.

Sophia weaved her fingers between Sophia's and squeezed her hand. "After your room, how about we get ready to go?"

Sophia swallowed. Then she forced a smile. "I'll tell you about the messenger on the way."

CHAPTER 4

"It's not spying."

Everett's assistant Kendra gaped at him, wide-eyed under knitted brows as she slowly shook her head at him. "Oh, it's not? What would you prefer to call it? A stakeout? Voyeurism? Or how about stalking? Creepy is what I call it. And I'm pretty sure it's against the law in most states." Her hands were planted on her generous hips, and she might as well have been pointing a finger for all the nope she was giving him.

"Listen, you know the house on Patton Place is going to hearing. All I'm asking you to do is check it out. Maybe have some lunch there. Relax while you listen to one of your audiobooks, or whatever it is you have on your phone. And if you happen to see Sophia Kent, just...let me know where she's going. I need to talk to her. Nothing else." It sounded completely reasonable to him.

He wasn't asking her to snoop around the property or peep into any windows. He just wanted to know where she would be so he could end up in the same place. How else was he supposed to find out if Mike was right about her?

"Uh-huh. Yeah, okay." Kendra rolled her eyes and pursed her lips as she sighed. "I better be getting paid extra for this, I know that. Because this is not part of my job description." She stomped off to her own desk in the lobby, and Everett could finally let loose his laughter. The woman was sassy and wild, but she was a team player.

Plus, he couldn't do it himself.

What would Sophia think if he showed up at her door without a package, or if he parked his car out front on Patton Place for inexplicable amounts of time?

This was crazy. Everett couldn't deny it, but there was too much at stake to leave it all to chance. He wouldn't give up on his promise to his family. The hearing wasn't far off, and if he was going to reclaim his grandmother's home with a clear conscience, he couldn't be in the dark about Sophia Kent.

An hour later, Everett still couldn't get any work done.

It was useless. He was a nervous wreck waiting to hear from Kendra, so he packed it up and headed home to grab Blue and let him burn off some energy at the park. And it worked. A little. Between the endless game of fetch and staring at his phone between throws, he was exhausted enough to stop fretting. At least for a while.

Everett tucked Blue's favorite tennis ball in his pocket and plopped down on a bench. "Let's rest for a minute, buddy. Give you a chance to catch your breath." He placed a portable water bowl on the ground and filled it from his own bottle. Poor Blue, in all of his furry brown splendor, rolled onto his side and let his tongue hang out of his mouth, panting with his belly up. He was out of breath and showing all forty-two of his dog years.

Everett slipped out his phone and pressed his thumb onto the pad to unlock it. His inbox lit up on the screen with yet another email from his half brother, Joseph Jr.

Joseph Monroe, Jr. 12:07 PM
Finalizing Dad's Estate
To: john.e.monroe@monroeproperties.com

Everett,

I've been trying to get ahold of you. I know you and Dad weren't on the best of terms, but there are some things here with your name on them. They're mostly documents, but there's also an engraved wooden box and some pictures. Figured you might want to drop by to pick them up. Either way, I'll be here until the end of August packing up the house for the sale. Then I'm heading back home in September.

You may not believe me, but I know how hard Dad was on you. He wasn't the easiest person to be around, but he talked about you a lot. We'd all love to see you and get a chance to spend some real time with you and Zora. No matter what, we're still family.

Hope to see you soon,

Joe

Everett closed the email and pinched the bridge of his nose. On a heavy sigh, he shook his head. He didn't have time for this right now. *His* family needed him—the ones who were actually part of his life, the ones who were always there for him. There were promises to keep to his grandmother, and his sister... "Shit. Zora."

What if Joe reached out to her, too?

Without thinking, he dialed her number. "Hey." The word came out rushed and he willed himself to breathe. He slouched onto the bench, stretching his legs out. "I saw your missed call."

Without so much as a greeting, his sister cut right to the chase. "Are we still on for next Sunday?" Relief flooded him. Joe hadn't gotten to her yet. "I've got a really good idea for a recipe." Last week they talked about having a low-key get-together to watch the Trailblazers in the fourth game of the western conference playoffs. The deal was she would do the cooking and he could enjoy basketball, as long as Everett picked up all the ingredients on her list.

Food, events, daily life, whatever...there was always a list with Zo.

"Yeah, we're still on. Text me what you need and I'll pick everything up at the farmer's market this week. What are you thinking about cooking? And how is it going with the agent hunt?"

Of course, as soon as he got relaxed, a pigeon decided to land right next to Blue, who, along with another chocolate lab he'd been playing with, pounced toward it, nearly causing Everett to drop the phone. Luckily, the leash was still around his wrist.

"You still there, Zo?"

There was a slight pause then he heard his phone ping against his ear. He could practically see the bullet points and check boxes lining the page. Then it pinged again. He checked the screen, but it wasn't Zora's list. Instead, there were several messages from Kendra.

Kendra: I'm downtown.

Kendra: She's with another woman. They stopped at an office building for an hour, and now they're walking on 20th by the Mediterranean restaurant and Java Hound Cafe. Am I done with my stalker duties for the day?

Everett held his breath as he reread the message. He was at Couch Park, which meant Sophia was only a few blocks away.

Everett: Yes. Thank you. I owe you.

Kendra: Indeed you do. I prefer my thanks in the form of dollars on my paycheck.

"Okay, you should have the list on your phone now," Zora said with a note of satisfaction. "As for Sunday's culinary masterpiece, you and Mike will just have to wait and see."

"I'm sure whatever concoction you come up with will be delicious. And I'm going to sit back and watch my Blazers deliver a beatdown in peace."

He got off the bench and led Blue back to the pavement, where they took off at a quick stride toward the shops.

"Heel, Blue." Everett tightened the leash as he waited for the pedestrian signal to cross over 20th. He paused for a second, trying to figure out how to get off the phone as he tugged on Blue's leash. "Okay, well..."

Zora sighed in his ear dramatically. "I got another rejection."

Damn, he hated to hear his sister sound so deflated. Especially when he needed to hurry up before Sophia moved on. He stopped, ready to give her a quick pep talk about why she shouldn't doubt herself and how these random people just needed a chance to taste her food first. He was going to drive home the point that pictures didn't do her food justice. And how all it takes is one agent to recognize the potential of her cookbook to make it a new food fusion phenomenon.

But he'd been so busy, stuck in his head, getting pumped up to deliver the motivational speech to his sister...that he failed to pay attention to where he was walking. Everett lost his footing and nearly tripped over Blue as his right shoe came flying off. As he wiggled back into his sneaker and tugged the back over his heel, he took a treat out his pocket.

"Good boy. Stay," he said firmly. When Blue sat back on his haunches, Everett set the leash down beside him with his phone still sandwiched between his ear and shoulder, and kneeled to tie his laces.

It might've been the second wind, or the simple urge that every dog gets at least once in its life to make a run for it. Whether for freedom or a squirrel, Blue bolted. In a fuzzy brown blur, he made a swift right and hightailed it down Vista straight toward Java Hound. *Dammit.*

"Zo, I'm going to have to call you back. Blue is on the move."

The rain let up only a little over an hour ago and already the streets were crawling with people. Not that rain ever deterred the residents of Portland, let alone the state of Oregon as a whole. Today, though, the sidewalk seemed unusually busy.

Everett was trying to keep up with his dog while he whipped through fast-disappearing openings in the crowd. He passed a few groups, all holding plates piled with food. Some were drinking what looked like wine or beer, and most carried totes emblazoned with the Annual Foodie & Brewery Festival logo.

Dang, it is today.

But this was no time to think about outings and entertainment. Heart pounding and breathing labored, Everett searched the streams and eddies of people, excusing himself when he bumped into someone.

"Stop, Blue!"

The dog couldn't be too far ahead. Though the farther behind Everett fell, the harder it would be to find him in the crowd.

It wasn't until he reached the Mediterranean cafe two doors away from Java Hound that he caught sight of Blue sitting just outside the entrance, his leash puddled around him. The years of training paid off—almost. He sat there like a perfectly well-behaved pet, the complete opposite of the one who ran away only moments earlier. To anyone else, Blue likely looked as if he was waiting for his owner to finish shopping.

Only the dog wasn't alone.

Sophia Kent.

There she was, crouched down beside him, petting his coat and cooing. Her face was at just the right angle, and there were those midnight eyes again—the darkest ebony with flecks of golden embers. They were curved into a perfect almond shape, suggesting a Dominican or Spanish family background. But those cheekbones and full lips were unmistakably Black.

He ambled toward the two of them, still trying to figure out what his angle should be.

Should he go for old friend? Or maybe, funny seeing you here? *Fuuuuuck.*

She still didn't seem to have noticed him as she leaned closer to check Blue's collar. While she did, he continued to study her. Images of her had played in his mind since yesterday, and he'd almost memorized her. She'd forgone the skintight jeans and barely-there tank of the prior day in exchange for pink pants and a dotted navy blouse. He wouldn't have called it fancy so much as preppy. But there was something about the understated way she paired the outfit with pearls. Shiny navy flats and light makeup gave the impression she was low-maintenance but well-kept.

Maybe she didn't require expensive vases or paintings, but she could just as easily be one of those women who'd spend obscene amounts on a single pair of shoes or a handbag. He scrutinized every inch, from head to toe, in hopes of figuring her out. If he didn't, it would keep bothering him, not knowing whether she was a pawn or running the whole game.

Taking a deep breath, Everett slowed his pace and composed himself, patting at his pants pockets for another dog treat. He allowed his shoulders to fall back as he settled into a strong stance and quietly cleared his throat. As his pulse leveled, he stood just behind Sophia and his furry traitor, who by now lapped up all the spare attention from a gorgeous woman.

Boy, would I like to trade places with you, buddy.

"Blue."

In one fluid movement, Sophia rose to meet Everett's eyes. "It's you. The messenger." One full brow raised in question. But she seemed genuinely excited to see him, which was…nice. Unexpected, but nice.

"Is this *your* dog?"

Everett gave a single silent nod without a word to accompany it…because the perfect approach still hadn't come to him. But "brooding and mysterious" was growing on him.

"You make a habit of letting your dog run free? You should try using the leash." Her lips were pursed, but he could see a smile creeping into her expression. She was warm and refreshingly down-to-earth.

He pressed his lips together and swallowed. For some reason, although she seemed to be joking, Everett felt the need to explain. "I, uh…only put the leash down for a second to tie my shoe and he made a run for it."

Sophia rubbed Blue's head, mussing his dark brown hair to his pure satisfaction. She lifted her chin and looked at Everett over the top of her nose, scolding him playfully. "Well…you take good care of my new friend."

"I'm sure Blue is pleased to make your acquaintance. He makes friends everywhere he goes." He squinted at his dog in mock disappointment. "If you ask him, he'll tell you this fine establishment is his favorite place. He's friends with the owner."

"Is that right?"

"Uh-huh. She bribes him with treats. Which is why he's sitting here pretending to be such a good boy. Huh, Blue?"

At the mention of the word "treat," Blue's tail wagged like crazy, and Everett lifted his brows to Sophia. *Case closed.* He proved his point, but now Everett needed to deal with a boatload of tragic whimpers and puppy dog eyes gazing up at him. "All right." He reached into his pocket and plucked out a Milk Bite, which sent Blue into a squirming frenzy.

As Everett lowered his hand to Blue, he shot an *I told you so* at Sophia, which earned him a soft, musical laugh and a prime view of the delicate line of her neck. He nodded his head toward the back of the store, where they could all see the owner was waving from the register. "Blue knows what he's doing."

Sophia gave the woman a quick once-over. "It's pretty low to blame all this on an innocent dog." She giggled, having way too much fun picking on him.

When the laughter died down, they stood there in silence, both looking at Blue.

But Everett was more afraid of how his body would react if he looked at her directly. Already he wanted to run the pad of his thumb over her full lips and trail his hand down the silky brown skin of her neck, not stopping until he reached her toes. His face burned. There was no denying he was attracted to her, which pissed him off. It was counterproductive, especially since his goal was to find out about her deal with Patton Place.

"Do you have a dog?" He was genuinely interested, but he was also eager to fill the silence.

She met his eyes. "No. I've always wanted a chocolate lab, though."

"Ahem."

When Everett looked up, another woman stood beside Sophia. There were some similarities around the eyes, but not much else. The woman who joined them sported big, curly hair, unlike Sophia's loose waves. Her skin was a little lighter, but it wasn't hard to tell they were related.

The woman stretched her hand between Everett and Sophia. "Since my cousin has apparently forgotten her manners, I guess I'll have to introduce myself." She shot Sophia a glare, then turned her penetrating attention on Everett. "I'm Julie. And you are?"

"This is the guy I was telling you about who was so kind as to serve me with papers," Sophia said loudly, carefully enunciating every word. Her eyes were wide, apparently sharing an inside joke with the other woman.

At this, Julie cocked her head at Everett, as if the information changed her entire view of him. *"This is the messenger?"* she shouted. "Damn. You said he was cute, but I didn't believe you since you usually have the worst taste in guys. But shee-*it!* You didn't tell me he's downright gorgeous."

A flush crept across Sophia's cheeks as her chin dipped to her chest and she froze. She fidgeted with her collar before lifting her eyes to meet his.

Everett bit back a laugh. He could see she was mortified, undoubtedly trying to figure out what to say that wouldn't further embarrass both of them. "Um. You'll have to excuse my cousin. She has no filter. Plus, she's very forward—" Sophia cut her cousin a sharp side-eye "—and also *almost married."*

On the outside, he was confident and cool, but on the inside he was giving himself high fives to the thunder of a roaring crowd. *She thinks I'm cute.*

"Engaged to be married." Julie clarified, winking at Everett. "Chill, Soph."

After a long and seemingly satisfying eye roll, she continued. "Since the two of you are just standing there like nervous train wrecks, seems I'll have to be the one who does all the talking. Now, Messenger. Mess. Again, what's your name?"

"It's uh...Everett."

Of course Sophia's quit-witted cousin didn't miss his hesitation. "Well, is your name Everett or not? You don't seem too sure about it. Should I be worried?"

"No."

"Okay, good then." Julie placed her hands on Sophia and Everett's shoulders to square them to each other. When they were face-to-face, she stretched Sophia's hand out. "Soph this is Everett. Everett this is Sophia." She grabbed Everett's hand and wrapped it around Sophia's. "Now you know another person in Portland, Soph, and you guys can be friends or...whatever."

A WAVE of people filled the sidewalk, edging Sophia and Everett close to the store window, where they squeezed into a small corner beneath the awning. As soon as Blue noticed their closeness, he snuggled up between them and Sophia watched while Everett endearingly ran his palm over the dog's soft head. But as she lifted her eyes, she also took note of a visibly harder head in Everett's jeans.

She bit back a grin and whipped around to see Julie wandering into the dog treat store before peeking up at Everett. "Do you, uh, know what's going on? Why all these people are here?" She craned her neck to see how many people were still crowding the sidewalk.

"It's the Foodie and Brewery Festival. They have it every year in June."

"Sounds amazing. I'm a full-on foodie."

A sheen of excitement illuminated his face. "Yeah? No kidding?"

Sophia felt a small zing of excitement settle in her chest. "I'm actually thinking about opening up a restaurant. It's why we're down here. I mean, we went to an appointment with my lawyer earlier and checked out a wedding dress shop for Jules, but now we're walking around checking out the empty store-fronts. I've only been here a little while, so it's kind of hard to know where to start. You know, in terms of what's a good area, if there are any other restaurants like the one I have in mind, foot traffic. You know, all the logistics."

"Awesome. What kind of food do you make?" He sounded genuinely interested, but the way he stiffened gave Sophia pause. It was almost like he didn't want to get too personal. But it was a little too late to worry about that—their bodies were pressed so close she could feel his breath and his heartbeat. She could smell his fresh scent, a mix of mint and ocean air.

Sensing his discomfort, Sophia changed the subject, but remained steadfast in her pursuit of small talk. "So...what do you do, Everett? I mean, is the courier service your main job?" Her voice was low against the harsh noise of the crowd. She glanced over her shoulder again. The sidewalk traffic was finally dying down.

When she looked back at him, he appeared to study her face. "I'm a real estate developer. Mostly commercial, but our residential end is growing."

"So you've probably lived here awhile then. You must know this place really well."

She could barely hear his answer. "All my life."

She waited, but he didn't say anything else. In the silence between them, suddenly Sophia became increasingly aware of her proximity, and in turn, of herself. Every nerve ending in her body stirred. The hair on her arms stood up, and though her posture was relaxed, her heartbeat pounded with an unsteady rhythm.

She craved to touch him—to close the narrow distance between them. She imagined how soft his honeyed skin would feel on her fingertips, him leaning into her gentle touch—and getting a good look at what was making that impressive impression in his jeans.

"So, Mess..." Julie barged in. "If you've been living here for forever, you can probably help us with two things. One, you can probably help us figure out a location for her restaurant. Maybe get us some information about the storefront we saw.

And two, you must know something about this guy, John E. Monroe, who's trying to steal my cousin's house."

Sophia snapped out of her daze.

Everett took a small step back, looking everywhere but at them while he slid his fingers under Blue's collar and tightened his grip. The crowd and the noise seemed to dissipate as Sophia's throat tightened and ached.

"Do you know him?" Julie pressed stubbornly, never knowing when to quit.

Sophia noticed the way Everett's shoulders tensed. He seemed to force a smile as he cleared his throat and centered his focus on Julie. "Uh, yeah. He's well known in Portland. What type of information you get depends on who you ask, though." All the emotion seemed to have drained from his voice.

Sophia didn't say a word, but she could still feel the weight of his stare as he turned to her.

Then, Julie let out a cynical gag? "What kind of sociopath doesn't have a picture online? Or, any social media accounts?" With the sidewalk all but clear now, she walked to the edge of the curb and allowed her head to fall back, seeming to absorb the sun peeking through the thin clouds.

Neither Sophia nor Everett moved an inch, but Julie was still running off at the mouth.

"He's probably some Scrooge who sits and counts his coins every day." She sighed loudly, releasing a frustrated groan. She lowered her chin and returned her attention to the two of them. "I mean, really. Where does he get off trying to swoop in and steal my cousin's house? If he thinks she's going to give it up easily, he's got another thing coming. Especially with the lawyer we've got."

Everett gave Sophia yet another thin smile before checking

his watch. Then he reached in his pocket, pulled out a gum wrapper, jotted down his phone number, and gave it to her before he clicked the leash onto Blue's collar. "I guess it's our cue. Come on, boy. It was nice meeting you, Julie." He flicked a glance Sophia's way. "And nice seeing you again, Sophia. I hope we can get together soon."

She returned his sentiments with a genuine smile. Sophia watched as he walked away, but he didn't look back.

CHAPTER 5

The Sunday after Julie left the rain finally let up for a few hours and Sophia was ready to take action on her dream.

A black Prius drove up to the curb and Sophia checked to confirm that the license plate number on the front of the car matched the details from the rideshare app. Through the window she waved at the driver Ahmed, a young, spiky-haired guy with thick brows and smokers' lips who looked similar enough to the nerdy picture at the top of her phone screen.

Sophia rang Kara to see if she wanted to go to the farmer's market with her, but she already made other plans. Apparently the time for wine-fueled boy talk and fun girly staycations was over. Kara was busy and Julie was back home in Vegas, so it was back to real life for Sophia. Which meant she needed groceries.

So here she was with Ahmed, who seemed nice enough, but not like they'd end up sharing recipes or texting on the phone all night. As she slid into the back seat and buckled up, he double-checked the destination and whipped his teensy hybrid car into traffic.

At some point I'm going to have to shell out the money for a car.

"Would you care for some music or a water?"

"No, I'm okay. Thank you, though. I'm just going to take in the sights." Sophia leaned against the door and stared out the window, hopeful Ahmed would get the hint that she wasn't in the mood to talk.

"Sure. No problem."

Outside, the city passed by in a blur of green and gray overcast day, but still she used her phone to snap a picture of a bridge among the clouds in the distance and posted it to Instagram. The caption read, *Rain, rain go away. Come again another day. Perhaps when I'm not headed to an open air #farmersmarket #portlandia #portlandfoodie*

Swiping to the rideshare app, she saw the estimated arrival time was thirteen minutes—enough time to just catch her breath. For four days she was an Energizer bunny, dragging herself around in nonstop fun with Julie and Kara. They ate out, shopped, danced, and talked till sunrise. Every morning, Sophia was positively buoyant about the prospect of the day, and every night she was love-drunk on having good girlfriends around to sample her new recipes and dissect the smallest little things about her new city life—although one way or another most of their conversations circled back to Everett.

Kara wanted to know every detail about him, and Julie was eager to describe him down to his very full, un-chapped lips. The amount of wine the two of them consumed while they scoured the Internet for his picture—and coming up empty—was obscene and impressive at the same time. They even searched for pictures of his dog Blue on the off chance Everett might be in the background. And even though they never did find him, Sophia reveled in the idea he was out there, in the same "weird" city, as the locals called it, while everyone vied for top honors in the informal keep-Portland-weird sweepstakes.

Why don't I just call him?

Based on the way his body reacted to hers on the porch the first day, and on the street last week, she harbored this sneaky feeling that behind his tight smile and his loose-fit jeans, he felt something for her too.

"Is it too cold in here?" Ahmed asked, yanking Sophia from her thoughts.

Sophia smiled and sat up straighter. "No. It's fine, thanks."

His tone was hesitant, but he seemed like he genuinely cared about his customers. "Not too much longer. By the way, this is Portland's best farmer's market. Make sure you hit the vendors in the back and try their biscuits. I promise you won't regret it."

"Thanks. I've never been, so I'll be sure to try them."

Ahmed returned his focus to the road and Sophia went back to her thoughts about real life. Which wasn't just about groceries, but suddenly also about lawyers.

Sophia was grateful Julie's friends rallied to help her find an attorney licensed in Oregon. Jacob Bornstein couldn't have been more than thirty-five, but he was graying already, although not a wrinkle marred his long, pale face. He wore a sensible navy suit, but he paired it with striped neon socks and tennis shoes. Right from the start, she suspected his unorthodox choice of footwear announced who he truly was to people who cared to notice.

And to say the guy was driven would be a gross understatement.

The walls of his office were covered with glass shadow

boxes full of autographed sports paraphernalia and framed pictures of himself with people who appeared to be members of his firm. Really, the place was chock full of all the things befitting of an up-and-comer. He seemed hungry for success and all the luxuries that came along with it. He seemed like a guy who watched way too many action movies with action heroes he idolized for being power players and score-settlers. And, lucky for her, not only did Bornstein know exactly who John E. Monroe was, he apparently was nursing a personal vendetta against Monroe's family.

She didn't have a clue where it stemmed from, but a few minutes into the meeting Sophia found out the Harmans and Monroes were basically a modern Portland version of the Earps and the Clantons—neither time nor space did anything to extinguish the flames of their families' hatred for each other. If anything, they seemed to be burning hotter the more time passed. And somehow, right on track with her luck, Sophia landed smack dab in the middle of the bonfire.

During their previous meeting, within seconds of handing Bornstein the Petition to Recover Property, Julie grilled him on what it meant as far as the validity of Monroe's claim. She wanted copies of everything from the date of the ownership transfer to the present. She listed off the deed, the guardian-ship and estate papers. She wanted death certificates. No stone would be left unturned. Before Sophia could think of anything else to add, Julie demanded Bornstein request a thirty-day extension.

Sophia gripped the arms of one of the uncomfortable modern wooden chairs facing the determined man across the desk. From what she gathered, in between piecemealing the conversation and watching Bornstein dance around Julie's questions, John Monroe was the guardian and executor for the estate of Barbara Monroe, John's grandmother. His claim contended that while John reconciled her estate he discovered the property was taken fraudulently from Barbara by Sophia's ex's grandfather, Henry Harman, nearly ten years ago.

By the time the appointment was over, Bornstein still wasn't sure where Sophia or Patton Place fit in John's master plan, or the Harmans', but given all the documents she and Julie provided, he accepted the retainer.

"I'll drop you here," Ahmed said, jolting Sophia back to the present. "This entrance is closest to the booths." Ahmed flitted a glance in the rearview mirror at her.

"Thank you so much. I'm sorry I didn't talk much, but I'll be sure to give you a great rating." Sophia stepped out of the Uber at the entrance of Shemanski Park.

The crowd was sparse, but there were still a good number of people and vendors out and about. As soon as she noticed all the full totes and bouquets, Sophia couldn't wait to immerse herself in the thick of things.

Near the entrance was a booth with barrels overflowing with eggplant and cabbage and cucumbers and kale and some vegetables she couldn't even name. The fresh, vibrant colors were inviting. Just the sight of them filled her head with new and different dishes she could make. There was definitely an extra bounce to her step as she walked. For Sophia, food was to her as paint or clay were to artists. No matter the ingredients, she could always make colorful art of a simple dish.

In this place, though, with all this inspiration, she could make a masterpiece.

Quickly, she grabbed her phone to snap a few pictures to send to Mom. Proof she was giving this city a real go. The farmer's markets in Vegas were improving, but could never match the beautiful, ripened cornucopia of this display. Snap.

Another two selfies, each with her smiling, head tilted to the right, her best side. Snap. Snap.

She aimed the phone at the farmer's market banner and centered it for the best angle. As she did, a small drop of rain landed on the screen, and she looked up to survey the sky. The sun peeked through the hovering clouds, warming the market and somehow elevating the sweet fragrances of flowers and food. Almost as a mainstay, a light drizzle began to sprinkle over the parade of canopies beneath the trees, but it didn't daunt her one bit.

Her fingers hovered over the keyboard as she typed a message to go with the pictures.

Sophia: Tell Otis I say hi. I'm out here making a life, singing in the rain, and picking good food. Hope your heart is open. Give him a real chance. XOXO Love you.

Mom: Love you too.

It was about as good a response as she could expect from her mom, considering she only knew how to do a glacially slow, one-finger jab text. Sophia smiled and tucked her phone away, unfazed by the weather. The more time she spent in this weird town, the less the rain bothered her. Somehow the air seemed cleaner, clearer. Certainly, cleaner than the dry desert heat of Las Vegas—clearer than her suffocating past, for sure.

Under no circumstances did she delude herself into thinking people in Portland didn't have to deal with the same kinds of problems she came with, but they just seemed freer. Here people weren't leashed to ideas of money and brands. They made things, grew things. They were holding up their end of the bargain with nature, giving as much as they took. More and more, she found she liked it.

She could see herself here.

Not because she was hung up on the newness of it all, but because she wanted to make something. Be a part of a community, which seemed to be in the middle of making the world a better place.

When she showed Julie the retail pad last week, something about having her cousin in her corner made the restaurant seem doable, and not so farfetched. There on the pavement Sophia imagined a small eat-in place, down to its bare bones, with one-of-a-kind recipes, where she knew her customers by name.

There'd be a Bob or a Lynn, and every time they came in, she'd ask if they wanted "the usual." And she'd know what "the usual" was by heart, because her place would be comfortable and familiar—the only kind of place she'd ever want to run.

Within twenty minutes of wandering the aisles of the market, Sophia purchased a tote with "Keep Portland Weird and Farmer Fresh" written on the front. It was perfect. Somehow it suited the new unbound version of her—new, improved, and a tinge kitschy.

It didn't take her long to load the tote down with two bottles of wine, one white and one red. Soon, a handful of the sweetest-smelling, vibrant yellow and orange tulips and fuchsia peonies, and an array of the earth's best fruit and vegetables accompanied them.

She'd just walked away from a booth boasting every kind of meat from chicken, turkey, and beef to yak, buffalo, and elk, with her own version of a sampler pack, when she smelled the irresistible aroma of fresh baked biscuits. She turned toward the mouthwatering smells, spotted a red umbrella and checkered tablecloth, and bee-lined straight for it. It was one thing to cook super-healthy food, but her nose knew no limits when it came to blowing the whistle on the hunger train.

"Oh. My. God. This is amazing."

With a savage bite and both cheeks full of warm, buttery goodness, she signaled a greasy thumbs-up to the bearded guy behind the table and closed her eyes in purest delight.

"They're the best, aren't they?" A deep, gratifying moan escaped her as a bass-filled voice interrupted her savoring.

Too stubborn to rush to swallow the biscuit, Sophia opened her eyes and stared, chipmunk-cheeked, at Everett standing beside her in all his splendor.

"Hello, friend." She managed a smile. "Funny seeing you here."

"IT IS, ISN'T IT?" An uneven smile flirted at the corner of Everett's mouth.

Sophia couldn't have known just how funny. It was not a coincidence, him being at the same place at the same time.

He started following her Instagram feed the day he served her with the hearing notice. More than anything it was a sparsely posted, collaged nutshell of her life. Mainly movies, bite-sized food, a lot of ice cream, family and friends, and throwback high school volleyball pictures. Then, in the last month, a photographer's dream portfolio of Portland.

When he saw her post today at the farmer's market, it only took him a short drive and a few aisles to find her.

And she was finally alone.

"How've you been? You never called." He let the words hang there between them, and he watched her wince at his bluntness. True, Sophia didn't call him, but he figured it was just as well. He didn't want to get confused about what he was doing with her.

Since he'd last seen Sophia, she'd been busy. This morning Mike told him about the extension, which he viewed as further evidence that she wasn't as innocent as she seemed. Although Everett needed more time with her to determine whether she was a pawn or a player, he still requested the denial of the extension. If she was a player, it was going to take more than a pair of wine-stained lips and midnight eyes to throw him off his game.

"I'm so sorry. I meant to, it's just my cousin you met—Julie —was in town." She frowned in consternation, her eyes wide. "She was here for four days, and we were packing in as much of the city and touristy stuff as we could before she left yesterday. I was her guide. Not that I know much about the place yet. Mostly downtown."

Of course Everett also knew this. Her cousin tagged Sophia and another girl online in an endless party-like story feed with celebratory stickers and hashtags.

At least he now knew she was honest.

"Is it your first time in Portland?" Everett nodded toward the loaded bags hanging from both of her arms.

He tried not to stare, but today she was absolutely mesmerizing. Adorable with her cheeks puffed out, full of...it looked like she'd raided the biscuit vendor...flushed with embarrassment. "Am I that obvious?" She threw her head back laughing, baring the soft curve of her neck.

Everett swallowed the remains of his own biscuit, genuinely enjoying the sound her laugh. He dusted the crumbs off his hands. "Can't say I've seen many locals stock for the season in one trip."

"Hey. I heard that." A playful grimace played across her face. "I *am* a local now. Remember, you came to my door?"

I wish I could forget.

He enjoyed her teasing, and he shouldn't be encouraging the feeling—he rather liked it, in fact, this playful side of her.

"Besides, this isn't like any of the farmer's markets I've ever been to. Vegas doesn't even come close."

As she spoke, he could feel her studying his mouth for the slightest moment, but it was enough to make Everett fall silent. Enough to force him to look at *her* mouth.

An obvious mistake, because he had to forcibly evict the image of her soft lips brushing his from his mind.

Instinctively, he licked his lips.

"Hold on a sec." Sophia squinted at him and scrunched her nose. "Do you mind taking a picture with me, for my feed? I really want my mom to know I'm getting settled and making friends."

It wasn't what he expected, and he had every intention of turning her down. What would Mike think if he saw a picture of him hugged up with Sophia? This was only the third time Everett had spent more than a minute with her, and already he was worried about the slight blurring of the clear line drawn between them. He was willing to do anything to save his grandmother's home—his family home—but something felt wrong about letting Sophia believe they were friends.

"Oh, no. I hate having my picture taken. I'm not photogenic at all. But if you want, I'll be happy to take one of you."

"Pleeezeee, I promise I'll only post it if we both look good. If you hate it, I'll delete immediately." She was looking up at him with those depthless eyes again, pleading, sexy, lip-biting. Her dainty hands pressed together in prayer.

Everett exhaled and let his arms slump by his sides. "Fine. Just don't tag me."

Sophia did a little shimmy, squealing with delight, her breasts bouncing. "Thankyou! Thankyou! Thankyou! You won't hate it, I promise. I'm actually pretty good. Or at least my food pics are fabulous."

Before, he could react to the shrinking distance between them or figure what she was about to do she lifted her free hand—loaded bags and all—just high enough to reach the side of his mouth. Everett didn't know whether to step back or lean into the warmth of her hand. "There. I got it for you. You were saving a little bit of biscuit for later," she joked. "As good as they were, I don't blame you."

Everything about her was easy and genuine, unassuming. Like she was completely unaware of what her proximity was doing to him.

Something about the innocent gesture left Everett unsettled. He was on edge. His whole body stilled and his heart paused for the tiniest instant. If his feet weren't rooted to the ground he would have stepped back or at least leaned away. Instead he stood there with a quiver in his stomach as a slight chill coursed through him.

Don't get caught up. She's still a Harman.

"Okay, say cheese." Sophia pressed her back against his chest and tilted her head up against the side of his neck. Her arms were outstretched, with the phone aimed down at them. On the screen the image of the two of them looked natural, like this wasn't their first time. Like they belonged together.

He examined every pixel, unimpressed with his ten o'clock shadow and thick brows. But at least he'd gotten a fresh fade and his teeth looked white. Sophia on the other hand smelled of sweet strawberries and cream and looked stunning without the least bit of effort. She puckered her pink lips. Her hair fell in waves over her shoulders, and, if he wasn't mistaken, there was heat in her dark eyes.

If he was really being honest with himself, they looked good together.

It was an image he wouldn't mind seeing more often.

CHAPTER 6

"See?"

Everett watched while Sophia studied the picture and then held it up for him to see.

"You look so cute. How can you possibly believe you're not photogenic? You could totally be a model for this farmer's market." She laughed and immediately quieted when she seemed to realize what she said.

"I mean...you look fine. You should have your picture taken more often." Her eyes were wide as she pivoted on her heel.

The awkward silence thickened.

"I...uh...should get going." Still he couldn't bring himself to walk away. "Unless you need a hand with those." It just felt like he should say *something*. "I think the circulation in your arms is being cut off from the rest of your body."

He laughed it off, but on the inside he was trying to gather himself—working to think with the rational head. Mike was right. She might be beautiful and sexy as hell, but this was his chance to gauge what he was up against.

He couldn't let a woman come between him and his family

home. This was about loyalty and keeping promises. The Harmans compromised both. If she was the only person standing between him and fulfilling his grandmother's last wish to reclaim the family property, Everett needed to know his enemy and her line of defense.

"Oh, my gosh. I thought you'd never ask. I feel like I'm carrying bricks." She smiled up at him, adjusting the bags on her arm to get out her phone again. "I better hurry up and call for a ride."

"Wait, you didn't drive?"

"I Ubered. This crazy idea entered my head to pick up some fresh produce for an amazing meal I was going to prepare, then burn a few calories walking back." She rolled her eyes. "Stupid, I know."

"Yeah. I'm still not sure why you thought it was a good idea." He joined in on the laughter at Sophia's expense. As she lifted her arms, Everett slid a few up his own arm and shouldered the rest. "What have you got in these things?"

She cringed. "You really want to know?"

"If I'm carrying these Santa sacks, I should at least get to know what's in them."

"Okay, but don't judge. I found my food processor last week, and I've been doing my market research and business planning, but now all I want to do is get my hands dirty. I'm planning on making this sort of stew with all kinds of meat. Throw in some red wine with a little gorgeous eggplant. Some bell peppers and rice—"

He interrupted Sophia's recipe, coming to a halt in the middle of the aisle. "Bell peppers. Damn. I almost forgot the bell peppers." He awkwardly fished in his pocket, balancing the bags, and brought out a crumpled piece of paper. "My sister. She gave me a list."

Sophia stopped just ahead of him. "Sounds like someone who knows her food."

"Please. She's pure drama. Miss one item and it's the end of the world." Everett threw his free hand up in exasperation. "Next thing you know I'll have a refrigerator full of food I don't know what to do with because she'll insist she can't make the meal without whatever it is I forgot."

"I like her on principal alone." A smile lurked at the edges of Sophia's mouth.

And there go those lips again.

Everett picked up his stride, browsing the vendors in search of the crucial bell peppers—anything to get his mind off those full, kissable lips. Bell peppers. "And it's never regular stuff normal people would know," he continued. "It's always something oddly specific, like horned melons or fiddlehead ferns. He rolled his eyes in mock annoyance. "She's actually asked me for both of those at one time or another."

He pulled Zora's list out of his back pocket and scanned it. There were ten items in all, and green female bell peppers were the only items he hadn't crossed off yet.

Sophia peeked over his shoulder. "May I?"

He stared at the list as he angled it toward her, trying to make sense of it. "See, this is what I'm talking about. How am I supposed to know the difference between male and female bell peppers? They're all green. It's about the extent of my knowledge on them. Normal people's knowledge."

She did a little bounce, and he thought she might actually break into a skip. "Actually, you're in luck. I happen to know the difference." She gave a smug nod, evidently pleased to be one of the abnormal people who knew the sex of a vegetable.

Or is it a gender? Is it a fruit?

"And...despite this being my first time sampling this lovely

Portland tradition, I happen to remember a booth with a great selection of both. This way, kind sir." Then she did a sort of skip-hop, stepping in front of him.

"After you, madame."

One aisle over and three booths down, the two of them were gaping at crate after crate of green bell peppers. Sophia picked up a couple of them, seemingly at random, and then turned them upside down and pointed out the number of bumps on the bottoms. She explained the female peppers were the ones with four bumps and were seedy, sweet, and better to be eaten raw, while the three-bump ones were male and tended to work best for cooking.

Everett was officially mind-blown. She might as well have just told him the earth was flat after all. "Get the fuck out of here. You're kidding, right?"

"Nope."

"Why do you know this?" He laughed. "No, seriously. I need to know why."

Sophia doubled over in stitches, but when she righted herself, Everett's stare did not waver. She smirked and lowered her chin in a coy, faux-humble move. "Did I mention I'm a renowned chef?" She promptly corrected herself. "Well, not *renowned*, but I can hold my own in the kitchen."

"Sounds like more than a dream in there somewhere, Sophia Kent. What the heck are you doing in Portland, then? You could be somewhere like New York or LA with your own restaurant. You could've stayed in Vegas at some five-star restaurant in a Strip hotel."

It surprised him. He didn't know what her food tasted like, but he didn't doubt her statement. And now, even more than before, he needed to know why she was here.

Why Portland?

"Honestly?" she asked, and he nodded, genuinely needing to know the answer. "There's a part of me in the house I can't let go of."

Everett paused for a moment to pay for the bell peppers before turning to her.

"I saw the boxes through the windows. How can you already have ties when you just moved in? And who would want to...steal the house from you?" The words wounded him to even say aloud, but the urge to ask overtook him. He needed to know what she knew. What or who was her tie beyond Austin Harman? And what part of her was in Patton Place that she couldn't walk away from?

"It's complicated," she muttered. The crease between her brows deepened, and Everett couldn't help but notice the easy innocence drained from her face.

"And this hotshot lawyer your cousin mentioned? Has he made any progress?" Even asking the question felt dirty and underhanded. If she wasn't loyal to the Harmans, Sophia was at an unfair disadvantage. More and more, he was learning exactly who she was, but she still hadn't figured out she was confiding in her own enemy.

"We'll see. I meet with him again tomorrow." Her voice was solemn, laden with worry. Almost as if the gods knew there weren't many more good places this conversation could go, the sky opened up and rain poured down onto the canopies, funneling water over them. Sophia dug into one of the bags Everett was holding for her and got out an umbrella. "Can't be too prepared. Want to come under?"

"Can I give you a ride home?" *Please say yes.*

She smiled with a resigned pucker of her lips. "If you don't mind."

"Not at all. My truck's not too far from here." Everett

ducked under the cover of her umbrella, trying not to think about how good it felt to be so close to her. He led the way toward Park Ave as they shuffled through the crowd. "Do you like basketball?"

Sophia gave him an incredulous look, though apparently grateful to have an end to the thick silence. "You may or may not believe it, but I'm a Lakers fan. It's been hard since Kobe left, but I still have faith."

She quickened her pace to match Everett's stride. "I'm waiting for the pendulum swing. They always come back every few years."

"If you want to save your stew for another night, maybe you'll want to join me for the game tonight. The Trailblazers are no Lakers, thankfully." He grinned, picking up the pace again. Her bags weren't getting any lighter. But when Sophia still didn't agree, he threw in the kicker. "My sister, Zora, and my friend Mike will be there, too."

She stopped mid-stride and asked, "The fiddlehead fern sister?"

Everett met her wide, magical eyes. "One and the same."

"Oh, yes. Count me in."

AFTER DROPPING SOPHIA OFF, Everett went straight back to his place. He was home less than ten minutes before Zora was all over him like white on rice. She scrutinized his every move as he took the groceries out of the bags, then proceeded to take over, as if he wasn't doing it fast enough or up to her standards. Then Mike not-so-discreetly offered to help her...which in and of itself was suspicious.

From the moment he walked in the door, he'd caught the

side-eye stares and hushed whispers between them. Now all of a sudden they're the awesome twosome? No way. Neither of them could do subtlety if it killed them.

"What's going on with you two?" Everett lifted his brows at Zora and Mike.

"Seriously Ev, I don't think the dentist has ever seen this much of your gums, and you're asking *us* what's going on?"

The ride to Patton Place couldn't have taken more than fifteen minutes, but it felt like a lifetime with Sophia only inches away from him. Aside from talk about the weather and Blue, they mostly drove in a comfortable silence save for the low hum of the radio. The whole time it was all he could do not crawl his fingers across the seat and entangle them with hers.

Everett could feel himself still grinning now, but at Zo's question, he cleared his throat and knitted his brows together. "What are you talking about?"

A rogue bell pepper fell out of the bag and Blue, who was splayed out on the floor. wagged his tail, leaping to his feet to sniff it. Everett swiped it from beneath his buddy's wet nose. "You don't want this." He mussed his chocolate brown fur baby. Unable to resist those big, sad eyes, he got out one of the gourmet dog cookies he bought at the farmer's market and bent down to give it to him.

Remembering his train of thought, he turned the spotlight on them. "I could ask you guys the same thing." Just the idea of Mike and his sister together was unsettling. For one, Mike was a player, and two, if they teamed up against him, game night or otherwise, he'd be the odd man out. But both of them could do worse. Even Babs had known there was something between them since they were kids.

As Everett stood and replaced the green pepper on the

counter, he bit back a laugh. He prayed he wouldn't think of Sophia every time he came across a four-bump bell pepper.

"Mike? Since when are you Mr. Helpful in the kitchen?" He looked back and forth between his friend and his sister. "And Zo? You don't have any demands, no wisecracks about what I picked up at the farmer's market? There's always something. I've just been hanging here twiddling my thumbs, waiting for the other shoe to drop."

Why am I being so defensive?

Even as he said it, guilt bubbled up inside him. He was deflecting and he knew it. But he couldn't let on to them about the war brewing inside him when it came to Sophia. He slipped past a guilty-looking Zora and grabbed a beer from the fridge.

"Uh..."

"Oh, this is one for the books. My bossy little sister is speechless. Now I know something's going on." He gave them another glance, shaking his head, trying to stifle his ear-to-ear, full-teeth grin as he strode out of the kitchen into the living room.

Everett settled onto the couch, remote in hand, prepared to turn on the television. For a second he'd almost forgotten he invited Sophia over to watch the game. A mix of nonsensical nerves and annoyance pummeled him. Yes, he wanted her to be comfortable enough to talk so he could get to know her, but what did it matter what she thought of his house?

Why did he suddenly care if she liked it?

When it came down to real estate, he could spot a jackpot on a street full of money pits. He could reconstruct, rebuild, and renovate like nobody's business. But deep down he knew when it came to making it an inviting place to live he only considered the basics. His house was well-built with top-of-the-line cabinets, fixtures, and gadgets, but it was bare. It was strong and clean, but plain. There were no decorative finishing touches. Nothing warm and fuzzy about it. Black and gray were about as good as it got in terms of his ability to experiment with color and texture. As far as paintings and accents making a house feel like a home went, he didn't have a clue.

Maybe because no house other than Patton Place had ever felt like home.

He reminded himself this was why she was coming tonight. Nothing else.

Everett shook off thoughts of Sophia and looked over his shoulder into the kitchen, where Zora and Mike were still standing around the island. They were locked in the middle of a telling look. Her brows lifted. Mike's eyes unnaturally widened. But it wasn't sweet and endearing like they were pillow-talking. They were...conspiring.

Mike and Zora shared a slight nod before they realized Everett's attention was trained on them. He turned and squared his shoulders, quiet for a moment as he read the situation. "What is going on between you two? Is there anything I should know?"

He thought his question would be met with fierce denial and backtracking and he'd get a good laugh. Everett could care less if they finally decided to be together and quit tiptoeing around, like it made any difference to him.

But, it wasn't what happened.

"See?" Zora pointed at Mike. "I told you."

"You told him what?"

Everett studied the way they stood on either side of island. Zora was beside the sink, while Mike stood in front of the barstool on the other end. Between them, a mammoth slab of granite nearing five feet in width. They weren't too close. On the contrary, what Everett found disconcerting was the distance between them.

Before he could ask any further questions, Zora cocked her head and smiled at him. "We were just wondering about your little trip to Shemanski."

We. Ugh.

"What about it?"

"Okay, before you go off the deep end, hear me out. Usually you take, what, fifteen, twenty minutes at the farmer's market? It's like you can't wait to get back. It's either the rain, or the crowds. Last time, it was the smell of the meat at the booth in the back. I can't shut you up about your list of gripes, right?" Zo held up her hands, palms down, signaling for Everett to be patient with her.

He nodded impatiently and sighed. She was allegedly getting to the point.

"Today, though? Not a peep. Not one word. You've been gone for hours. And..." she sang out the word, holding one finger up. "And. You got exactly what I needed. Every vegetable. Perfect. Ripe. Beautiful." She pressed her hands on the counter and lifted herself up onto her tiptoes on a level of excitement it seemed she could hardly contain.

"So, we think you might have solicited some help. Maybe from a newcomer to this little town?" Zora went straight for the juice.

Dammit, Mike!

One mention of a good-looking woman and he was all ears, and apparently mouth. Couldn't keep a lid on it.

Zora and Mike mirrored each other with smug grins smeared across their conspiratorial faces. It could have been an evasion tactic to steer Everett away from his suspicions about the two of them, but his sneaky little sister had ways of putting her feelers out. Ways of knowing when anything remotely good happened to Everett.

Is this good?

He needed to say something. Otherwise Zo would count his silence as an admission. Whatever he came up with, it better be good if he was going to stand any chance of going up against a woman who knew him inside and out and a lawyer.

Avoidance seemed his only real chance of escape. Everett glanced at his watch, then over to the television, grinning like an idiot, but he couldn't hide it. "You better hurry up with whatever it is you're making. The game is coming on in like an hour."

On a volume level only meant for small dogs and insects, Zo released a high-pitched squeal. It seemed to erupt from every part of her body. "Yes." She shrieked. "I knew it. Where is she?"

It was pointless to deny the effect Sophia had on him, especially to these two, but Everett refused to just cave. No matter how futile. He stood and made his way past Mike, who it seemed had decided to keep his thoughts and hands to himself for the time being rather than risk a beating worse than the one already coming.

"Who, exactly, are you talking about? I went to Shemanski by myself." He laughed despite himself.

"Ev, seriously? You're going to act like I can't see right through you? With the goofy grin?" She planted her hands on her hips and looked at him sideways. "Ugh, you're killing me. You might as well spill."

He cracked his IPA open and threw his head back in a long satisfying swig. Half the fun in this was seeing her squirm. He knew every second he withheld, Zo was growing ever more impatient. With a mischievous smile, he came up for air again and shrugged. "I don't know what you're talking about."

Take the hint.

"So that's the story you're sticking with? You really want to play it like this? Because I have ways of finding things out. I have resources." She paused, but if Everett thought it was the end of it, he was sorely mistaken. "Mike?"

Blue's head popped up and his tail began slapping against the tile as his eyes flickered between Mike and Zo. Rather than get involved, Mike raised his hands in surrender.

"Okay, Mike. I thought we were on the same team, but now I know where we stand," she said. "I was going to play nice, but since you assholes are sticking to your little man code—Everett, Mike already told me you got all soft for Sophia Kent, so quit playing."

Everett slouched into the cushions of the couch and turned the TV on. "Why don't you ask her yourself when she gets here?"

CHAPTER 7

The image of Sophia's face on the phone screen was zoomed in close enough to see the pores on her nose and cheeks. God she hated how FaceTime always gave her a funhouse mirror look with her forehead elongated and her eyes so close together.

She took a few steps back until the camera framed her entire body.

"You know Portland has like fifty million farmer's markets, right?" Julie's voice sounded like she was talking around a mouthful of grapes.

"Actually, I didn't know." Sophia was so happy to have one nearby, she hadn't thought to see if there were any others.

"Either way, let's get this straight." Julie cleared her throat and then the image on the screen bobbed up and down until she appeared to have propped the phone up. She was farther away now, and Sophia could see her cousin curled up in the bed. She was getting comfortable for whatever point she was about to drag out. "It was raining. You and Everett's fine ass were just standing there with no umbrella, basically all up in each other's faces, dripping wet, talking about the female anatomy of a fucking bell pepper? Then he asked you to come watch basketball at his house? With his sister?"

Give or take a few details. That's about the size of it.

Sophia gave a noncommittal yes, deciding it was easier to agree than go through the infinite details of her cousin's editorializing.

Julie squinted at her, seemingly determining how else she might torture her. "Okay, yes. Then this is definitely the dress to wear. Turn to the right again."

"Did I tell you I talked to Mom today? She still won't stop sending the countdown emails. I shouldn't have told her I was filing for my business and food service licenses. It's sent her into overdrive. But she did admit things are going okay with Otis."

"Girl, you should see those two canoodling and holding hands and stuff. They went on a double date with Mom and Stan last week. She won't admit it to you, but she's so into him."

"Good. Maybe she'll stay out of my love life. If I ever get one." Sophia inched to her right per Julie's instructions. "Can you see it now?" she asked, shifting slightly until the bite-sized image of her appeared at the top right corner of the screen. Her phone was propped on top of three books on top of the bed, facing her, as Julie tilted and turned her head on the screen. It didn't take a stretchy funhouse mirror version squeezed into the frame of the phone for Sophia to see the dress was far too tight.

Still, after she saw the Instagram photo of the two of them, Julie insisted on approving her clothes for her visit with Everett. So, while Sophia primped and preened for her on FaceTime, Julie judged and nixed just about everything in her closet. They were either too loose or too homely, or just plain frumpy.

"Yes, I definitely think this is the one. Might get you a love life tonight."

Sophia groaned. Of course Julie would vote for the article of clothing most closely resembling dental floss. Sophia preferred comfortable clothes with some semblance of class. Something loose, so, say, if she dropped her purse and needed to pick it up, the hem wouldn't hike up and put all her goods on display.

"I'm thinking this one is a definite no-go. It's got groupie written all over it. Besides, this is the sixth outfit I've tried on. I'm going to stick with my jeans and T-shirt."

Much to Julie's chagrin, Sophia was sticking to her guns.

"Oh, my gosh." Julie expelled a lungful of air. "You have no clue how to play the game, Soph. You've got to dangle the right bait if you want to catch the right fish."

Ever since Julie locked Nico down, anyone would swear she wrote the how-to book on dating and marriage. There were still about two months before they would walk down the aisle in late July, and already she was the authority. Although it was true, Julie and Nico's relationship was the sweetest thing ever.

Suddenly Sophia lost the motivation to put on airs. "Well, if the right fish wants to catch my bait, they better know what they want, with or without all the shiny frills."

She wanted to be comfortable and relax, and maybe make some new friends. This was what she'd always hated about dating. It was too much work. It required too many outfit changes. All the more reason why she agreed to something so low-key. It was a basketball game. On television. In a house. "It's the Trailblazers. Game four of the finals. I'm not going clubbing."

The dress was red and skintight. Didn't exactly say kick back and relax. "And anyway, how's he going to concentrate on the game if I'm wearing this...thing?" She spat the word, "thing," as if it tasted nasty.

"All's fair in love and war."

"Correct me if I'm wrong, but one does not wear a skintight red Band-Aid of a dress to watch basketball." Sophia shifted on the bed, tugging at the scant hemline. As she fell back onto the mattress, she leaned her phone against the pillow at the headboard so she could still see her cousin.

"One does, if one wants to catch Everett, which one should, if one was not blind and crazy."

The thing was, Sophia wasn't entirely sure she did want to catch Everett. He was kind of cute and obviously chivalrous, but she wasn't sure she really wanted to put her heart back out there on the line. Especially with the whole house situation and Mom probably conspiring with the universe for her speedy return.

"What kind of woman wears a skanky dress to watch basketball? Really?"

Julie didn't have any qualms about her answer. "Hopefully the kind who puts out." Her picture began to shake and a loud rustling noise came through the receiver. Sophia could see the walls pan by in the background until the screen went black.

"Ew, that's just nasty. His sister and his friend are going to be there."

"Not in the living room, fool." Julie's voice burst through the darkness. "Go in his bedroom. Turn up the TV, and use a pillow to muffle your moans," she whispered. "You need this."

"I don't even know what to say." Nasty wasn't even the word. Not the part about having sex with Everett. Sophia could totally imagine that part. But she felt dirty just thinking about his friend and sister down the hall, trying not to hear her screaming in ecstasy. She brought the phone closer and squinted at the screen. "And what the heck are you doing? I can't see you anymore, and now I can barely hear you."

"Shh. I'm in the closet. Now keep it down."

Sophia lowered her voice and watched the dim lit picture of Jules come into grainy focus. "Why are we whispering?"

"I'm hiding from Nico. I don't want him to hear us."

"Why? He doesn't know you're a freak already? I mean, I'm not going to ask, and I'm not going to judge, but you sound like you're speaking from experience, nasty." Sophia teased. "Did you put out on the first date with Nico?"

Julie's face might as well have been pressed against the screen she was so. "Come on, now. Please. Are we talking about the same guy, here? The messenger?" She sucked her teeth. "Shit, if Nico hadn't come along, I would've taken the position up there in Portland so fast and landed me some sexy-ass messenger Everett."

In the distance, Nico's voice echoed through the phone.

"Dammit. He knows I'm gone," Julie whispered.

"Again, weirdo. Why are you hiding from him? Is this some kind of strange engagement hazing ritual, or do you guys always act like five-year-olds?"

"Unless you want him getting all up in your business with detailed questions, then be quiet," Julie whisper-yelled. "If he hears us talking, he's going to have all kinds of advice. He'll be trying to Google this guy. He won't find anything because I've already done the digging. Just...don't even go there."

After that hiss/whispered mouthful, it was no surprise Nico found her. A door swung open and the screen flooded light into the closet where Julie was hiding.

"What are you doing? I didn't know where you were." Nico's shaky voice vibrated with worry.

Sophia could see his legs from the knees down, then his arms as he lifted Julie up onto her feet.

He must have seen the phone's illuminated screen, because the next thing Sophia knew, Julie was being interrogated about why she felt the need to talk on the phone in the closet. In seconds flat, he went from anxious inquiries about her safety to suspicions of cheating.

Before she knew it, Julie was telling Nico the whole story about Everett. No detail spared. Down to his dog and her exaggerated estimates of his...uh...personal measurements, Julie clued Nico in on the man. She either didn't care that she'd left Sophia hanging on the line, or she'd completely forgotten about her.

But some ten or so minutes later, both of their bright-eyed smiling faces appeared in the camera.

"Well, thanks. Since we're all up to speed on Everett, can we please get back to me?"

"Are you wearing that?" Nico asked.

His tone was level and even, but the inflection on the end? There it was. The judgment. The label. People always said what's on the inside counted, but the flawed human need to categorize kicks in and there it is. The Look. It says women who wear tight dresses to watch basketball games are asking for it.

"I don't think so."

Nico's brows gave the slightest jerk upward.

It said it all. She wouldn't wear the dress.

"Yeah. No matter what his wishy-washy tone says," Julie interjected. "Nico and I both agree you need to go ahead and dust off the cobwebs. Asshat didn't have shit on this guy, and he certainly didn't have any rhythm."

"Would you please not bring him up?" Sophia said with a little too much edge in her tone.

"I'm just saying. Ask Liz. The best way to get over an old guy is to get under a new guy. Just think of this new guy as a gift to your vag. It'll be so happy."

Sophia couldn't help but laugh at her crazy cousin. But, all this talk about her vag, and sex, and Everett, left her running hot under the collar. Her stomach clenched and she squeezed her thighs together.

"He is pretty delicious, isn't he?" Sophia admitted.

"Yes, so please. I'm begging you, for my sake as your cousin, and as a personal favor to your dusty vag. Please don't wear the baggy Lakers shirt and those raggedy jeans." Julie's face twisted into an exasperated grimace.

Maybe not the Lakers shirt...

Sophia looked up, staring at nothing in particular. She imagined herself face-to-face with Everett, the way he would be looking at her with hungry eyes. He'd meet her curbside and open her door for her, only to see the dress. Except— "But it's still raining."

There was nothing sexy about freezing in the rain. Goosebumps were not the best look for a sort-of first date.

"And you don't own a dang umbrella? I know you have a trench coat," Julie said. But before she could get the rest of her thought out, she seemed to latch onto an idea with iron claws. "Yessss! Better yet, wear just the trench coat and nothing else."

Sophia heard all she needed to hear from "the authority." Hah! Julie was the authority on how to be a groupie tease. So much for her help. All she'd done was activate Sophia's raging libido. Now, while she should be comfortably watching basketball with a group of new friends, she was going to have to do everything in her power not to jump his bones on sight.

A pair of skinny jeans and a long sleeve, button-down striped T-shirt later, Sophia's driver crept down a tree-lined street and stopped in front of a gorgeous split-level Craftsman-style home with window boxes full of flowers.

Even under the cover of night, through the glistening translucent mist, she could see lush, richly colored shrubs. She couldn't be sure whether the house was blue or a light shade of gray, but there, beside the green door under a dense canopy of maples and elms were the house numbers he'd given her.

Just to be sure this was it, she compared the map app on her phone to the address Everett texted earlier.

This was the right street.

She rolled down the window and craned her neck out to get a better look at the place.

For some reason she couldn't quite pinpoint, she couldn't imagine him living in a full-fledged family home. He wore jeans, but the brands were high quality, with even higher price tags. His truck, though it was clear he used it for work, had a custom paint job and all the premium accessories, which didn't scream family man.

The house was beautiful, and probably showcased all the luxuries anyone would want in a home, but somehow she'd imagined him living in something modern—some kind of contemporary loft or a high-rise.

This place? This was where people raised kids. People who lived in these kinds of homes threw dinner parties and spent their summer holidays on the water.

More than anything, Sophia couldn't imagine a bachelor living here. Especially not an excruciatingly hot bachelor with only man's best friend as his roommate.

Hell. He's probably got a girlfriend. Or, a fiancée. Oh, my good-ness. Sophia's breath shallowed and her heart pounded against her ribcage. *Hence the reason his sister and his friend are coming. He's just being nice.*

Oh. My. God.

Sophia sat back in the seat with her head pressed firmly against the headrest. "Shit!" she said aloud, only then remembering she wasn't alone. "I'm sorry."

The driver, a young guy with glossy black hair and blinky eyes, turned to face her. "Is this it?"

She was still deciding whether to tell him to take her back home or suck it up for one night, still trying to convince herself it was just a get-together. To just go in and make some friends and keep on keeping on. "Yeah." She breathed the word, getting it out before she could change her mind again.

But she still didn't get right out. Instead she peeked at the Craftsman once more, pumping herself up to do this—to see Everett again. Only when it was too awkward for her to keep stalling, she grabbed the bottle of merlot she'd chosen from the wine cellar and got out of the car.

As her rain boot-clad feet squelched toward the front door, she absorbed the peaceful sounds of crickets chirping and flashes of lightning bugs twinkling. Nightfall did not do the sprawling lawn any justice. Up close, Sophia smelled the sweet perfume of roses and azaleas and wisteria, and the slick, stone-paved walkway was peppered with fallen petals and sun-washed leaves. But the house itself hovered over her, grand and even farther-reaching than it seemed from afar.

She got so caught up in the garden landscape and the gape-worthy sight before her, she nearly ran into a woman. "I'm so sorry," she said, trying to maintain her footing on the slick, wet ground.

"You must be Sophia." The woman was bubbling with excitement, completely unaware of Sophia's silent prayer this was indeed his sister and not some girlfriend Everett failed to mention.

A forced smile crept at the corners of Sophia's mouth as her eyes darted down to the woman's left hand. No ring. An audible exhale escaped her as her eyes fell on the woman for the first uninterrupted moment. She was stunning. The same flawless brown skin as Everett's, with hazel eyes. In the place of what Sophia imagined would be sweeping, long locks was a sexy, sweet pixie cut styled in the latest trend of spikes and tapered edges. She was exactly the kind of cool woman who made women want to be friends with her and men fall all over themselves for a chance to be with her. Down to her boho bell-bottoms and threadbare, sleeveless tee, her grace and class were only enhanced by endless style.

Please be the sister. Please be the sister.

And now she wished she'd taken Julie's advice and worn the red dress. Maybe she would have a fighting chance over this bohemian goddess, if by some horrible stroke of luck she wasn't the sister.

"Hi," Sophia managed. "This is for you." She handed over the wine, but it took Sophia off guard when the goddess gave her a tight hug.

"Come on in. I'll take your coat." She tailed Sophia into the house. "You're right on time. Ev and Mike are in the kitchen."

As Sophia stepped into the house feeling a little lighter, she let her trench slide off her arms as she took in her surroundings. Out of nowhere a blur of brown fur came rushing toward her. "Hi, Blue." She crouched down and mussed the dog's short hair. His tail whipped through the air as he nuzzled into her hair. "It's nice to see you again, too."

"I see you and Blue already know each other. I don't know where my manners are. Here I've been talking to you for five minutes and haven't had the decency to tell you my name." She bounced on her toes and stretched her hand out. "I'm Zora."

Hallelujah.

Sophia got to her feet and went in for another hug. "I'm so glad to meet you. From what Everett told me about you, you share the same love of food I do. I can't wait to pick your brain."

"Should we go uncork this?" Zora asked with a nod toward the kitchen. But then she turned and stared at Sophia like a bug was on her.

"What?" Sophia asked.

"Oh, my gosh. Are those Hunters? I *love* them. They're on my list." She looked down at Sophia's feet, then back up to her eyes.

Sophia turned, blushing. "Thanks. Yeah. I got them a while ago." She glanced down at her navy patent leather rain boots.

"Ev! These are the exact rain boots I want for my birthday. Take notes."

As soon as Zora yelled "Ev!" Sophia turned, and there was Everett. She'd seen him only a few hours before, but somehow, in some inhumanly impossible way, he was more handsome than she remembered.

Her mouth fell open, but words refused to roll off her tongue. Instead she pressed her lips together in what she hoped was a warm smile, for fear anything else might give away the fact she was practically panting like a dog in heat on the inside, thanks to Julie and all her sex talk.

"Noted," he said to Zora while his eyes remained locked on Sophia. "You clean up well." He closed the distance between them and gave her a light kiss on the cheek.

Oh, the stars! His lips were as soft as she imagined, and it took every ounce of her self-control not to turn her face and taste them. He was still talking. Something about fajitas and a tip-off, but she couldn't get past the warm, tingly spot on her cheek where Everett's full lips grazed her skin. She'd gotten a whiff of his clean, minty, ocean scent and a close-up view of the way his clothes clung to his lean, muscular body.

Suddenly, she was hyper-aware of him and what his presence did to her. Her heart raced and her skin pulsed. And for a quick second she seriously considered blaring TVs, moan-muffling pillows, and a gift to her vag.

IN NO TIME AT ALL, Sophia warmed up to Zora. The two of them, and Blue, were three peas in a pod. The women talked about city life and food, of course. As soon as the topic of the farmer's market came up, they agreed bell-pepper-gender nonbelievers just didn't know what they were missing—and likely couldn't cook. Meanwhile Blue might as well have been in Sophia's lap, at least if he'd gotten any closer. *Traitor.*

Everett sighed. The urge to do something overwhelmed him. He needed to get her alone. "Sophia, did you have enough to eat? There's plenty left if you're still hungry," he said, getting to his feet. "Or I can get you another beer."

She looked up at him, and he saw something behind those eyes he couldn't decipher.

"Uh...no. I'm okay, thanks."

He stood there for a second. What else could he say? *Meet me in the kitchen so I can finally get you alone, because my sister's been hogging you all night?* "Sure. No problem. Just...let me know."

What the fuck was that? Let me know?

Before he could do or say anything else embarrassing, Everett stalked into the kitchen and got himself another beer. Purposely, he leaned on the island and stood right in his sister's line of vision, so when she looked up, he shot her a death glare. One he'd given her many times over the years. Apparently an effective one, too, because Zora excused herself and ambled into the kitchen, all wide-eyed and raised shoulders until she was standing beside him.

"What? What did I do?"

On the screen, the Trailblazers shot a buzzer-beater from half court to close out the half. Everett ground his teeth. "Who's she here to see? Who invited her here?"

He didn't have to look at Zora to feel the wide smile spreading over her smug face. This was exactly what she wanted, probably part of her plan. "I thought you told me to ask her myself." She tilted her head toward him, but he refused to look at her gloating smirk and raised brows. "I thought...there was nothing to spill. So, what you're saying is, Mike was right? You are going all soft for Sophia Kent."

"What's there to spill, when she and I haven't had a moment alone so I can get to know her?"

Zora's giggle bubbled up, and it was all he could do not to stick her face in his armpit and make her say uncle.

"Admit you like her and I'll see what I can do about arranging some quality time for the two of you." Now Zora squared her body to him and folded her arms. She was positively glowing with I-told-you-so as she bit back a shit-eating grin.

"Fine." *Uncle.* He sighed and rolled his eyes, practically pouting. "I'm interested. Hope it makes you happy. But, it's not what you think." Bold-faced lie. Whether he wanted to admit it or not, Sophia Kent affected him. She bothered him, and awakened something dormant within him. Just being near her made him feel unhinged, unsure of how to be or what to say. Her warm eyes and the soft curve of her cheeks drew him in. With every word she spoke, he wanted to cover her lips with his and feel the low rumble of her laugh against him.

"She's Austin Harman's ex-wife. Sophia Kent is living in Patton Place. That's why she's here." Everett turned to Zora now, a pointed expression on his face. "Mike thinks it's a 'birds of a feather' type thing, but I still don't get the same vibe. I'm just trying to feel her out, see where her head is. I think she's the one being played."

Zora's hand flew to her mouth and her eyebrows were practically in her hair. Her mouth was wide open, but she said nothing.

"Yeah. Exactly how I felt, too. I couldn't believe it, but Mike is so hell-bent on her name. He can't get past the fact she was married to Austin. You know how he is. *Once a Harman, always a Harman* to him. But I don't see it with Sophia. What do you think? You're the one whose been talking to her all night." Everett pinched the bridge of his nose and waited, but when he looked at his sister, it wasn't the flabbergasted, shocked expression from seconds earlier.

Her mouth was still open, but her brows were dipped into a deep vee. Not shock—disgust. "What the fuck are you doing, Ev? Does she know who you are? That it's been our family home for generations?"

He didn't expect Zora to go right for the gut. All the air rushed out of his chest—gut punch.

CHAPTER 8

"**D**amn, Zo. I'm not doing anything shady. I just want to know if she's like them or not. Can't you understand where I'm coming from? I don't want to be the one who helps a Harman wrong anyone else. I've been looking over the documents, and I'm pretty sure the only thing she got out of the divorce was the house. Austin knew we were in the right and we'd get the house, so he set her up and let her think she'd won."

Zora closed her eyes and exhaled, deflating against the counter. "That's just so fucked up. I've always known he's an asshole, but how do you screw someone you once promised to love forever? That's low, even for a Harman."

She got lost in her thoughts, staring off into nothing. But then she squinted her eyes at Everett. "Man, I can't believe this is the reason you've been stuck in your head. I thought you were probably still reeling about the email from Joe."

"Wait, you know about the email?"

"Yes, fool. He sent me an email too. I just don't let it ruin my whole world like you do. He said most of the stuff has your name on it, but I know Babs's recipes are there. They're all I really want, but you better figure out if you're going to get her box. I'm pretty sure it has some papers she wanted you to have and her ring."

Everett rested his face into his steepled fingers. Zora was right, but it didn't change anything about his feelings toward Joseph and his family. Or the house. He couldn't just go there and act like everything was all right. As if for most of his life the unwelcome mat hadn't been left out, and aimed specifically at him.

From the island, they watched while Mike talked to Sophia, but he and Zora stayed in the kitchen. Everett couldn't wrap his mind around Sophia's situation. And now the prospect of setting foot on Joseph's property left him feeling uneasy. He couldn't make out what Sophia and Mike were saying, but she looked uncomfortable. Her posture was rigid, and she was fidgeting.

Everett moved to go back in the living room, but Zora grabbed his arm.

"There's just one thing I don't get." She narrowed her eyes at him. "The Harmans are loaded. Why is the house the only thing she got in the divorce? Did she ask for anything else, or was it all he let her have?"

The same question had nagged at Everett since they met on the porch at Patton Place. What was in the house she couldn't let go of—what was so complicated?

"No." The sound of Sophia's voice jolted Everett from his thoughts.

He slowly moved toward the living room, Zora on his heels. Mike was leaned back in the chair, angled away from the television. Every point on his body faced Sophia, his breathing deep, slow, and measured. His sharp chin lifted as he stared at her with narrowed eyes, appearing to size her up, read her.

Everett knew Mike's guards were up when it came to Sophia. To him, she was the enemy, a willfully blind outsider who couldn't begin to understand family, loyalty, and what it meant to own property in the Pacific Northwest as a person of color. She was an interloper, and he was treating her as one.

But what did he say to upset her?

Sophia clasped her hands together and shot Everett a nervous smile while Blue stood guard beside her. Mike's face was blank, but something in his eyes seemed off, the way he blinked slowly, holding Everett's stare before turning back to Sophia.

Dammit. Don't mess this up, Mike.

"You're here with us, in my friend's house, but we don't know anything about you," he said. It was blatantly aggressive and unapologetic. As he leaned in toward Sophia, with his elbows on his knees and his hands clasped beneath his chin, while she rubbed Blue's fur and shifted in the seat. Worry glazed her eyes.

Everett should have stopped it. Wanted to stop it, but he needed to know. These were his own questions being fired by Mike's lethal lawyer's tongue.

"What I want to know. What we all need to know"—he gestured toward Everett and Zora, his jaw muscles rippling —"is what brings a woman to Portland alone? You don't know anyone. You have no ties here, and the house is all you've got."

Sophia clutched her purse and stood. Everett knew she was justified, but his feet were cemented in place. He wanted to hear her answers. Maybe if she met him halfway. If she would just tell them the truth, they could get past it. Maybe she was tied to the house, or it was dream or something. Whatever it was, he hoped it wasn't about the money. Because it if wasn't, maybe...just maybe...they'd be free to get to know each other on a deeper level.

Sophia's eyes met his, begging him to rescue her. Be in her corner. Tell Mike he was wrong.

But Everett didn't move. He stood at the entrance to the living room, on the cold, hard kitchen tiles, watching. Heart pounding. Mind racing. Blood storming through his veins. His muscles like lead. He was stuck in panic's grip while those dark, deep, luminous eyes blinked, giving way to a stream of tears as she ran for the front door.

"Ev? What the fuck?" Zora cursed him as she ran after Sophia. She grabbed her coat and followed Sophia through the door, leaving it ajar.

Everett ran his hands over his face and through his hair. "Fuck." He clenched his fists. What did he just do?

Through the open door, a cool whisper of air whipped through the curtains and the sound of rain tapped against the windows. He could see his sister outside on the porch with Sophia. He could hear her sobs, but he couldn't see her.

The strangest feeling overcame him. It was as if everything would somehow be all right if he could just see her face. Surely he'd get lost in her eyes, but the truth would be there.

"I shouldn't have come," she said. "I don't know why I came." The sound of muffled cries between shallow, hitched breaths came through the door.

"Mike is an asshole." Zo consoled her. "Don't worry about him. And my brother? He really is a good guy. He just has a hard time showing it sometimes."

Lightning cracked, loud and sharp, and the dark sky behind Zora lit up briefly. "I'm so sorry. You came here to make some friends, and we made you feel unwelcome." Zo drew Sophia into a hug. "Please don't leave."

The side of Sophia's face lay on Zo's shoulder, but her red-rimmed eyes found Everett's through the door. As he walked toward her, he focused on her and only her.

His voice obscured by the rain, he muttered, "I'm sorry. Please stay."

Zora released Sophia from their embrace and eyed Everett with warning in her glare.

"Please stay," he said again, once his sister was gone.

Sophia's chin dropped to her chest. "Is it true what he said? Do you feel the same way about me?" she asked. It was a simple and honest question, but pain smeared her face into a blur of fear and anxious anticipation.

She was waiting.

When she lifted her eyes, he knew there was nothing else he could do. He slipped his hand behind her, to rest on the small of her back, guiding her back inside. He still didn't have the answers, but deep down, as he met her gaze, Everett already knew what he needed to do. Straight-faced, he lied.

"No."

THE NEXT MORNING, Sophia shimmied on a pair of jeans and a T-shirt and whipped her hair into a messy bun. After gliding on some pink gloss and adding mascara, she dropped her shades over her heavy lids and dragged herself to her appointment with Bornstein. Her bedhead look better be good enough, because she could barely keep her eyes open.

She'd stayed up practically all night trying to make sense of what happened the night before. Why was Mike being such a dick to her?

He'd been aggressive and his questions were straight-up rude. The only reason she stayed as long as she did was because he was Everett's friend. But even friendship only got him so far.

'What brings a woman to Portland alone? The house is all you've got.'

Ugh.

Thinking about it, she got pissed all over again. Where did this random guy get off interrogating her? Seriously, *we don't know anything about you?* Obviously. It was the whole reason she went there in the first place, to get to know new people. It took a lot of talking, raised voices, and firm "no's" to talk Julie down from flying back to rip Mike a new one when Sophia told her about it this morning on the phone. Heck, even Everett was at risk of Julie's wrath until Sophia mentioned the ride home.

Everett refused to let it go. He apologized for the way both he and Mike acted, insisting he and Sophia try hanging out again. This time it would be just the two of them over coffee. And soon. He didn't want to wait, so they settled on noon at Revolución off Sixth.

She couldn't deny the thought of seeing him again, of a do-over, made her giddy. She bit back a grin and pressed her hand to her cheek. Her skin still blazed where his lips brushed lightly over it.

"Something you want to tell the class?" Bornstein asked, a cold splash to startle Sophia out of the warm memory.

"Uh...I was just thinking about the restaurant I'm going to after this meeting."

The amusement in his eyes said he didn't believe her either. Although now Sophia was thinking about funny stuff she didn't plan to share with the class, she gave him a once-over. His suit was still pristine, but gray this time. And while she should have been squarely focused on whatever updates Bornstein reported about the petition, at the moment all she wanted was a glimpse of today's socks.

Before it threw her off, but today for some reason his crazy sense of style soothed her nerves. Like he was going to fly his freak flag as high—or as low—as he wanted because he had zero F's to give about what other people thought of him. The last pair were neon stripes. And this was Monday. Something told her starting a new week was just the occasion he needed to go hog wild with his foot accessories.

She cleared her throat, inhaling before she slouched against the hard wooden chair, tilting her head to the side to get a glimpse beneath the desk. A little lower. Bam!

Sure enough, dad sneakers and purple socks dotted with mini red and yellow pizza slices.

She barely managed to stifle a giggle. "I love your socks."

Sophia guessed the deadpan expression was supposed to make her think he didn't care one way or the other, but the little lift of his chin was all she needed to know he was pleased. This was the Portland she was slowly falling in love with—the teensy details and quirks.

Bornstein flipped through the pages stacked in front of him and stopped a quarter of the way down, adjusting himself in the chair. "This isn't going to be easy." He scratched the back of his neck and straightened his posture. His chin was high, but it put her further on edge.

Her stomach was all tied up in knots and she felt dizzy for a moment. "Should I be worried?" She uncrossed her legs and re-crossed them, trying get more comfortable, but it was useless. There was no way she'd find comfort in any of this. If anything, the only solace would be to gather as many details about this Monroe character as possible and see if she could reason with him herself.

CHAPTER 9

In so many words, Bornstein said this was mostly about reclaiming ownership, loyalty, and family for the guy. All things she could get behind. After all, weren't they the same things she wanted? At least that was what Sophia thought she was trying to do—for her, and for everything Ainsley meant to her.

It's not like she was trying to deprive anyone else. The house meant those same things to Sophia.

"It doesn't look good," he said, again. "There's no point in sugarcoating this. We have a case, but *he* has all the cards."

"But the house is listed in the divorce decree." Even to her own ears, Sophia sounded breathless and desperate.

"I'm not saying a quitclaim deed is worthless, but we need to be realistic here. He has the original deed to the property, and our motion to dismiss has been denied. Monroe's got an edge going for him, if only because he's got time on his side, but he hasn't won—"

"Yet," Sophia snapped back and immediately felt like an asshole. "I'm sorry." She wasn't mad at Bornstein. He was on her side—her only hope, really. But the whole situation felt hopeless. She knew nothing about real estate and deeds and petitions. They were all foreign to her because Austin usually took care of the paperwork and told her where to sign.

Bornstein leaned back in his chair, crossing his arms. "Denial of a motion to dismiss doesn't mean he's been awarded anything," he said soothingly, seemingly catching on to her tendency to jump to conclusions.

"We've got our work cut out for us on this. The deed is important, but it's not what worries me most," he said, slow and measured.

"There's more." It wasn't a question. It was acceptance. What she expected all along. She ran her hands along the nape of her neck and turned away, waiting for him to just say what he had to say.

The window, spattered in raindrops, gave only a blurred view of the sun covered in a blanket of clouds and mist. Sophia listened for the most worrisome part, as one after another, the drops streamed down like tears.

"Barbara Monroe was seventy-three and showing signs of middle-stage dementia," he said.

Sophia sighed and closed her eyes. She didn't have any idea where this was going, or how it related to her, but Bornstein was right. At the mention of the word dementia, her worries expanded exponentially. Nothing about this felt like it was going to be easy.

"Before she died, as her power of attorney and guardian *ad litem*, John Monroe was in the process of having her clinically diagnosed. He has letters from physicians signed prior to the date of the deed transfer." He spoke softly and carefully, the way people do when they explain grave situations to children.

Although he couldn't have known just how fragile the situation was for Sophia. She could still remember hearing her mother in the other room talking to a friend, unaware Sophia was listening. They were drinking wine and playing Pokeno, when Mom laughed. "Lord, it's like Charlie has dementia," she'd said. "He doesn't remember a damn thing about where he came from. Old fool. Up and leaves his wife and daughter, and to do what? Find himself out in the great big world? No, nothing. That's what. Can't remember a damn thing. No clue where he's going, either. We're better off without him."

But they weren't. Nothing was better without him.

He erased himself from their lives, took everything with him, and Sophia learned to rely on herself.

The silence enveloped her as she blinked back tears, never saying a word as she allowed Bornstein to continue.

"The time limit for Action to Recover Real Property in Oregon is ten years." He let the words sink in for the faintest moment. "This is bigger than claims of rightful ownership. We're talking about mortgage fraud and elder abuse. These are criminal implications."

"What?" She gasped. "Against me?" She felt life a knife had been rammed into her back. "I had nothing to do with my ex's business affairs. I mean, I just got the house in the divorce settlement. This is fucking crazy."

Her heart pounded at the thundering of her own voice, and her blood raced with a mixture of anger and defeat. What was she even doing? Did this house mean enough to her for her to be willing to jump through so many hoops?

She hadn't signed up for this.

If Sophia wasn't certain before, she was now, more than ever, sure Austin was behind everything.

Fraud? Elder abuse?

Her mind didn't work the same way, but Austin was definitely a *by any means necessary* kind of guy. Easily, and without an ounce of remorse, he would take down anything or anyone standing in the way of what he wanted. He was spelling it out for her. Whenever it came to a head between Austin and Sophia, she always came in second. He made sure she knew she would never make it anywhere worthwhile without him—and would never get anything from him.

Tears continued to burn her eyes as she stifled a sob, heat rushing to her neck and cheeks.

A stark white blur crossed her line of vision as Bornstein handed her a box of tissues. She yanked one out and dabbed at the corners of her eyes, swiping beneath the lower lids for any traces of smeared makeup.

"Listen, Sophia. Right now this is a civil suit. We've still got three weeks until the hearing. I've requested closing documents from the mortgage company and the health records for Barbara Monroe. We're at a disadvantage at this juncture, but don't write us off just yet." Bornstein's tone was even and matter-of-fact, but gentle.

Sophia's eyes were still lowered while she absorbed his comments. The fight ahead of her suddenly felt real, tangible— its grip tightening around her. She swallowed hard, gulping back the catch in her throat. She sat taller despite her insides sinking. "What should I do?" she asked. "I can't just sit back and do nothing while this guy takes the only thing I've got left."

A severe expression smoothed the lines of his face. "We have to prove there was no fraud. Either we come up with an original deed, or show beyond a reasonable doubt that Barbara Monroe was of sound mind at the time of the transfer."

Just the thought of it made her feel tired to the bones.

He sighed loudly, lost somewhere in his head. "Might as well be the Hatfields and McCoys all over again. The Harmans and Monroes have been at each other's throats for generations, competing and stealing. Land, houses, women." He leaned back in his chair and pressed a finger to his top lip, staring at Sophia. "This all started over a woman. Maybe we can end it with one."

Wait a second. Bornstein also mentioned the family feud at the last appointment. He could work on getting the documents his way, but she'd rely on her own instincts. Maybe what she'd been missing in her search was what started the grudge.

First she'd do a little more digging about Barbara Monroe.

Next, if John Monroe was anything like Austin Harman, she'd follow the money and the inflated ego.

Shouldn't be too hard to miss.

EVERETT SAT in the far corner of the coffee house. He'd managed to nab two seats at the bar facing the street and already ordered one large black coffee, no sugar, no cream. It was still an hour and a half before he expected Sophia.

"You've got thirty minutes. What was so important it couldn't wait until later?" Everett swiveled on his stool and leaned his back against the bar. "And what happened last night?"

"Oh, you mean when you just stood there with your mouth hanging open while I asked Austin's wife the hard questions?"

Everett narrowed his eyes and crossed his arms.

"Whatever, man. I didn't come here for this shit." Mike shifted his weight onto his hip and hauled out a wad of rolled papers from his back pocket. "Since the motion to dismiss was denied, she's up against the wall. She's either got to prove there was no fraud, which is going to be damn near impossible considering we have the original deed, or she has to prove Babs wasn't in the middle of her battle with dementia."

Everett tucked his feet beneath the footrest and let his weight teeter. He opened his mouth to speak, then immediately thought better of it. Somewhere in this rant he hoped he'd hear an actual update.

"Listen, man, all I'm saying is they've got nothing, and we've got three weeks to coast until this hearing. So what do you want to do?"

Everett's chest tightened as heat crawled up his neck to his cheeks. "Do? What do you mean, what do I want to do?"

"That's why I'm here. It's not just about the house anymore. The deed was sent to you by Austin Harman, which basically removes him from the equation, but it still leaves Sophia and the Harman Estate," Mike trailed off.

The way he settled back on the stool, overdoing the casual air, it was hard not to notice the cocky tilt of his head and the smug jut of his chin. It was an intentional pause, a pregnant pause.

"Okay. I'll bite." Everett shot him a pointed look and held his cup closer. Slowly, he savored the robust aroma of his dark roast, then sipped.

Mike must have noticed his curiosity, because he was no longer sitting at a bar while Everett drank flat, lukewarm coffee. The attorney in him reared its devilish head as he let the silence drag. He was in a courtroom, zeroing in on the infinitesimal doubt still lingering in the back of Everett's mind when it came to anything related to Sophia.

At all costs, Everett was determined to avoid his friend's knowing stare. He cursed under his breath. "Try to get to the point sometime today." He released a deep, weighted sigh.

Mike drilled down his list of counts in his favor. "You were seeing red, you wanted this so bad. I could see it on your face every time you visited Babs at the hospice. You said someone would have to pay for what they did to her. And I'm saying it's not too late."

A hardening in Everett's stomach paralyzed him while he replayed the days and nights of those last few months of his grandmother's life. Instead of helping her remember their Christmas traditions or her favorite donuts from Ed's bakery, he'd been in and out of doctors' offices, working to get her legally declared. He was the one stuck with pawing through piles of paper and medical records, her things—all the little things that made up her life.

The Harmans kicked her while she was down.

He wanted to sag, but didn't dare with Mike-the-shark watching him. "What about the estate?" He took the bait.

"Henry Harman is dead, but we could prove his history of targeting elderly homeowners with financial difficulties. He promised to take over the payments and allow Babs to stay in the house. At least five other similar claims were settled out of court. Who knows how many more people there were? How many more didn't come forward?"

Everett struggled to find the right words. "And Sophia?"

It seemed lost on Mike, but Everett could hear it in his voice. The small inflection. The unmistakable tinge of hope. Though he didn't owe it to her, deep down Everett needed her not to be involved. He needed to not be wrong about her—for the tiny flip in his heart to not be wrong about her.

"Honestly, I don't know if she was involved," Mike reluctantly admitted. "What I do know is I started doing some digging into Austin Harman's personal and business finances, both before and after they were married. There were similar claims against him long before she showed up, but one in particular stood out."

Mike skimmed through the unrolled papers he'd brought with him and took out one from the middle. He took a long swig from his cup, his Adam's apple bobbing as he swallowed, and slid the page in front of Everett. "An accusation of embezzlement was reported to a local Las Vegas news station. Guess who the tip came from?" He pointed to a line toward the top of the page.

It wasn't Sophia's name, but the words "the accused's wife" glared back at Everett.

Everything in him slumped. "Sophia."

For some reason he couldn't fathom, a hesitant pang struck through him at the taste of her name on his tongue in such a compromising context. The questions stacked like bricks, rebuilding the walls around his heart.

He didn't know why, but he couldn't look at Mike at first.

"A quickie move. No family or friends here. Then there's the mystery surrounding why she's hell bent on living in such a huge house for one person."

Everett looked at his friend now. His attorney.

A satisfied smile settled on Mike's face as he covered the seed of doubt with fertilizer and mulch. "Makes you wonder who's really trying to remove themselves from the equation."

It took Everett ten minutes after Mike was gone to text Sophia. He needed more time.

Everett: *Hope I caught you in time. Can't make this after-noon, but how about dinner tonight?*

Her reply came quickly. *Dinner tonight. Patton Place.*

CHAPTER 10

"**I**s everything all right, Everett?" Sophia asked.

Across the table, he gave a tight smile that failed to reach his eyes. His mouth was full, but still she expected more than another half nod. It was the latest of about five or six he'd given her since he arrived. All in all, he'd managed a few "fines," a couple of "goods," and an especially rare "um hmm" between bites of boeuf bourguignon.

In her spare time this the afternoon she started her search for information about Barbara Monroe, and actually got a few nuggets about her relationship with Henry Harman. Still on a high, she'd cleaned and cooked up a storm in anticipation of Everett's visit to the house.

In the back of her mind she imagined the night unfolding differently. They'd ended the evening on such a good note the day before, and when he replied immediately to her invitation it was reassuring. Tonight, though, his silence took her off guard. Sophia hoped he wasn't freezing up again.

What happened between last night and today?

Unblinking, Sophia stared at Everett pointedly and allowed

her silverware to clank loudly as she placed them beside her plate. The second he took his last bite she stood and blew out the two standing candles at the center of the table.

"I'll take your plate. I don't want to keep you." She seethed, picking up his dish and padding to the kitchen before he could respond.

No sooner did she turn on the water, Everett appeared on the other side of the center island.

"I had a nice time." She barely heard his low whisper.

It took everything in her gut not to lash out at him. A nice time? "Oh. Did you?" she asked. *Let's see how you feel about a few goods and fines.* "Good."

"Sophia?"

Something about the urgency in his tone tugged at Sophia's heart against her will and she looked up at him.

"What really brought you here? To Portland, I mean?" he asked, his tone on edge as if this was the question he'd being dying to ask.

Her heart raced and her throat closed. She couldn't seem to catch enough breath to reply.

"I served you the papers, so I know how you came upon this house, but what's keeping you here? There are restaurants everywhere, so I don't buy it. You have no family and no friends here. And what about this place? It's huge. Way too big for one person. So I'm asking you again, and I hope you'll be honest with me. What brought you here, Sophia?" Desperation chased his words. "Or at least why are you making this particular place your home?"

He stood there with his arms folded.

She'd been asking herself the same question since she turned the key. Her mom and Julie, they'd questioned her, too. And she even had a stock answer: I have to do this on my own.

To an extent it was true, too. She did need to learn to rely on herself, but not because anyone said she couldn't. Because life had proven it to her over and again. It taught Sophia that loving completely only left her hurt in the end, weakened her. And she was still paying for her weakness. But this house, if she could be here and make it on her own, it meant she was strong enough—without Austin, and for Ainsley. *She* was, simply, enough.

But the same question coming from Everett, she wanted to answer him. Somewhere deep down inside her, she needed him to really understand the depths she'd crawled out of to make it here.

"You really want to know?" Sophia's voice broke, shattered by raw emotion. For so long she hadn't allowed herself to linger on the reason. Inside, she warred with herself. Who was Everett to her, and why did he deserve to be let in? Would he understand?

This time he didn't nod. He uttered a simple, "Yes."

In silence, they climbed the winding stairs until they reached the landing. Sophia led Everett to a closed door on the right. With her hand clasped around the knob, she paused briefly and looked at him, willing herself not to turn back now.

The memory of darkened, honey-brown eyes bored into her, urging her to open the door. She'd brought him this far, but all she could think about was what he would think of her after. It felt strangely like she was on one of those crazy, adrenaline-driven game shows. In the midst of her frenzied nerves, she'd volunteered to share with him the whammy she'd kept hidden behind door number one.

Sophia opened the door and switched on the light.

She watched while Everett walked into the pink-walled room with the yellow polka dot accents and stopped next to the untouched, pristine white crib. All the simple, necessary things with a few luxuries sprinkled in. Her mother's rocking chair. The plush yellow duck with the rosy cheeks. The ruffled-edge quilt with Ainsley's monogram embroidered in pink satin thread.

"This is it. This is my reason." Sophia shrugged, biting back the rising lump in her throat.

Everett exhaled as if he were still taking it all in. He ran his hand over his hair, figuring. "You're pregnant. That's why you're here?"

"No."

"I don't get it." Everett pinched the bridge of his nose and squinted at Sophia from under furrowed brows. "Why wouldn't you want to be near your family, your friends, your support system? It can't be easy going through all of this alone."

She swallowed hard. "Everett, I'm not pregnant...anymore." The last word was a whisper, the last straw.

Glossy eyes met his.

"I'm sorry. I'm such an asshole. I didn't know. I just saw all this stuff and figured..." With every inch of his sunken shoulders and crestfallen expression, Everett seemed determined to atone. Recognition and understanding sharpened his focus on Sophia.

She ran her eyes along the lines of the chevron-patterned rug. "When I got pregnant, Austin and I decided we were going to move here and put down our roots. He'd been working so much, and I could feel we were growing apart. This place was going to be more than a house. It was finally going to be a home...you know what I mean?"

Everett gave her a reassuring smile.

Sophia sighed and walked over to the changing table beside the crib, where a few folded blankets were stacked. "I moved here first to get things ready for the baby. Her name was Ainsley," she said, straightening and smoothing the pink chenille blanket on top. "I got to be her mommy for about twenty-nine weeks, but then I got preeclampsia, basically high blood pressure. Runs in my family on my dad's side. With the level of stress I was going through with my now-ex, my body wasn't strong enough, and she was a stillborn."

She swallowed hard and exhaled, pushing a loose hair behind her ear then turned to face Everett with a forced smile. "Anyway, I didn't mean to get all depressing on you, but it's just, this is the only home she was ever a part of. I never prepared anything in Vegas. I just assumed we would be here."

"I'm so sorry, Sophia. I didn't mean to pry."

"It's not your fault. Don't worry about it." She fingered the gold-winged, pink pearl charm on her necklace, holding it up to him. "She's still with me all the time."

Without a word, Everett closed the distance between them and hugged her. Kissed her hair gently.

And with his heart beating next to her ear, she felt her wall coming down.

For a brief, sweet moment he held Sophia there, absorbing her warmth and the softness of her skin against his. But as her heartbeat slowed, his seemed to synchronize to the same staccato rhythm. They clung to each other, unmoving, until her sobs subsided.

Everett no longer doubted for a second that Mike was wrong about her.

"I'm sorry."

When they slowly parted, they paused when their faces were only inches apart. He met her gold-flecked gaze first, then trailed down to her full, bee-stung lips with traces of the red gloss she'd worn earlier. Suddenly, the urge to touch them was too great and, without thinking further, he leaned in and pressed his lips gently over hers.

He wanted to quiet her nerves, make her feel better, but all he'd done was open his own floodgates.

A toxic combination of anger and desire combusted within him. She was the only woman he wanted, and he was the one man she couldn't trust. His skin prickled with anticipation. He could barely control his breathing in the face of his overwhelming need to protect her from everything she'd already gone though.

Everything he was now putting her through.

The urge to back away ticked inside him, but with Sophia so close, he wanted to stay, and let his hands run wild over her body. He wanted her in a way he'd refused to let himself want anyone in a long while. Somehow, in spite of the short time he'd known her, more than anything he wanted her to want him.

Goddamn, Mike. Why did Everett let him get into his head?

He kissed her softly now.

Everett didn't want to be another person who betrayed her. She didn't deserve it. She didn't deserve to be lied to by him. As he peppered her lips with small pecks, tasting her sweetness, it occurred to him the kiss was one-sided, and he hesitated, but the second he began to withdraw, he felt the urgency in Sophia's lips pressing back.

A fierce heat warmed his insides and spread south.

No. "No," he managed.

He gently ended the kiss, and Sophia's eyes snapped open, desire darkening their brown irises. The kiss ended, but he could still feel the warmth of her, shallow breath soft and steady, brushing against his chin.

Then Everett lifted his chin and stepped back.

"Thank you again for the dinner. It was delicious." He flexed his fingers, then balled them into fists, cracking his knuckles as he bit the inside of his cheek. "I'm going to get going now. I'll just let myself out."

As much as he wanted to, he didn't have the nerve to turn around. Not at the nursery door or the front door. Not as he climbed into his truck and drove away.

An hour and too many whiskey cokes to count later, the broken look in Sophia's eyes finally began to fade from Everett's mind.

"Jack. Give me another one," he slurred to the bartender.

"Okay there, big guy. We're going to have to cut you off." Jack was the slender, tattooed woman with a shock of black hair standing a few feet down the long, glazed mahogany bar. From what Everett could still see, her arms were ripped and those skintight little black short things she wore gave more than a glimpse of the junk in her trunk. And her rack? Every time she leaned over the bar to set down her drink orders, he'd gotten the bird's-eye view.

"You booting me out?"

She gave him a crooked smile. "You don't have to go home, but you do have to get the hell out of here," she crooned loudly over the din of the neon-lit room. "Want me to call someone for you? A cab? Uber?"

Everett laid his head on his folded arms on the bar top and closed his eyes. "I've got a big, big, big problem."

The bartender scooped ice from a freezer below and poured it into a line of three or four glasses he could see from where he was sitting. "And what's that, hon?"

"I don't think I'm going to make it." His eyes fluttered open and shut again. "I need help."

She appeared in front of him with her hands on her hips. "Well that's for damn sure."

"I've got blue...balls," he slurred.

This time, the woman erupted with laughter. "Well, here's a new one on me. I guess you're just going to put it all out there in front everyone, huh? You're such a hot mess, Ev," she managed through a fit of giggles. "About all I can do for you is give you a Dixie cup and show you to either the men's room or the exit."

"I need help," Everett mumbled again.

His barroom confidante squinted her eyes, as if considering how to counsel him. She took the towel hanging from the side of her waistband and began wiping down a wet spot on the bar. "If it's so bad, there's at least two thirsty women in here whose eyes have been on you since the moment you walked in. I'm sure you wouldn't have to do much to get their support. Hell, the one with the red hair might help you out in the restroom right now."

Everett didn't look to see which women she was talking about. In fact, he ignored her comments altogether and continued enlightening her with his current dilemma.

"This woman. She's gorgeous. I'm talking even without a stitch of makeup. Got the kind of flawless, smooth skin you just want to touch. Soft-spoken. Moves like a goddamn gazelle." He grimaced. "I've got to wear boxer briefs just to keep my friend down there under control."

"Ah, so there's a woman behind your royal blue balls?"

"*The* woman." Everett jolted upright. "Second I'm near her —" he pinched his index finger and thumb together "—I'm all over the place. Can barely put two words together into a proper sentence because I'm thinking about basketball and polar bears, trying not to get a hard-on."

Jack scanned the room before returning looking back at Everett. "So what's the problem? "She's not into you?"

"What's the problem?" He clapped his hands together in exasperation. "I'll tell you what's the problem. She's the enemy, that's what's the problem. Montagues and Capulets. Hatfields and McCoys. Same shit. We're not supposed to be together. We want to two different things." He sliced two fingers through the air. "Cut from two different cloths."

Everett closed his eyes and shook his head. "Besides, this kind of thing never works out. Starts off great, but eventually you end up not being enough and they move on to the next person. Passed up. Replaced. So why even go there in the first place?"

Again, the way it did in Sophia's sad, tragic nursery, the image and sound of Everett's mother weeping filled his mind. Joseph hadn't thought twice about leaving his wife or his kids. He just moved on. Found a new family.

His eyes popped open, and Jack was staring at him with a smarmy smile.

"I'm sorry to tell you, bud, but you've got it *bad*, my friend. Sure you don't want the Dixie cup?"

CHAPTER 11

Sophia: Is everything okay? I've been trying to reach you, but I haven't heard back. Hope to talk to you soon.

This was it. Hint taken. Sophia drew the line at three texts. If Everett didn't want anything more to do with her, so be it. Because she was *not* desperate. She'd just...give it ten minutes.

She stepped to the edge of the sidewalk, out of the way of passersby, hiking the bag of ice cream pints tighter under her arm as she thumbed through the icons on her phone. She tapped the one for settings and scrolled down to messages, swiping on her read receipts, just in case, before checking her most recent messages received. There was nothing wrong with her phone, but she did have a new message from a 503 number she didn't recognize.

503-555-0437: Hey, it's Zora. Want to go to a bar tonight with a couple of friends and me? 7:30 at La Moule. Let me know if you want to come with.

Slipping her phone back in her pocket, Sophia turned down Broadway headed toward the post office, still deciding. A girl's night out did sound like fun. Maybe she could invite Kara to join them. Based on her last conversation with Kara, she was about as tired of driving around all day to make ends meet as Sophia was of dealing with the whole house debacle.

But, as fun as it sounded, it involved Zora, Everett's sister. They'd be laughing and drinking, having a jolly good time, then inevitably he would make his way into the conversation and there would go her night. Besides, she had a date with some mint and chips ice cream and the new horror flick on Netflix with the killer clown.

Dang it. What is the name of that movie?

Sophia hauled her phone back out to check the app and absently looked up. She walked aimlessly toward the post office to drop off a package return and somehow ended up right in front of the vendor pad she'd shown Julie as the perfect place for her restaurant. It must have been a sign.

It might have been the coincidence making it feel like there was magic in the air, or the daily emails from Mom, counting down to Sophia's imminent return to Vegas, but a fire lit in her belly, and the thought of calling the number on the sign suddenly didn't seem like such a bad idea.

She punched in the numbers.

"Hi, yes. I'm at your building downtown off SW Broadway and saw your sign in the window. I'd like to inquire about leasing," Sophia said, wringing her fingers as she paced. She stood in front of the vacant pad in a dilapidated plaza. It wasn't much to look at now, but from what she could see, it embodied everything she wanted. It was a quaint, comfortable place to serve up bites of home cooking with a bit of a Vegas twist.

"Yes, thank you so much. I'll hold." A bluesy rendition of a Coldplay hit played in the background. As she waited to be transferred, she admired the modern architecture of the building. Slipping the phone between her ear and shoulder, she cradled both hands on the window to block out the glare as she peered through the glass at the exposed ceilings and brick walls. Based on the glass display cases and ornate shelves, it could have either been a nail salon or a clothing boutique.

It definitely wasn't part of Portland's upper echelon of retail pads, but the place spoke to her. What she saw were good bones. Her imagination immediately went to work filling in her mind's blueprints with a row of bistro tables alongside the far-right wall and family-style seating intermixed. She imagined colorful pendant lights and local art warming the atmosphere. And maybe a fireplace to give it a cozy, welcoming feel.

"Thank you for calling Monroe Properties, this is Mike. How can I help you?" The man's voice echoed a deep bass and rang vaguely familiar to Sophia, but more than anything, she couldn't shake an eerie feeling that coiled around her when she heard the voice.

"I'm sorry. Is this Monroe Properties, as in John E. Monroe?" Sophia squeezed her eyes shut. *Please say no.*

"One and the same. Kendra said you were interested in leasing our SW Broadway pad, correct?" Sophia's breath lodged in her throat and sort of hung there. "Hello? Are you still there?"

Mike.

Well, no wonder.

A shiver of recognition coursed through her and she could

feel her eyes bulge and her mouth fall open. She was more than a little light-headed and chilly. The world narrowed for a moment and she was in one of those cold, sketchy-looking, horror flick hallways that stretched farther away by the second. One minute it was the buzz of fluorescent hospital light dark around the edges, and the next, boom! The bad guy smack dab in front of her. *Holy shit.* If this Mike was indeed the Mike from Everett's house, then everything finally made sense.

Sophia pressed her ear firmly to the phone as he spoke again. She needed to hear his voice and remember his face. She listened so closely she could hear the minute din of static prickling on the line. Her own name on his duplicitous tongue reassured her. No wonder he was out to get her. Mike was Everett's friend, but he worked for the man who was working overtime to put her out on the street.

On the off chance he would remember her from the short time they were in each other's company at Everett's the week before, Sophia altered her voice until it sounded adenoidal and pitchy. "Uh...sorry. I think I have the wrong place," she said quickly, disconnecting the call.

With a heavy sigh, she took one more look through the window. This was definitely the beginning of an ice-cream-and-horror-movies phase.

THE KILLER CLOWN did not have the calming effect she'd hoped.

The rest of the afternoon, Sophia spent with her computer researching restaurant occupancy limits, sign costs, and menu items, which only led her to Google...and back to the Monroes.

Her search for information about Barbara was trumped by

Mike's connection to Monroe Properties. It was a public company, so she began her search on the county assessor's page and weaved her way through to the county clerk and recorder's pages. The business itself, described as a real estate development company according to the land registration office, gradually bought up real property, commercial and residential, over the past few decades.

And the list was only from the time they incorporated.

There were a bunch of documents with the names Winthrop Monroe and Barbara Monroe. John only showed up in the past ten years, give or take a few.

Sophia scooped a spoonful of mint and chips ice cream and stuffed it, along with an Oreo, in her mouth and chewed absentmindedly, deciding there must be something she missed. Deep down, she could feel she was getting close to uncovering something big.

As she clicked on one of the most recent filed deeds, a title transfer, there at the bottom of the second page was the name Michael Kennedy. He'd signed as power of attorney for the business. Attached was an Oregon Real Estate Power of Attorney, on which, Michael, or rather, Mike was appointed to represent the company on behalf of John E. Monroe.

"Shit."

Sophia leaned back in her chair and stuffed two more cookies into her mouth while staring into the distance. She crunched hard into the creamy center as her mind whirled.

"Why do you want this house so bad, Michael Kennedy? What are you up to?" she said to herself as she picked up her phone and found Julie in her favorites.

"Hey girl, hey," Julie chirped into the phone.

"Jules. You know how I told you Everett's friend Mike was being such a dick to me?"

"Am I supposed to understand what you just said when you sound like some kind of Jurassic freak with rocks in your mouth?"

She chewed the rest of her cookies and ice cream and washed it down with milk.

"What are you eating, anyway?"

"Ice cream, Oreos, and milk."

A muffled movement sounded in Sophia's ear. "You know they make cookies and cream ice cream, weirdo. What flavor ice cream?"

Sophia sighed. "Mint and chips. Now, can we try to stay focused here? I'm trying to tell you something."

"Oh, okay. As long as it's only mint and chips, fine. Go ahead."

Sophia wasn't what you would call picky. She didn't discriminate against any ice cream flavor, but she started to pick up on a pattern indicating certain ones worked as cures for different moods. It was sort of like essential oils, but creamy and delicious. She used ice cream the way people use lavender for insomnia and inflammation, or juniper to strengthen nerves and ease gout symptoms. Mint and chips when she really needed to think, or rainbow sherbet when she was really happy and wanted to keep the good times rolling. But if the problem was really serious, strictly for heartbreaks and flighty, scatterbrained thoughts of offing herself, there was Strawberry Cheesecake ice cream.

Her whole family knew this, and sometimes they spazzed with over-the-top flavor reactions.

"Listen Ding-Ding. Everett's friend Mike, the one who was all up in my face the day at his house. He works for John Monroe."

"As in the fucktard trying to take your house, Monroe?"

Mike's words echoed in Sophia's head. *"One and the same."*

"Oh, shit. How do you know?"

Sophia sat up straight. "Girl, I've been digging and diving on the Internet all afternoon. Today I was downtown by Broadway and saw the cute storefront for the restaurant we looked at, so I called the number on the lease sign posted out front."

"Please say you put down a deposit."

"No. Just listen. Guess who answered the phone when I called?"

A loud screech came through the line. "No."

"Yes. The receptionist transferred me to someone for leasing and Mike answered. I could not believe it. So anyway, after I basically hung up in his face, I got on the Internet and bam! Right there on the screen was Mike's name. Rather, Michael Kennedy, I should say. He's the damn attorney. The power of attorney for Monroe Properties, the bad guy's company."

"What the—"

"I know." Sophia shook her head and pursed her lips...as if Julie could see her.

Julie whistled. "So you know what you've got to do now."

"Uh, no," she dragged out the last word. The document only proved what she already knew, but there must be more. She didn't know what she was going to do with this tidbit of information. Heck, she didn't even know if she should still talk to Everett. Not like he'd replied to any of her messages since their dinner last week anyway.

"Soph, try to pay to attention. You're going to have to pick Everett's brain. Use him to find out more about this Mike character."

"The thing is...he hasn't called me at all this week. Even though I've messaged him, um, once or twice."

"Is that why you're roaming the streets looking for properties by yourself instead of letting his fine ass take you?"

Sophia cursed silently. Somehow she'd hoped Julie wouldn't pick up on the little slip of the tongue. "Yeah," she said hesitantly.

"What happened now? I thought you guys were good after he drove you home."

"Yeah, about that. I might have shown him the nursery...and cried. Bawled."

"Lord, have mercy. What the hell is wrong with you? One dinner and you're already telling him your life story, complete with baggage. Seriously, you need to get this under wraps. As your wiser, older cousin by a month, I need you to promise me now you won't keep unloading on this guy. *If* he ever wants to see you again."

Sophia rolled her eyes, wishing she could go back to the night and maybe show him a photo album or a tchotchke from her childhood instead of dragging him into the doldrums of her life on their first date. Well, sort of date.

"On a side note, his sister, Zora, did invite me for drinks at some bar. Let me look at the text again," she said, holding up her phone from her ear and scrolling through the messages.

"Yep. Right here. At seven thirty. I probably could use a stiff drink after all this."

Ice cream and horror movies weren't going to cut it.

AGAINST THE NIGHT SKY, the black décor and dim candlelight of the restaurant made the room feel shadowy and obscure, like it was guarding secrets. Which was why Everett chose La

Moule—to both feed his gloomy mood and drown it in alcohol. Over a week passed since he last saw Sophia, but seeing her now, across the bar and having a good time with Zora, knotted his insides.

After rereading Sophia's texts, he turned his phone facedown on the table and slouched into a more comfortable position in the taut leather booth. He propped his arms over the top, letting his knees fall open. This was where the blue balls came in. Just thinking about her made him hard.

However, regardless of what his body wanted, his moral compass was still pointing due north. Avoidance might have been immature, but it was the only safe way to ensure the compass (not his dick) remained pointing up. It wasn't right to let Sophia keep thinking they were anything other than two people at odds over a house which meant the world to each of them, but for very different reasons.

He watched as she threw her head back laughing, and the urge to walk over to her left Everett seething. He gritted his teeth, the tightness in his jaw almost painful. He should be the one making her laugh, taking her out, and buying her drinks.

As soon as the idea hit him, he bit back the temptation.

I'm doing the right thing.

As the young waitress passed by, he caught her attention and gulped down the rest of his Pilsner. "I'll have another one, and uh... send one over to the lady at the end the bar, please. The one in the black dress." He lifted his chin toward Sophia and waited for the waitress to single her out.

"Sure. Should I say who it's from?"

"No. I just want to watch." And then he did.

A few minutes later as she accepted the drink, Sophia's back seemed to go rigid. In a slow, nervous turn, she looked over her bare shoulder and scanned the room until her attention landed on Everett. The look she gave him wasn't quite what he'd hoped for, but a potent mixture of knee-jerk excitement lit up her eyes, followed by telltale signs of annoyance. Tight smile. Raised brow. And of course the slow folding of her arms saying *your move*.

He was pretty sure the memory of his cowardly exit from the nursery was scrolling across the screen in her head.

On the outside Everett was cool as a fan, confident, and smugly confident he was winning the staring game. Unblinking, he took a swig from his glass, remembering the kiss they shared while she poured her heart out to him. Here was this strong, beautifully flawed woman who'd suffered unthinkable tragedy, and yet she'd endured. Survived. On the inside, he was both mesmerized by the mere sight of her and appalled at himself because he was about to add to her troubles. *Damn the right thing.*

He slid over the bench and out of the booth on a beeline for her. "Sophia." He gripped the bar with both hands without facing her.

Matching his even tone, she muttered, "Everett."

"What are you doing here, Ev?" Zora squealed and wrapped him in a bear hug from behind.

"Hey, Ev," his sister's friends cooed in unison.

Any other time, he might have shied away, acknowledging them with a nod or a wave, but the opportunity of the situation was not lost on him this evening. Ignoring his happy drunk of a sister, Everett wriggled out of Zo's clutches far enough to greet her friends. "Hey Oli, Remi. How've you guys been doing?" He kissed them each on their cheeks, lingering a little too long to be casual. He layered his efforts on thick with unwavering eye contact.

If he wasn't mistaken, when he turned, he thought he might have noticed Sophia's smile tighten.

In his best Denzel move, he leaned against the bar and allowed his stare to travel from Sophia's legs up to her eyes. "And how've you been?"

Sophia tossed him a quick glance and immediately turned back to about two fingers of a neon green cocktail and the untouched Pilsner he'd sent over.

"Okay. I deserve the cold shoulder. I should have responded to your messages." He bobbed his head in admission, but this time when she met his look, a giant "no shit" sign flashed across her forehead.

"Don't worry. I won't bother you anymore."

"Fine. I'm an asshole. I admit it. I shouldn't have ghosted you, but I promise, I had my reasons."

"Oh, well then, of course that makes everything all right." Sophia folded her arms.

Zora squeezed into the narrow space between Everett and Sophia. "I love how you guys are arguing like some old married couple," Zora slurred, nudging her brother's shoulder. "Might as well skip all the pretense and just go get a room."

Not helping, Zo.

His eyes darted to Sophia's cringeworthy expression, which no doubt equaled the one he was sure twisted his face. Zora let loose a roar of laughter as she turned back to her friends, and the two of them burst into snickers.

"Can I get you another...what is it? An Amaretto sour?"

"A Midori sour," she corrected him.

"I see you didn't touch the pilsner I sent you.

Sophia sighed. "I don't like beer."

It came out louder than she might have anticipated. A light

flush crept over her cheeks as she tried to laugh it off. "Did you come over here for any particular reason?" she deadpanned.

Everett was at a loss. He couldn't very well tell her he'd been a coward and she was the only thing he'd been able to think about since he walked out of the nursery. But he could show her. A loud riff in the music pierced the noise of the crowd, and he took it as a sign.

"I was hoping you might want to dance with me." He leaned close to her ear and whispered, "Or you could stay here with my sister and talk about her latest recipes. Did she have a chance to tell you about all the ingredients in my grandmother's gumbo yet?"

Everett raised a brow at her.

Sophia's attention flickered from him to Zora and her friends. She seemed to consider her options. After a short pause, she stretched her hand toward him and let him lead her to a small space in the corner. Over the chatter and clanking of dishes, he could barely hear the music, but he didn't care. This was his chance to hold Sophia again. Hidden in plain sight among the crowd, he rested his hands on the small of her back with enough pressure to keep her steady against him. For a moment, the music rocked them, and as they swayed to the melody, Sophia allowed her head to rest on his shoulder.

"You are going to look at me, aren't you?" he asked.

She didn't respond immediately, but after a few beats, she raised her gaze to meet his and twisted her face into a smirk. "There. Are you happy now?"

"Is it too much to ask for a real smile?"

She stared at him, blank. He wasn't sure whether it was uncertainty or her guard was back at full attention, but the indecision was plain. Then Sophia unraveled her expression, and for a second she was herself.

"Just tell me one thing. Are you really so afraid of a woman's tears?"

The tracks of his mother's tears when Joseph left were scarred in his mind.

Everett didn't have time to conjure up a good lie, so he told the truth. "Yes. What man wouldn't be?" He raised his hands in defense before replacing them on the small of her back. "Really, I don't know what I was expecting when you took me upstairs. I mean, I was hopeful—"

Sophia elbowed him in the ribs and he caved inward in mock agony.

"I know. I know," Everett laughed at his misjudgment of the situation. "I'll tell you one thing, I wasn't expecting something so meaningful to you, so raw."

"All I could think about at the time was, 'man, I don't even know this woman.' It took me a couple of days to realize what exactly the problem was. I don't know you. I don't know anything about you, but the first time you let me in and show me who you are, what made you who you are, I run." Everett shook his head, wishing he could lose the memory altogether. She was listening intently, allowing him to say his piece, but he was running in circles trying to get to the point, trying to figure how to say it. He moved his hands to her arms and fixed her in place, steeling himself. "I want to know you, Sophia," he admitted on a low whisper.

Everything in him urged him to tell Sophia the truth so they could work together to find out what Austin was up to, because he wasn't lying about wanting to get to know her.

"Say something," he said.

"The thing is—" She swallowed hard. "I've been through so much, and I'm still trying to find my way back to me. I feel like *I* don't even know who I am. I thought coming here, doing this on my own—for me and for Ainsley—it would help me see clearer, be stronger. Everything in me told me not to let you see the nursery, but another part of me needed to just rip off the Band-Aid, you know?"

He nodded. "Yeah. Mike is always telling me not to get caught up in my head. Just let the past lie."

At the mention of Mike's name, Sophia winced.

"Don't worry about Mike. He's still paying for what he did to you."

"What's his deal? I know he's your friend and all, but tell me about him, because I wouldn't let my friends treat my guests the way he treated me. And I wouldn't let my guests mistreat you the way you allowed him to do."

"I know and I'm sorry. I can't tell you how sorry I am. It's just he's been a friend for a long time, and he's an asshole. He's protective and looks out for Zo and me. I look out for him, too. What do you want to know?"

Everett caressed Sophia's back, feeling the tension subside.

"I don't know..." she hesitated. "It's just. Something didn't feel genuine about him. Like me being around, somehow infringed on his friendship with you." She shook her head, as if she still didn't quite get to the crux of the matter. "It was like I was his enemy. I know it sounds crazy, but the way he treated me was the way you'd treat someone who'd personally wronged you."

Everett gave a noncommittal nod. Was this it? Was Mike using Sophia to get back at Harman, or was there more to it?

"I'm sorry he made you feel unwelcome. He's probably just trying to have my back."

She nodded. "Yeah."

Everett cocked his head back to look her in the eyes. "Do

you want to get out of here? I was hoping you'd let me take you somewhere. There's a place I want to show you."

He liked the idea of him and Sophia finally talking, but he didn't drudge through days of blue balls to get this close to her and talk about Mike.

CHAPTER 12

"**D**oes it glow in the dark? Is it a star?" Sophia guessed. "You have a telescope and you want to show me the constellations?"

Everett shook his head, appearing to stifle a laugh as he turned into a parking lot a couple of blocks from the river. "I hope you haven't had a chance to see it yet. It really is amazing at night."

Sophia sighed. "Why can't you just tell me?"

She watched as he peered out the window at the car on their left. "Why can't you just relax?" He held up his palm toward her with splayed fingers. "It'll be worth it, I promise."

Sophia leaned back against the passenger seat door and studied him for clues as he backed his truck out of the space...only to pull back in again. "Fine. Since you won't tell me where we're going, and I still have no guarantee you're not an axe murderer, if you *are* planning to kill me, can you at least let my mom know I love her?"

She flashed him a smile before turning to the window as a

mist sprayed the glass, the mirrored glare magnifying her full lips.

Lord, the man could not park to save his own life. Everett backed out of the space again and corrected his alignment before inching back in straight. She bit back a giggle. "I think you're pretty straight now."

She watched as a smirk twisted his mouth, leaving behind a lopsided grin. He shook his head, rolled his eyes, and turned off the ignition. "Let's go."

As soon as she was out of the car, Everett lifted the lever on the side of the driver's seat, sliding the backrest forward, and fished out what looked like a black blanket.

"What is it?" she asked, stepping back.

"Calm down. I keep a few spare jackets with me at all times. The weather here is unpredictable, as I'm sure you've noticed. Plus, we're going to be on the water." Everett leaned over the front seat and held out one of the jackets for Sophia. "Unless you want to freeze."

Reluctantly, Sophia took it. "Thank you."

Everett shut his door and pushed his arms through the sleeves of his jacket, stifling a bout of laughter. "I didn't think you'd refuse, given the dress you're wearing." It was quick, but she heard the slight emphasis he placed on the word "dress."

"Why'd you say it like my dress is a disgusting eyesore?"

"It's a nice dress, but—"

"But what?" Sophia cut him off, walking around the bed of the truck.

"It's a bit formal for a night out for beers? Oh, excuse me. A night out for amaretto sours," he corrected himself. He was teasing her.

"Whatever, funny guy. I wanted to look nice. I wanted to make a good impression on your sister and her friends."

"Ah, so this was all for them. It makes sense now."

"Can you just say what you're trying to say instead of being all cryptic?" Sophia folded her arms.

"I'm not trying to say anything." Everett shrugged. "I just...I think you're beautiful without all the fancy hair, the makeup, the dress. You don't have to change for anyone."

Sophia stared down at her hands to avoid meeting his eyes. Suddenly she felt shy, and she couldn't ignore the flip her stomach did at the compliment.

"Thanks."

A kind of awkward silence fell between them. She wasn't expecting flattery. After a few beats, Sophia slid her arms into the gigantic fleece jacket. Drowning in warmth as she pushed up the sleeves over her hands to her wrists, she settled herself beside Everett and looked up at him. Without saying a word, she linked her arm in his.

"So, you say we're going to be on the water? Does this mean you have a boat or yacht?"

The minute they rounded the corner toward the waterfront, Sophia's mouth dropped open. "Oh, my goodness. Is this where we're going?"

"Uh-huh."

"It's...spectacular," she gushed. "I mean, I saw it in the daylight, but how is it this amazing at night?"

Everett looked straight ahead. "I know. I felt the same way when I first saw it after they built it a few years ago. Now it's one of my favorite places. The lights. The music. It's just whimsical and beautiful."

"What's it called again? I know it's the something crossing bridge."

"The Tilikum Crossing. 'The bridge of the people.'" He held his hands out in front of him in captions at the larger than life structure before them. "It's what Tilikum means. It's the Chinookan word for family or tribe. People."

"I read about it on a trip planner site last year, but none of the pictures showed it at night." She blinked in awe. "Nothing like this."

"I know. It's kind of like a hometown secret. There's so much to this city, but this is my favorite place to be when I've got a lot on my mind, or if I just need to sort through some things."

"I can imagine. It's amazing." A gust of wind whipped over them and Sophia held on tighter to Everett's arm, tucking her face into the soft, damp fleece.

"And you know what's the best thing about it? No cars. No traffic. They built it for the MAX orange line light rail, but it's more like a good hiking trail. I love the fact it's for people to be together," he continued, undeterred by the rain picking up. "Look around. People come out here all hours of the day and night. If you want to take in the sights or get in a good bike ride, the TC is like...a twenty-four hour open-air oasis. My grandmother never got to see it up close. Man, she would have danced and twirled to the music."

"I'm sorry. She passed away?"

"Yeah. But even before then she was suffering from dementia. She was in hospice because she would just go walking and get lost. Or hop in the car and drive somewhere she'd been at one time in her life. Once Zora and I spent a whole day searching for her, and you know where she was? Mount Hood."

Sophia laughed. "I really want to go there one day."

"I'll have to take you, then. I'll bring Blue."

It wasn't necessarily what he said. It was a mountain open

to the public. But there was promise behind his words. Tonight wasn't the last time she was going to see Everett.

Her heart drummed in her ears, and she could feel the tremor of her pulse speeding up.

"Anyway. She remembered a time we'd all gone hiking when Zora and I were younger, and we couldn't find my sister. She went back there to look for her." Everett lowered his chin. "Anyway, I don't want to dampen the mood, but I could see her doing her dance on this bridge."

"I love that. I can tell she meant a lot to you."

He nodded and a comfortable silence fell over them.

They'd been walking in comfortable silence for a few minutes, but then he stopped just after they reached the water. Sophia could feel the weight of Everett's eyes fall on her. She didn't turn to him, but every cell in her body responded to the almost physical touch of his attention. Butterflies fluttered in the pit of her stomach. Her fingers and toes tingled. Her heart? It was a bass drum, pounding in her ears.

"I'm hoping maybe it's a good place if you've been an asshole and you want to get back in the good graces of a beautiful woman," he trailed off, grazing the pad of his thumb over her cheek.

Sophia leaned into his touch.

"Maybe," he continued. "Just maybe, she'd agree to take a midnight stroll with you across a bridge coming alive with lights and music."

When Sophia looked up at him, heat ran down her spine and lingered. She didn't say a word, but the expression on her face must have conveyed the yearnings of her mind and body. Everett closed the narrow distance until there was only a whisper between them. If magnetic fields were possible to see with the naked eye, it would be thick in clouds all around them. Sophia's mind raced, but her hands and her lips were uncontrollably, involuntarily attracted to him.

She couldn't exactly explain what happened in that moment, but once their lips touched, all else—time, thought, and distance—ceased to be. Heat and light and music danced around the sweet, minty taste of his hungry mouth over hers. Her hands roamed untamed over the muscular cords of his chest and arms. He smelled of fresh lemons and ocean-drenched cotton.

It seemed far away, but the faint slap of rain over the surface of the water roused Sophia from her trance. The light drizzle morphed into heavy drops splashing on her forehead.

"It's raining," Everett said without loosening his hold on her, his gaze unwavering.

"But I don't want to go home yet." Sophia lifted herself on tiptoe to brush her lips against his once more. Looking up to the breathtaking bridge glittering in the night sky, then back to Everett, she nodded toward it. "You want to get caught in the rain with me?"

The question itself was innocent, but deep down Sophia knew she was asking him for more. She was asking him not to run away.

THE FOLLOWING morning Sophia stared out of the passenger seat window of Everett's truck, biting back a grin. There wasn't much to see outside. It was gloomy as always, raining and overcast. But the second he'd driven away from her house, he flashed his devastating smile and a fresh wave of desire slammed into her. Immediately, her mind flooded with images of the night before on the bridge.

They kissed.

And not just any kind of kiss, it was the panty-dropping, tonsil-hockey kind of kiss. It left her overheated and hormonal.

"So how many places are we going to see?" she asked. As previously promised, Everett was taking her to see a few retail pads for her restaurant, followed by lunch at some place he swore would take Sophia's love of food to a level of obsession.

Here she was, trying to make idle conversation, but her mind was still reeling with all her fantasies about last night. And Everett? She watched his reflection in the window glare. They'd been in his truck for about fifteen minutes and he'd barely looked at her. He was calm as ever, as if nothing had happened. Meanwhile she was on the verge of spontaneous combustion just sitting next to him.

They weren't even touching, but heat built between them like a stoked fire. She squeezed her thighs tight and bobbed her feet, which were crossed at the ankles.

"Three today," he said as he hooked a left turn. "Maybe two more. I'm having my guy run the numbers now. They've all been on the market for a few months with no bites, which might work in your favor."

To avoid being rude and avoid eye contact while he was talking to her, Sophia stupidly veered in his direction. Of course, for the first thing she saw was his full lips. She could still feel how they blazed over her skin under the cold of the waterfront. The light stubble of his beard rubbed rough against her cheeks and her neck, driving her hormones wild.

"Uh...okay. Are they all downtown?" Her attention still glued to his lips, she bit down hard on her bottom lip.

God, there must be somewhere else to look.

To avoid his disarming smile and those luscious lips, she

looked down...and unfortunately found something else to hold her attention—something thick and hard. Her breathing shallowed and her heartbeat stuttered to a frenzied rhythm, sounding in her ears like the ebb and flow of the ocean. Quickly, she jerked her eyes away from his lap and stared straight ahead for fear of what other trouble she could get into just looking at him.

As the green light turned yellow, Everett slowed beside a street trolley to allow a group of pedestrians to cross.

"Yeah. Two of them are just off Tenth and Eleventh, although they're kind of pricey because of the prime locations. The other one is not too far. It's on the southwest end of Broadway. But it's pretty reasonable and close enough to grab some foot traffic."

He was still staring ahead as his thumbs tapped the steering wheel to the beat of some classic eighties song on the radio. The bass echoed in the truck cab, and for a second she thought he might break into song.

"Is this your jam?" she asked, a smile quirking up the corner of her mouth. "I used to love this song. My mom loved blasting dusties on the highest volume. Or, do you guys call them oldies but goodies?"

"I hope you're not making fun of me. The best music came out in the eighties. Michael, Prince, Madonna, Whitney, Bon Jovi, Wham," he began ticking artists off on his fingers. "Don't even get me started. Def Leppard, Journey, Queen, Duran Duran, Hall & Oates, Guns N' Roses. Stop me any time, because I can keep going forever."

Now Sophia burst out laughing. "Wham?" she asked, her eyes widening.

As the light turned green, finally Everett did look at her.

Study her was more like it. And something about his smile was genuine and boyishly innocent.

"Don't even try it. What kind of music do we have now? A bunch of emo kids singing about death and gold chains."

Sophia was doubled over now, gasping for breath.

"It's all right. Make jokes, but there are only a handful of people who actually make good, important music anymore, and you know it. People these days are unoriginal. They remake and remix everything, music *and* movies. I don't really have a choice but to play the old stuff."

"No," she said, dragging the word out for emphasis. "There's plenty of good music out there, but it's not on the radio. You have to keep your ears open and get out of your ancient box. Maybe download an app instead of having people choose your playlist for you."

Sophia rolled her eyes wistfully. He sounded like Mom and Aunt Marian. "How old are you anyway, oh, ye judger of good music?"

"I'm thirty-four. Born in the eighties, and proud of it."

They were nearing Fourth Avenue, but by the flow of traffic, it would be at least five more minutes before they reached the first location.

Everett pressed his finger on the radio dash a few times, setting the mode to auxiliary. "I'm going to play you a song, and I dare you to tell me you don't feel something when you hear it." On his phone he pressed an app and fanned through songs before landing on one.

The truck cab filled with the first tinkling notes of the keyboard mixed with low bass. Even before Luther Vandross's familiar, silken voice matched the honeyed melody of *So Amazing*, tears pricked at Sophia's eyes.

CHAPTER 13

S ophia was still fidgeting with her purse zipper, staring at her fingers, praying the tears wouldn't fall. When the first one tracked down the curve of her cheek, she met Everett's compassionate gaze.

When he wiped away her tear and pushed a flyaway strand of hair away from her eyes, Sophia explained the tears away as nothing but old ghosts coming back to haunt her. She told him her father dedicated the words to her mother at their wedding. She said this was the song her parents played on repeat while they danced in the living room when times were good.

What she didn't tell him was, out of all the songs in the world, this one reminded her she was replaceable.

The words were well-meaning and melancholy as they ripped into the air, taking her heartstrings with them. He hit the hook and Sophia's mind drifted to the last time she saw her father and all the things she was willing to do to make him stay back then.

Over ten years had passed since Sophia heard the song. Her mom stopped playing it the day her dad left. The day he chose his shiny new life over Sophia and her mom. While he begged Sophia to believe his leaving could never weaken the love between a father and daughter, she knew better.

The hurt was written in her mother's eyes.

Luther belted about love bringing him and whoever he wrote the song about together, the rhythm faster now, her heartbeat faster still.

"How long has it been since you lost your dad?"

His tone let on that he thought Sophia's father died too, and she did nothing to correct the assumption. To Sophia, he died the day he left. He went away, and with him he took her mother's happiness, his money, and Sophia's innocence. He took the ability to deny the truth she'd been reminded of ever since: All good things come to an end.

As Everett drove, he found every way he could to continue touching her. A squeeze of the hand followed by interlaced fingers. Finally, lifting their hands to his lips to kiss the back of hers. Her skin blazed beneath every inch of his kiss.

When the truck came to a stop in front of the first commercial space on Southwest Broadway, Sophia gasped.

Her window was closest to the curb, and she was turned away from Everett, but she sensed him sliding near her, so close her back was against his chest. "How did you know?" she asked, her breath catching in a throat still thick with emotion.

She pushed all thoughts of her father to the back burner and let Everett's question about losing her father hang out there unanswered.

Luther's voice faded away, but his words stuck with her. The man she was with was so amazing. The empty storefront was the same place she visited with Julie. The same place she called Monroe Properties about when Mike answered the phone. She hadn't seen the other two locations, and the warning signs were in plain sight, but already, deep down, her heart was set on this kitchy little spot.

Everett slipped his arms around her waist and nuzzled his chin into the crook of her neck. His body heat warmed her, his clean, fresh scent intoxicating. "You told me that day on the street. I was waiting to tell you until I got them down to a reasonable offer."

She could feel the stubbly tug of his beard on her face as the corners of his mouth curved up into a smile.

"So, what do you think?" he asked.

Her answer was undeniably in favor. Sophia twisted in his arms and met his smoldering eyes. Every nerve ending in her body danced with anticipation as her heart raced. Without another word, without thinking about what last night's kiss meant in the light of day, without second-guessing herself or the hidden meaning behind his lovely gesture, she closed the narrow distance between them and pressed her lips over his.

"ALL THIS TALK about your food, it's making me hungry." Gently, Everett brushed his lips against Sophia's, lingering for the slightest moment as her eyes snapped open, warmth brightening their brown irises.

After the realtor left, Sophia and Everett stood outside the remodeled historic building, her small hand comfortably nestled within his. She leaned in close to him, and he could tell by the faraway look on her face she was imagining all the possibilities for her restaurant.

He, on the other hand, was still trying to figure out how they got here.

What am I doing? Why was he helping her put down roots here?

"I could eat," she said, oblivious to the war going on in his head.

"Good," he said, helping her step up into the cab. "because I made us reservations at a nice quiet little place with a decent view. Might be a bit early since I didn't expect us to bypass the other two buildings altogether, but we should be fine."

He rounded the front of the truck, got in, fired up the engine and glanced over at her as he veered into the lane. She was watching him with those hopeful eyes, her back against the passenger door and her head leaned against the headrest. One knee was tucked up against her chest, and the other leg sort of hung open, her jeans hugged her long legs, and the simple green sweater seemed to snuggle against her curves, but she might as well have been lying there naked.

Fuck. Give me a break.

The temperature in the truck went up at least fifty degrees, and he could feel the heat crawling up his neck to his cheeks.

"Don't look at me like..." he trailed off, shaking his head. He stifled a low growl. "Am I supposed to be able to drive with you giving me those eyes? With you sitting there like...that?" He looked over at her again, and now the corners of her mouth were turned up.

"How am I looking at you?" she asked. It was an innocent question, but the low, husky way she said it was anything but vanilla. He never saw this side of her, this flirty, uninhibited version. And as much as he knew he needed to draw the line somewhere, his body seemed intent on crossing it.

Everett switched hands and steered with his left, freeing his right hand, he lifted the center console, configuring the layout into a three-seater bench. "Come over here next to me," he said, keeping his eyes firmly on the road. Out of nowhere easiness drifted down over them and he weaved his fingers together with hers.

He'd tell her soon—maybe today, over lunch.

The night in the nursery, Everett knew what he needed to do—the right thing to do. He went to Patton Place to find out her motives, Austin Harman's motives, for the house.

But what he found there was a broken woman who'd somehow latched onto to the walls around his heart and brought them crumbling down. As her eyes welled and she flushed, standing in the pale pink room, he couldn't unsee her —the woman behind the mask. Her lush lips, the tawny, blushed, high cheekbones framed by dark brown waves. Glowing, depthless dark eyes hiding all the hurt. Yet he hadn't been able to tear his gaze away. She was fragile and beautiful all at once. A colorful, mesmerizing mosaic of the pieces her father and her husband left scattered in their wake.

He'd wanted to tell her everything would be okay eventually. Assure her the numbness would soon wear off, and one day, though the pain would still be there, it would be dormant, and she wouldn't have to remind herself that others' mistakes didn't define her. Then again, he realized how much more lies hurt the longer they remained unspoken. And so, against the fiery urgency in his heart, he'd held her soft against his chest for a moment, kissed her head, and left.

With every intention of never going back, he let her go, determined not to be yet another person who hurt her. He meant to untangle her from his lies. That while he told himself he was fine, after a while she'd fade, too. Seeing her under the low lights of La Moule, then under the star-studded sky at the bridge, he couldn't let her go.

Once more, he kissed Sophia's hand and smiled at her, but

she didn't seem to notice his smile was frayed around the edges.

"So we have a little extra time?" Her soft voice crept into his thoughts. He watched her in his periphery. There was hesitation in her voice as she continued staring at him.

"Yeah. We can just drive slowly. It's nice out. I'll let you pick the music." As Sophia scrolled through the songs on his phone with her free hand, she scooted in closer to him. Suddenly, Steve Perry from Journey was crooning *Faithfully*.

Everett squeezed Sophia's hand. "Good choice."

For a moment, they both sat there listening to the song, the meaning and emotion, reveling in their closeness as the morning crowds moved in currents along the sidewalks. This was exactly what he wanted. The easy, quiet settling between two people, where there wasn't anything to prove. But even then the irony of it wasn't lost on him.

As Perry belted out the words, Sophia loosened her hand from his. This song did completely different things to her.

He flicked a glance at her replacing his hand on the wheel. "Everything okay?"

"Yes," she breathed. Her turbulent expression was centered on him now, the way it was the night on the bridge. And like he did then, he felt the same tightening of his muscles and the fire burning through him.

He'd been jealous of the wind and the rain getting to wash over her soft skin. He'd kissed her. Hurried and ravenous, he'd deepened it, allowing his worries to ebb away. A small voice inside warned him to stop, to tell her before they went any further, but he'd tuned it out then, instead choosing to listen to his body, the soft, tingling sensation pulsing over his skin. His racing heartbeat as it pounded in his ears. The hardening of his groin.

"Keep your eyes on the road, please," Sophia smiled at him.

Fire burned everywhere Sophia touched him, as every inch of his body relived how he felt on the bridge. He'd caressed the soft curves of her face and inhaled the tangy sweetness of her perfume and shampoo. As her hands dipped beneath his jacket, roaming untamed, he allowed his tongue to explore the depths of her hungry mouth.

Something dormant inside him surged to life that night. It was almost as if she awakened every nerve ending in his body. He'd forgotten what it was like to want, and to be able to have. He begged for his body to forget.

When Sophia got in his truck this morning, Everett pretended the feel of her soft, sweet lips didn't fill the long-standing void within him. He knew he didn't have the strength or the will to let her go again, so he stayed away.

Today, the plan was to renew his resolve to resist her, but the way she was looking at him now, his plan was shot to hell. Those warm ocean eyes darkened like a turbulent storm, and it was feeble to deny the magnetic force, the irresistible pull between them.

He felt it now, electric and insatiable.

"Both hands on the steering wheel please," she instructed. Her words were in direct contrast to the reserved, softhearted person he knew thus far. She sounded forceful and stern, despite the smile curling up the corners of her mouth. She also sounded a little ragged, the words hitching on her shallow breath.

Sophia was still watching him, but she was sitting ramrod straight. Slowly, she crawled her dainty fingers over his thigh and Everett released a surprised gasp. He wasn't sure whether to be shocked or overjoyed, but he stilled in place.

"So, it's safe to say this music gives you the feels, huh?" He quirked a nervous smile, but as she carefully eased down his pants zipper and dipped her blazing hand inside, all the humor was smashed to smithereens.

Everything Sophia knew about him was based on a lie, but with every second he was near her, it became clearer that the lie was so much better than the truth.

CHAPTER 14

S ophia glided her hand over his smooth, warm cock straining the seams of his tight jeans. Where she got the nerve or the audacity to do this she couldn't say in a thousand years, but he felt right. This moment between the two of them, it was right.

It had nothing to do with the leggy brunette who showed them the retail pad. Realtors often wore skintight dresses with slits running the length of their thighs. It wasn't unheard of for them to be drop-dead gorgeous, either. Aquamarine eyes and Angelina Jolie pouty lips were commonplace.

Apparently it was completely normal for real estate developers and realtors who often worked together to hug way too long and kiss each other on the cheek.

Even if said kiss was closer to Everett's lips.

"Do you want me?" Sophia stroked harder, just the thought of that woman touching Everett searing through her. No, it had absolutely nothing to do with the way the realtor's long, skinny fingers wrapped halfway around his bicep.

Sophia was *not* jealous.

She trusted him, and wanted to feel so much more with him. Be impossibly closer to him. Really, when she thought about it, she wasn't sure why she held back. Who was she holding back for?

Encircling his cock with her fingers, she stroked his full girth. Up and down, slow...then fast...until he stiffened and expanded within her grasp. A low growl spilled from his parted lips and the throb between her legs pulsed with need.

Her sex life had only ever been regimented and missionary at best. The time was planned. The place was always on the bed at night with the windows closed and the lights off. But with Everett, his kiss made her feel wild and alive. Like she couldn't wait to find out what other ways he could jumpstart her body.

He'd sparked an uncontrollable flame within her. And here they were, in broad daylight, in the middle of the road, driving without tinted windows while she jacked him off. It was more than empowering. It was fucking hot.

As his chest rose and fell, hard and hurried, she was emboldened to keep going—to bring him to his peak. With her right hand, she unfastened her seatbelt and the top button of her jeans. The anticipation left her heart racing and an ache low and tight in her belly.

Slowly she unzipped her pants and removed his right hand from the steering wheel.

"Sophia?"

"Yeah?" she breathed, biting her bottom lip.

"Sophia?" he said her name again, as if there were no other words in his vocabulary. "Ummmm, I'm trying to drive, here—avoid a head-on collision." Thank God he had remarkable reflexes.

Panting, Sophia said what she tried to say ever since his lips touched her. "I need to feel you." Her lids lowered, and she slid forward onto the edge of the seat, lifting her hips. Without another word, she guided his hand into the opening of her jeans. Sliding his large fingers deep into her panties, she pressed his middle finger all the way in between her folds before adding another finger. Heat seared through her. She guided his hand, riding its rhythm while she continued stroking his cock with her other hand.

"Everett?" she called to him, not giving a damn about the way this made her look or where they were. "Take me somewhere. Please."

He looked over at her now with darkened eyes as his hand pressed inside her lace-rimmed pink panties. His fingers deepened slightly and Sophia thought she might explode right there. She was practically coming apart at his touch.

He could barely keep his eyes on the road.

In what felt like a flash, the truck was moving at lightning speed, other cars going by in a blur as he barked orders at her, now taking over command. "Kick off your shoes," he said. His eyes roamed over her from head to toe. As she obeyed, he continued. "Now the jeans," he said, licking his bottom lip.

Sophia did not hesitate. With the engine roaring beneath her, she shimmied her hips, allowing the pants to come down, only her underwear puddled around her ankles too.

"Oh, my God. You're so fucking hot." Everett jerked his hand away from her as he overcorrected to keep the truck from swerving off the road. "Are you trying to kill us?" he barked, his heated stare flickering between the road and Sophia.

A hungry smile curved his luscious lips, and Sophia's stomach flipped.

"Pull over," she said. "I don't care where. Just stop the fuckin' truck." Sophia sighed, squirming on the bench seat. Her body ached to feel all of him inside her. "Please." She moaned for him.

Given the urgency of the situation, Everett banked a left down toward the zoo and veered off to the side of the road.

The street was tree-lined and provided as much cover and shade as they could have hoped for, although privacy was sketchy because of passing cars. But this was where they were going to do it, she decided. Her first time with Everett was going to be roadside in his truck.

It was about as far from safe and regimented as she could get.

If all good things do come to an end, please let me have this one thing first.

He swallowed hard as he turned to Sophia. She was practically writhing as the car skidded through the shrubbery to a halt.

"Do you have anything?" she breathed.

He stared at her for the slightest second before yanking his wallet out his back pocket and slipping out a condom packet. "You sure you want to do this?" he asked, though by the ravenous look in his darkened gaze and the thickness in her hand, she could tell their bodies were on the same page.

With a push of the hazard button on the dash, Sophia lifted her right leg to straddle him. He reclined the seat slightly. As his large, deft hands grasped her behind, she released the length of him from his jeans and rolled the condom down.

Oh, my Lord. Thank you.

She nodded. Her poor little rabbit wasn't even a decent stand-in. His cock was thick and long, with smooth veins, and she couldn't wait to feel him inside her. "Definitely," she said, as she lowered herself, allowing his cock to fill her insides. Her folds clenched warm and tight around it.

"Say something dirty to me," Sophia whispered.

She clasped her fingers behind his neck and covered his lips with hers. His tongue glided against hers as his hands slid beneath her sweater. With one hand, he unclasped her bra and her ample breasts fell free against the cashmere.

"I want to fuck you hard," he said, complying with Sophia's request for dirty talk. Although it was hot as hell, almost pushing her over the edge, the words didn't sound natural on his tongue.

But what he lacked in the way of smut, his long rod made up for tenfold.

Sophia let her head fall back as he thrust deeper, in and out as she raised herself up and slammed down along his length. His lips blazed a trail from the sweet spot behind her ear and down the curve of her neck, until he lifted her sweater, removing the last barrier between them.

When his hot, wet lips suckled her hard nipple, she let out a gasp, digging her nails into his back. Riding wildly on top of him, she bucked. He pressed her breasts together and buried his face between them, giving each one the same amount of attention.

"Everett, you feel so good. Harder. Please, harder," she begged. Sophia dragged her tongue over his thick neck.

With his hands pressed firmly on her hips, he thrust himself harder to meet her fall, pounding against her throbbing ache. "Oh, fuck."

For a few more incomprehensible minutes, they continued this way until they were both short of breath, shuddering with sated pleasure, and their bodies spent and limp.

"Sophia?" Everett whispered into her hair as she collapsed on top of him.

"Yeah?" she moaned.

"Are you okay?" She could feel his body stiffening beneath her. His hard chest crushed against her. Unmistakably, his worries were getting the best of him.

"I'm more than okay," she said, sitting up, still straddling him. "I'm...on freaking cloud nine." She was bubbling and buoyant, and she couldn't remember the last time she'd felt this way. Not about herself, or any man. "Please don't overthink this, Everett. You gave my body what it needed. You gave *me* what I needed. I don't want you to spend even one second thinking this was a mistake."

A giggle escaped her, sputtering into a full-on laugh, and she threw her arms back around him. "Instead I want you to be thinking about when we can do it again."

But he still said nothing.

"Everett, would you say something? Is this like the nursery thing for you again? Did I freak you out?" Sophia leaned back against the steering wheel, searching his wide eyes.

"Sophia, this was amazing, and I don't know what I did to deserve you, but—"

"Don't." She pressed a finger to his lips. "No buts. Don't ruin this. At least not while you're still inside me. It was perfect and beautiful, and I don't want to rain down on it with worries about mistakes, and second-guessing." She leaned in to kiss him harder now. "Plus, I already want you again."

As if on cue, her stomach gurgled, making a croaking frog sound. "Well, maybe after we eat."

"This is where you made reservations?" Sophia was practically bouncing out of the seat when Everett backed into a parking space beside a Japanese Garden sign. The plan was to take the shuttle over for lunch and a little sightseeing.

"I've been wanting to come here for a while."

"Yeah? I was hoping this would kill two birds with one stone: tourist attraction and sustenance all in one." He shrugged.

As they exited the truck and headed over to the MAX station, she twined her fingers in his and nuzzled her face in tight near his neck. It was early, but the crisp breeze picked up, fresh with the scent of pines and flowers.

In Portland, it was almost perfect.

"Look how smart you are. Good thinking." Sophia scrunched her nose at him and dragged him by the hand.

By the time they made it over to Umami Cafe, they were just in time. Apparently reservations were usually for parties of six or more, but because Everett used some kind of secret power connection, the rules didn't apply to him.

"So do you make a habit of deflowering girls on the side of the road and then schmoozing them with VIP treatment at iconic gardens?" Sophia stifled a smile, but he did not appear amused. She held her hands up in defense. "What? I was just checking."

She said it only in Everett's earshot, but just the idea of the hostess overhearing her sent a surge of heat up her spine again. Who was this new person she was becoming, this hot and bothered seductress? Whoever she was, she definitely shocked the hell out of Everett. If anything, this new sex-crazed thing she found buried within did a number on her, too.

A shiver coursed through her as images of them in the truck flashed in her head, especially the way he filled her so completely. Sophia waggled her brows at Everett.

"What am I going to do with you?"

"I could think of a lot of things." She winked playfully, but his question was just as much serious as it was sexy. "Please stop thinking so much. Last I checked, amazing sex was a good thing."

Basically ignoring her comment, Everett reached across the table for her hand and held it, rubbing her fingers. It wasn't hard to tell where his mind was going, but she didn't want to go there. She wanted to stay firmly rooted on the fun, carefree, hedonistic side of things. Having no expectations was turning out to be strangely freeing. Going blind equals less to lose. Plus, she did the straight and narrow, the safe way. But now she'd gotten a taste of the other side, and she was in no hurry to go back.

As it turned out, also in no hurry to get back to the straight and narrow: her raging libido.

"I talked to Zora the other day," she said, trying to push the conversation in a different direction. She stuffed a forkful of her deep-fried avocado, crab, and cream cheese roll into her mouth.

"Yeah?"

"Uh-huh," she muttered, staring out the window at the garden in autumn bloom. Trees in varying sizes and all shades of red, green, orange, and yellow painted the horizon. "I was telling Zora my cousin's wedding is coming up in September. She was helping me with catering ideas since I'm basically going to be doing the food as well as jumping in as a bridesmaid."

"You should really consider letting her help you with the menu for your restaurant. She's pretty talented. Learned from my grandmother."

The second the words left his mouth, Sophia couldn't believe she hadn't come up with the idea herself. Zora was as crazy, if not crazier, about food than she was—a complete foodie. Plus, as a blogger, she knew the suppliers and the locations, the best farmer's markets. They'd talked for over an hour about everything under the sun, and they got along like long-lost sisters who actually liked each other.

With her cheeks bulging as she chewed, Sophia nodded and mumbled, "I just might."

"Although, I don't know if I like the idea of you guys spending so much time together without me." Everett flashed his devastating smile and a fresh wave of lust slammed through her.

"Well, then. If you want me to keep you around, you're going to have to make it worth my while."

In record time, Everett waved their waiter over while they finished their food. By the time he signed the merchant copy of the receipt and placed it—along with a generous tip to make up for their abrupt exit—in the leather check presenter, Sophia was standing by the door, ready to go.

She winked. "Round two?"

As it turned out, rounds two, three, and four were all as mind-blowing as the first, effectively erasing the last of Everett's blue balls. He couldn't get enough of Sophia, and she was insatiable for him, dragging him behind trees, taking him in the truck on the way home, and back at his place again. He couldn't remember the last time he wanted it nonstop with the same woman. For years sex was just sex, a way to meet his most basic primal needs. With Sophia, he wanted her every time with more urgency than the last, and he was hard-pressed to turn her down, no matter how misplaced his morals were at the moment—or his spent body. Which was nestled beside her in his bed.

Snuggling for Christ's sake.

She felt like some kind of test or prank between God and the devil to have something so wrong feel so mercilessly amazing. The kissing and hand-holding were nice, tame. But having her naked body molded to his beneath the sheets wasn't exactly where he thought he'd be when he agreed to show her retail spaces.

When did the initial lust ever fail to wane?

When did the sun come up?

Sophia lazily pressed her butt against his hard-on. "Morning," she moaned.

"Good morning." Everett pressed his finger into her warm, slippery folds, a move that was nearly his undoing. *Fuck.* She was already wet for him. As he penetrated her, gliding against her slick hollow, he groaned with satisfaction. "Fuck. Am I ever going to get enough of you?"

She covered her breast with his hand, arching into him as he slid in and out again and again, keeping it smooth and simple, letting the rhythmic friction do all the work. "I hope not. I can't imagine feeling this good without you."

He should have freaked out at her admission. Made up some excuse and told her to pack it in and go. But Everett's ego flared at the idea that only he could give her this kind of unrelenting pleasure. He drove deeper inside Sophia, filling her up until she quaked and trembled, squealing his name.

Still, he wasn't finished. He pulled out and turned her flat on her back so he could see her eyes. It almost hurt to see how beautiful she was. Long curls fanned over the pillow, framing the soft curves of her tawny brown cheeks. Her lids hung low over those warm, depthless eyes, and her lips were rubbed pink as she sucked on his middle finger.

Slowly, he lowered himself down her body, sucking the hard peaks of her breasts down to her trim belly. When he was just low enough, he centered his tongue at the meeting of her thighs and laved it over her pink bud. He lingered there, stabbing it repeatedly like a jackhammer until her toes curled.

She squirmed and writhed against his tongue while his hands weighed her down and pried her legs open. She gripped the headboard, lifting her hips for his access. And when he was done, her body bucked and jerked and jolted upright.

"I'm in heaven," she breathed. "Can we just stay like this forever? Let's never leave the house. Forget about the restaurant and your business. We could just stock up on food and water and ice cream, and hole up in here until we overdose on mind-numbing sex."

"Ice cream, huh? It's an amazing plan," Everett said, crawling up her body.

Now she was completely sated, he settled between her thighs once more. This time he was slow and gentle while he allowed his eyes to wander over Sophia. She was stunning and kind, and sexy as all hell. She was more than he ever wanted in a woman. And for however long he could have her, she was his.

Slowly, he lowered his face to brush his lips over her soft pout. He drove deep and tight until he steadied his full length inside her. Then, he lifted himself up onto his elbows. He stayed like this for a few minutes, staring into her eyes, letting her in. "I'm crazy about you, Sophia," he said finally.

It was more than he should have said, but it was true—exactly the kind of secret that claws at the caged heart until it's free.

Right then, he should have told her the truth, while they were naked with nowhere to run or hide.

While their hearts and eyes were open, he should have told her about the house.

He should have helped her see how Austin wronged both of them. Surely there was a way they could make it all work out in the end.

Instead, he stroked until he came and watched her doze until she fell asleep in his arms. He studied her without a care in the world, as her light breath feathered in soft ripples over his arm.

"I'm sorry. I don't want to lose you," he whispered, thankful she wouldn't hear him.

CHAPTER 15

A week later, with the help of Blue, Everett continued his personal tour guide services for Sophia with a trip out to Mount Hood. They started early on the Paradise Park trail, headed for Ramona Falls. For the first quiet, crowded three miles they held hands while Everett led the way. But as the trail cleared, he found himself dragging his feet, lost in the war in his head.

For every day he spent with her, the harder he knew it was going to be to unravel the lies. At some point, whether he wanted to or not, no matter how good it felt just being with her, he needed to tell her the truth. Every fiber in his being was dying to touch her again, to kiss her again, but he didn't want to get lost in the haze. The last thing he wanted to do was hurt her, but more and more he knew the hurt wouldn't be Sophia's alone.

Just tell her.

"Sophia. I want to tell you something." The words struggled against his throat.

Up ahead, she stared at the beaming horizon in the distance. "It's gorgeous."

Everett moved closer to her and loosened her backpack straps from her shoulders, dropping it on the ground. From behind, he began massaging her arms and neck, which were warm from the high sun and thick humidity, as he took in the clear view, mesmerized.

Though he'd hiked this trail at least a dozen times, seeing it again through her eyes was very different in the best of ways. Over her shoulder bright oranges and evergreens were set amid a dusty blue skyline. Lush alpines peppered the meadows. Water cascaded down stair-like rock columns. It danced and splashed in an ethereal shower.

How did he ever overlook such a natural beauty? Was it simply because Sophia's presence magnified its brilliance the way she breathed life back into his world? She was changing something in him. In the short time he knew her, she'd given him comfort and ease. He'd been rejected and replaced many times, but Everett didn't know if he would be able to bounce back from losing Sophia.

He turned to face her. "Yeah. Definitely can't beat this view." She was the sight he wanted to wake up to every morning. The truth was the only thing standing in his way.

Everett swallowed over the lump in his throat. *It's now or never.* "Soph?" He braced himself.

"Hmm?"

"I want to share something with you." Sophia nodded, indicating she was listening. "The day when you were telling me about your dad, I knew what you meant. It's been two years since my father died. We weren't close, but it did hit me hard because I was still mad at him. He was unfaithful to my mom, and she took her own life because of it. But, on top of losing

Mom, he abandoned Zora and me. So it was like we lost both our parents even though my grandmother took us in. He started a new family and we weren't part of it. I spent so many years trying to be good enough for him. And I realized how much his lies hurt our family—how much we lost because of him."

She squeezed his arms tighter around her waist. "I'm so sorry, baby."

Everett's throat tightened and he could feel the sting of tears in his eyes. Before he thought about what he was risking and couldn't get this out, he continued. "When he remarried and had more kids, he cut us off. So my grandmother, Babs, was everything to us."

"Her name is Babs?"

"Well, Barbara, but we all called her Babs." Everett smiled despite the memory of her. "She passed away a few years ago, and Zo and I took over the family real estate development business. It's basically just me, though, because she's concentrating on building up her food blog and a cookbook." Sophia turned in his arms to face him, and already he felt his nerve waning.

"What made you think about this?" she asked. Concern braided her brow as she looked up at him.

"Soph, I need to talk to you about the house."

A burst of shivers ran down Everett's spine and every nerve ending on his skin prickled.

"What's on your mind?" she asked, her voice low and sweet, but the tone was thick with worry.

"I know why you got the house in the divorce." The words sort of skidded out fast. Almost too fast, but they needed to be for him to lose his grip on them.

Her brow pinched together. "What do you mean? I told you

it was the only thing I asked for. The only thing that meant anything to me." She let her chin drop, and Everett could tell she was thinking about the baby she lost.

He wondered if she really thought everything pertaining to the house was so cut and dried.

"Babe, you don't think it was too easy? I mean, from what you told me about your husband, he doesn't seem like the kind of guy who would just give you what you want without a fight," Everett reasoned. "If the house was all you wanted, I would bet it's the one thing he'd be unwilling to give you."

Sophia looked up at him, and he could see the war in her eyes. Their usual warm brown color darkened beneath her narrowing lids. "You're right, but you don't know him. You don't know what I went through. I agreed on mediation, with the house as the only contingency. If he didn't agree, we'd still be going back and forth. I'd still be fighting because of how much it means to me."

"I know all about how much a home means."

Everett brushed his thumb over the pad of her lip and cupped his hand over the curve of her cheek, resting it there. For the slightest moment, he gazed at her, contemplating his inevitable loss once he explained his connection to Patton Place to her. As much as he loved her, he couldn't be the person who caused her more pain.

Softly, he brushed his lips over hers, lingering, tasting her sweetness. He squeezed his eyes shut, taking in her familiar scent of coconuts and sunset. He waited until his heartbeat steadied before breaking their kiss. And in the moment, he couldn't bear to tell her he was the one standing in the way of her dream, for fear of losing his.

Everett twined his fingers with hers and guided her back on the trail. Their feet crunched down over rocks and twigs as they navigated the rough terrain. He looked down at Sophia again, and as he did, he stumbled over a raised tree root and fell facedown. With the slope of the hill, he rolled with the descending momentum a few feet until the path leveled off.

He groaned at the fierce pain stabbing at his knee.

Sophia came running behind him and bent down to check his injuries. "Baby, are you okay?" she asked, panic lacing her tone.

He moaned and held tight to his knee. A pained grimace smeared across his face as he took account of the damage. Dirty scratches and scrapes mostly, but on his right leg, a bloody gash covered the dusty kneecap. "I'm fine." Everett rolled to his side and tried lifting himself up, but a sharp hollow ache rendered him helpless.

"Let me take a look at it," she said, assessing his knee. Gingerly, she squeezed her fingers around the bone, tapping and poking. "It's not broken or fractured, but the bruise is going to be pretty nasty."

Everett rested for a couple of minutes before he insisted they get going. At the rate the shadowy clouds were moving and by the moisture thick in the air, a storm was not far off.

Sophia wrapped his arm around her shoulders and used a boulder to help hoist him upright. A piercing pain shot through his leg and he winced, his grip tightening on Sophia's shoulder. "Put your weight on me," she said, "I can handle it." But it was obvious he was weighing her down.

Everett met Sophia's eyes just as a sprinkle of raindrops sprayed over her face. "Don't worry. We're almost there. It's not too bad, but I definitely need to get this cleaned up, and I don't want to do it here. If we stop now, we'll get caught in the downpour." He limped, stifling the urge to moan at every step.

As they hobbled down the hill, the rain began falling in

sheets. The sun was hidden behind a dingy cotton blanket of clouds, and a sidewinding breeze picked up. The ground muddied under their feet until they were practically sliding downhill with trees blurring beside them and nothing to hold onto but each other. They were drenched and clinging with slippery grips, bursting into laughter as they fumbled toward the bottom.

In a crashing ball, Everett fell with Sophia still tucked under his arm and the weight of his body. They were a soaking wet mess of grass and mud and happiness.

"Ouch," Sophia squeaked out between giggles. "Where in the hell did all this rain come from?"

"This is Oregon. There's always a possibility of rain." He chortled, shaking his head. "I love getting caught in the rain with you." *Love.* He loved everything about his woman. Everett propped himself up on his elbows, staring down at Sophia. With his free hand, he slid the wet hair stuck to her face out of the way. "You're so beautiful," he whispered.

He'd said those words to her every day they spent together, and he wanted to tell her every day for the rest of...

She stared back at him now, her laughter waning as she met his serious expression.

"I love you, Sophia."

As her lips parted, he kissed her again, his mouth crashing down on hers. This time he kissed her relentlessly, hungrily. Deep and exploring, his tongue roamed her mouth. He drank from her. He tasted her. Until her lips were swollen and pink.

He kissed her like it might be the last time.

"I say we shower, then order some pizza, because at this moment cooking is out of the question." Sophia untied her other shoe and kicked it off before tossing her muddy socks into the hamper. They were back at her place, in her bedroom, and she was still on cloud nine from his confession.

He said he loved her. Then, he'd kissed her senseless.

She was still reveling in the euphoria as she slipped into the closet, leaving Everett still standing there, a dirty, sexy, hot mess in the middle of her pristine room. He was looking around, stunned by his surroundings and she just wanted to rip his clothes off right there.

As she stripped out of her wet pants and long sleeve T-shirt, she peeked out of the door of the walk-in closet. "Are you just going to stand there, or are you coming in the shower with me?" She winked and he shuddered as she stepped out wearing nothing but a lacy red panty and bra set.

Everett was gorgeous and kind and everything she ever wanted in a man. More than she ever thought she'd have. Not to mention he was driving her libido crazy. What wasn't there to love? Why was she holding back?

He took a step closer, meeting her halfway.

"You can't go in the shower in those?" He lifted his chin toward her brand-new lingerie, which was apparently the best purchase she ever made, given the blazing hot look it earned.

It was almost as if the second she decided to forget all the pretenses, forget about Austin, forget about the hearing, and just let go, everything simply fell into place. Bornstein got back to her, saying things were looking good with the case and she'd likely get the house. Things were lining up with the retail pad on Broadway, and she was brimming with ideas for the restaurant. And to top it all off, Everett loved her.

Sophia walked up to him, leaving a few feet between them. "Ev. I lov—"

"Don't." He pressed a finger to her lips. Then, using both

hands, he cupped her face. "It's okay. I want you to say it when you're ready."

Her insides flooded with a mixture of urgency and relief because finally, here was this beautiful man who loved her. He was her unanswered prayer. Maybe she didn't have to rely on herself alone. The notion made her feel empowered. And the thing about power? There was nothing sexier.

She chewed her lip and turned so her back was facing him. "I can handle these..." She bent over, sliding her panties down her legs until they puddled at her feet, then righted herself. "But, I was hoping you could help me with my bra."

Playfully, she pushed her hair over her left shoulder, out of the way, and eyed him seductively behind lowered lids.

Everett didn't say a word. He leaned in and trailed his lips over the nape of her neck, unclasping her bra at the same time. On the small of her back, she could feel his cock growing hard, the warmth of his hands lighting the fire low in her belly.

She reached her hands behind her back and rubbed him through his jeans, wanting him inside her. Needing him now. When she pressed a hand over the rim of his pants and found him ready for her, she stroked him, circling her thumb over the soft head. Before she spontaneously combusted, she moved slowly toward the bathroom.

"I'll see you in there."

An hour later, they were both thoroughly satiated and starving for food for a change. Sophia whipped a blanket up into the air, letting it billow down over Everett on the living room couch. She'd propped his leg up with two throw pillows and bandaged the scrapes.

"I'm going to take care of you. Here's the remote." She gave him a quick kiss, then walked over to flip the switch to turn on the fireplace and close the mesh curtains. "What do you want on your pizza?"

Everett snuggled into the blanket and aimed the remote control at the television. As soon as the Home Network buzzed to life on the screen, he changed the channel to ESPN. Without looking away, he replied. "I'll take pepperoni, banana peppers, and extra cheese. What do you say we watch a movie? I've been wanting to see the new paranormal killer one."

"Ooh. The one where the ghost haunts and kills the politicians who murdered his family? It looks so good. Yes, it's a plan. On the pizza too, minus the banana peppers, but I'll swap it for jalapeños unless you can't handle the heat."

He playfully raised his brows at her in challenge.

"Okay, then." Sophia tapped on the app for the local Italian restaurant she found a few weeks ago when she was walking the neighborhood. She ordered the food and added sodas and a brownie pan, which would go perfectly with the salted caramel ice cream in her freezer. The flashing bar on the phone screen said their food was in the oven and would be delivered within thirty minutes or it would be free.

With the food taken care of, she set the phone on the coffee table. Keeping an eye on his knee, she carefully squeezed in beside Everett on the couch. When she was safely passed the danger zone, she rested her head on his shoulder and her hand over his heart.

Everett tightened his arm around her and flicked through the channels.

The glow of the television highlighted the sharp lines of his face, creating a white silhouette at the edges of his dark brown skin. He looked like he was carved and created just for her.

"What?" Everett asked without meeting her eyes, though

she knew he felt her looking at him because an adorable dimple popped out.

She was staring, but she made no effort to explain it away as she trailed her fingers over the sharp curve of his jaw. "I love you too," she said. Her voice did not waver and there were no questions in her tone.

He'd been lying on his back, but now he shifted onto his side so they were facing each other. She could feel his soft breath lightly graze over her cheek and his heart chasing hers. The kiss they shared was unhurried and soft. Like all the time in the world was theirs. Like time didn't exist before this moment.

Suddenly Sophia was aware of all her senses. The feel and pressure of his hard muscles wrapped tightly around her. His fresh, clean, soapy scent combined with the minty taste of his tongue as it freely grazed over hers. Even with her eyes closed, she could see he was the man she didn't know she needed.

Just beyond their moans and his muffled growls, Sophia heard the doorbell ring. "Pizza," she mouthed into the kiss.

"I don't want pizza anymore. I just want you."

Sophia struggled against his embrace. "I want you too, baby." She smiled, opening her eyes. She licked the tip of his nose and he peeked at her beneath hooded eyes as he thrust his hard cock against the pulsing ache between her legs.

"Hi," she giggled. "I love you, but I'm hungry," she said, planting a chaste kiss on his lips before climbing over him. "I'll be right back." At her words, every horror movie she ever saw flooded her mind. "Or, um…I'll just be a minute."

Everett sighed and adjusted himself on the couch, wincing at the pain in his knee. "Okay, but don't leave an injured man waiting too long. I need my medicine."

Sophia walked to the door, still laughing. Ever since they

got back from Mt. Hood, he joked about sex with her being the best cure for his pain, since all the blood rushed to his penis. He said it rendered his brain and the rest of his body helpless against his need for her.

She grabbed her purse on the table in the foyer, digging for her wallet as she opened the door. "Give me just a sec while I get you a tip."

Finally, when she found the five in the wallet pocket, she looked up. "Here you g—"

"Hello, Sophia."

She could feel her eyes widen and heat rush from her neck to her cheeks. She swallowed and blinked, hoping she was dreaming and her ex-husband wasn't really standing on her doorstep.

Indeed, the forecast was correct: the chances for the storm to be a big one were great. What was she going to do with Austin at the door and Everett on the couch?

Her luck did not change.

Austin was on the second step. Given his height, their eyes were level.

"What are you doing here?" she asked, a mixture of annoyance and panic creeping into her tone. She stuffed the money back into her purse and quickly glanced over her shoulder. She didn't want Everett to see Austin. She never wanted them to get within a thousand miles of each other.

Just leave me alone. Please go away.

"I'm glad I was able to surprise you." Austin's baritone was playful, but the expression etched into the pale, hairless lines of his face held the same stern flatness. He wasn't smiling. He was searching, studying her. Inspecting her changes.

Sophia was doing the same.

She was learning she wasn't the same spineless, weak-willed woman.

Austin stood completely erect, his arms flat at his sides with his fingers hanging loose, rain dripping from the tips. His face seemed rounder, pudgier, like he'd gained some weight, though his features were sharp and angular and soured with disdain. The deep-set, stark blue eyes she once considered airy clear skies were now overcast and icy as they peered back at her.

Despite the downpour soaking into his tailored black suit, she didn't invite him in, nor did she hint she would. Instead, Sophia backed into the doorjamb, holding the handle and blocking the entrance.

"You're not welcome here," she managed.

She expected shock or embarrassment, but his reaction fit neither of those descriptions.

Now a wicked smile chiseled a thin line across his face as if her rejection humored him. Like she was a child daring not to obey. He got off on being dismissed, but instilling fear in people fueled him. Intimidation was his favorite tactic.

He stepped up onto the porch landing, towering a head above her as he flattened his large hand on the face of the door. It squeaked as he pried it open further.

She stilled her stance in case he lurched forward. "What in the fuck are you doing?"

"This is my house," he chided her.

Sophia stood tall and lifted her chin. She was trying to keep her voice low for Everett's sake, but she couldn't let Austin show up and show out. Not on her doorstep. Her backbone was definitely stronger.

"No! This is MY house now," she roared, her voice thundering, echoing against the hollow of the hallway.

CHAPTER 16

Everett's phone buzzed in his pocket. As he dug it out from under him, he saw it was a text from his sister.

Zora: Did you tell her yet?

It was only the tenth time she asked him in the past week. This was just like her. Talk about old habits dying never. Even when she was a toddler, if she wanted something, she'd harp on it until she got what she wanted. In this case, there was only one answer she'd accept.

He tried telling her he was working on it and he needed more time—needed to wait for the right moment. None of which were the correct answer for his little sister. Still he staved her off for a little longer.

Paired with a few glasses of wine and a couple of slices of pizza, tonight seemed like the right time and place to unload the truth. Only, would Sophia still be his once she knew everything?

Everett: I see you're still minding my business. This is how I know you're adopted. Love you.

And three, two, one...

Zora: You're a small child, you know that?

Everett: Say you love me back. What if I die?

Zora: Don't be such a brat. Just tell her already. And fine, love you.

Works every time. Everett smiled to himself, pleased with his ability to rile his sister up. It cracked him up to be able to get under her skin. He shouldn't enjoy it, but she just seemed to walk right into his trap. It was too easy.

Everett: Laying it on thick, are we?

He hated to do it, but she left herself wide open, and teasing her was so much more fun than making promises he wasn't sure he could keep.

Everett picked the remote control back up and pressed the guide button. As he scanned through the available movies, three rows down, he saw the *Paranormal Vigilante.*

"I found the movie. It's on OnDemand," he called to Sophia. As he listened for her response, he realized she'd been really quiet. Too quiet, and it was taking way too long for a pizza delivery.

"Baby, you need me to—"

"This is my house." He heard Sophia's voice boom from the hallway. *Aw, shit.* Quickly, Everett swung his feet over the side of the couch and limped toward the front door. The pain was wearing off, but it was kind of nice having her tend to his needs.

From her tone, he couldn't tell whether she was an angry mess of hunger, or if the delivery guy was trying to force himself inside. Although, given her level of hunger, he was willing to bet on the former.

"What happened? Did they get the order wrong?" He laughed as Sophia's back came into view. It wasn't until he was directly behind her when he saw her body wedged in the door, her foot planted in place like a doorstopper.

Then, he noticed who was standing on the other side of her. *Fuck.*

"Austin," Everett said, shocked.

Almost instantly Everett's body tensed and his jaw clenched. Unblinking and singularly focused on the unwanted guest, Everett saw red as he urged his antsy fingers not to ball into fists. The sight of the man alone left him on defense. He wanted to push Sophia behind him and protect her from everything Austin did to her, and all the horrible things he knew a Harman was capable of beyond the terrible things the man had already done to her.

"Wait, you two know each other?" Sophia said, pivoting toward him. Her eyes flicked back and forth between him and Austin. She looked confused, and rightly so. He shouldn't have waited to tell her. Now he didn't know whether he would get the chance to before he was cut off at the pass.

Everett ignored Sophia for the time being. "Can we help you?" he asked Austin. "Because if not, I'm pretty sure this is trespassing."

A smug grin stretched the edges of the asshole's mouth, and Everett wanted to smack it off.

Everett was imagining all the ways he could teach this guy a lesson. He felt the hardness tightening his expression, but then Austin turned to Sophia and looked at her sideways.

"Oh, honey, John and I go way back. Our families go back even further," he said. He was clearly sensing that Everett hadn't disclosed just how many ties their families shared over the decades.

"I'm not your honey," she spat, and glared at Austin before fixing her evil eye on Everett. "And what is he talking about?" Her narrow look seared through him as she folded her arms and looked up at him. Her brows shot up expectantly.

Nope, he definitely wasn't going to be able to put it off any longer.

Everett cleared his throat and spoke, slowly and tentatively —another pair of ears were just waiting for him to get it wrong. "Remember when I told you about my grandmother?" He was talking to Sophia, but Austin straightened at the mention of Babs, matching Sophia's folded arms while Everett got to the point.

Austin leaned on the doorjamb. His ankles were crossed, like he was settling in for a good storytelling. A tale which Everett was sure he would be quick to fill in any holes.

Sophia inhaled and sighed impatiently, as if she vaguely remembered. Seeing how fast she downshifted and turned on him, an agonizing pang pierced his heart. It really sucked to be on this end of the stick.

At her slight nod, Everett continued. "Well, what he's referring to is the short-lived relationship his grandfather, Henry, shared with Babs."

"Oh, putting it mildly, don't you think? I'd say sliding in on someone else's bride, no matter how long the relationship lasted, is foul. I'm sure you'd agree."

Austin's words weren't minced. They never were.

On the surface, he was talking about Everett's grandfather, Winthrop Monroe, and the choice he made decades before. How he willingly gave up friendship for love. Barbara was so close to being a Harman herself until Winthrop swept her off her feet and she called off her engagement to Henry. Everett was sure it would be the version Austin would tell—the betrayal sparking a feud and burning the bond between rival families. And of course, beyond the surface, the whole *sliding in on someone else's bride* comment, wasn't lost on him. But Sophia was no longer Austin's bride.

The stories weren't old. Babs warned Everett against the red fire blazing in Austin's eyes now. She said she saw it in Henry, and in Joseph, Everett's father—the anger and the greed-fueled need for revenge.

Babs's choice was the same as Sophia's. She would have to choose: money or love. Or rather, house or love.

Everett's level tone and his volume teetered along with his restraint. "Maybe, but we're not our fathers, and we're certainly not our grandfathers." His neck thickened beneath the pressure of his clenched jaw and tense shoulders. "So why don't we just draw the line in the sand here? She doesn't want you here, and that's all there is to it."

As Sophia squared her body to Austin, he backed away from the door without breaking his stare. Everett stood directly behind her and settled his hands on her shoulders, caressing and massaging them.

They were finally a unified front facing their common enemy.

Austin glared as he watched Everett's hands moving rhythmically over Sophia's body, but then the mystified look transformed into amusement. "Oh, shoot!" He fisted his hand and blew into the small hold his curved fingers made. Laughter pinched at his brow and his face reddened. "This just keeps getting better and better by the second. John? I see you're still enjoying my leftovers."

Sophia's eyes widened. At first, Everett assumed she was outraged by Austin's reference to her as a leftover.

Nope, and the implication of the word "still" made it seem like this had happened more than once. But then the rims of her eyes filled and her lips quivered.

"What, baby? He's an asshole. Don't listen to him," Everett pleaded with her.

"Bottom of the barrel, huh, Soph? You're so weak. I knew you were nothing without me." Austin shook his head and continued snickering, nourishing the doubt he'd planted with sly sublety. "I'm sure he'll leave you soon, too, just like I did—if he's smart. Like your father did. But, I don't know…"

She swallowed, seeming to bite back emotion. "John? Why does he keep calling you that? Tell him it's not your name. Tell me John is not your fucking name." Her words caught on her breath as she blinked repeatedly, waiting for the truth.

"Baby? I love this." Austin was relentless at his taunting, throwing gasoline on the deteriorating situation.

"Actually, I've been meaning to—"

"Actually what? Your name is *Everett.*" Sophia stepped away from him, and he reached for her, but she jerked away, looking at both of them like they were one and the same. Like they were both monsters.

"How about I introduce you two? Sophia Harman—"

"It's Kent," she said through the tears now freely flowing. "I gave the name back in the divorce too, if you recall."

"Okay." Austin shook his head lightly and smirked as if to say, *whatever. It doesn't matter either way.* "If you insist. Sophia

Kent meet John Everett Monroe, the man who's going to take this house away from you. Can't blame me for this one, I'm just taking my cue from you guys."

Sophia's shoulders deflated and her chin dropped to her chest. "John E. Monroe."

Austin threw his hands up in the air, washing his hands clean of the shitstorm he created. With a theatrical spin, he pivoted and walked away.

This was his intention all along, and Everett and Sophia played right into his hands. He was right. It just kept getting better and better for him. The outcome would have been the same for Austin either way, but they added the cherry on top by falling in love.

"Tell me it's not true," she whispered through her tears.

"I was going to tell you. You have to believe me," Everett said. But his answer was weak even to his own ears. His voice was uneven and shaken. "This was my grandmother's house. The Harmans stole it from her. For years, they've been searching for a way to retaliate for her leaving Henry, they knew she was suffering from dementia, and they tricked her into signing over the deed to them. I'm just sorry you ended up in the middle of this mess. You have to believe me. Sophia, I love you."

"It all makes sense now." Her voice was just above a whisper. She was talking more to herself than to Everett—her attention fixed on something in the distance. "I should have known. All of it was right there in front me, and I was too weak, too stupid to pay attention to the clues. Barbara 'Babs's Monroe. Her early onset dementia. Monroes and Harmans. The family feud. Mike working for Monroe Properties, *your* real estate development company," She mumbled.

"You're not making sense, sweetheart."

"It makes perfect sense. You were at my door serving me the papers for the hearing. You've known this wh-whole time." There was a catch in her throat, but the accusation in her tone was unmistakable. "You let me fall for you and cry on your shoulder while you listened to everything I've been through. I met your family, and I thought we really were something worth all the pain, but you were lying all along. It was all a lie."

The knots in Everett's stomach tightened. The thought of Sophia believing what they shared was anything less than a miracle, a gift, crushed him.

"Please don't say it." He ran his hands over his hair and pressed his palms against his temples. He'd never felt so helpless and afraid. His heart hammered against his ribcage and he couldn't catch his breath. "I love you so much. I just didn't know how to tell you about the house. This doesn't change anything about how I feel about you. Please, Sophia."

She swiped at her tears and looked at him.

The ocean in her eyes was calm as a tremble ran over her.

He recognized the look, broken and betrayed. He'd been there too many times to count. He could feel the shards of his shattered heart cutting him from the inside out as she held the door. When Everett set foot out onto the porch, she inhaled, standing taller as she centered herself in the frame.

Then she uttered the words with the power to cut the deepest.

"I don't ever want to see you again," she said, and slammed the door in his face.

SOPHIA WAS nine movies deep in a forty-eight-hour Netflix horror movie marathon. Granted, the bloodshed on some of them was a little much, even for her, but their logic comforted her. To be precise, three logical steps.

One: there were no happy endings. Right now, happiness equated to tears, and fear was better than bawling herself into a catatonic state.

Two: if there was any sex in it, it was mostly B movie bumping and grinding, and they ended up getting killed off almost instantly.

And three: she was too scared to move, which basically justified her unwillingness to relocate from the couch.

"Oh, don't go in there," she yelled at the TV as she carved out another heaping spoonful of double scoop Strawberry Cheesecake ice cream and stuffed it in her face. As the tangy sweetness melted, she shook her head at the woman who decided waiting for her boyfriend in the Jacuzzi was a good idea.

Nestled into a comfy corner of the couch, Sophia was warm from the heat of the fireplace and the mound of blankets clouded around her, but the cold of the ice cream balanced into a feeling of coziness.

"Open your damn eyes, idiot. It's not Tyler," she screamed at the bikini-clad woman on the screen as she finally took note of the callused, bloody fingers on her wet skin. Surprisingly, she was able to get out of the water.

"Run!" Sophia continued to yell. She was fully aware this was a movie, the filming wrapped, thus allowing her to watch it on the couch in three-day-old, slightly dingy fluorescent pink Lily pajamas. But she did not reserve one-sided TV talk just for movies. Jeopardy, Friends re-runs and reality shows were not exempt. Her TV-talking skills were long since honed as an only child, then as a woman in an empty marriage, and now after a post-betrayal breakup.

"Not toward the woods. Oh, my gosh. Seriously? Go ahead and fall while you're at it."

As if on cue, the woman tripped over a teensy mound of ground cover. Pretty much grass and flat dirt. And somehow the magic bathing suit miraculously managed not to reveal even a nipple despite all the woman's running and falling. Sophia burrowed into the blanket, peeking through her fingers. Sure enough, the masked murderer caught up with bikini girl in no time flat. *Maybe it's because she was running around in circles?* He hovered over her and took equally slow steps forward as she crawled backward.

The second he cranked the machete up over his head Sophia braced herself. It was either going to be an ear-to-ear slice like Tyler, a watermelon whack over the head, or the hang out to dry gut-drop. She slid down into the covers a few more inches. Her eyes widened and her heartbeat thudded in her ears as she held her breath.

"Please don't hurt me. Please. I'm begging you," the woman pleaded—as if he'd brought the blood-smeared machete to slice cold cuts.

Just when Sophia thought he was going to go watermelon on her, he leaned down and grabbed her by the ponytail, hauling her up in the air. *Gut-drop? Really?*

He brandished his machete right next to her as the woman reached for his mask.

Then the robotic, adenoidal chirping of Aqua's song, Barbie Girl burst into the air.

Sophia screamed and yanked her covers up over her head when she heard the music. She jumped to her feet, bouncing on the sofa cushions as she looked around. Her phone buzzed and rang with her cousin's ringtone.

"Not now, Jules. Not now. It's Kevin Killian." She pointed at the screen, jumping frantically. "Kevin fucking Killian is the Machete Man," she yelled to the phone as it danced across the tabletop. "I *knew* it."

After a few seconds the ringing stopped. Killian dragged the lifeless redhead's body to his shed just as the virgin who'd been hiding in the attic opened her eyes. Then, buzz. Buzz.

Ugh. Barbie Girl's world again.

"Your timing is the worst. What?" Sophia snapped into the phone, while she craned to keep her eyes on the TV. Her voice trembled with both fear and irritation as the virgin stepped on a squeaky floorboard. "I'm busy."

"Seriously? What are you even doing? You can't hide from your family."

It was true. Though the truth wouldn't stop Sophia from trying, even knowing it was futile. They were going to descend upon her eventually.

Sophia sighed and plopped down onto the couch, burrowing back under the covers. "I'm not hiding from you guys. I'm hiding from Machete Man." She could still see a blurred version of the action through the threads.

A series of beeps sounded in her ear. She held out the phone to look at it. "I don't want to FaceTime right now," she said, putting the phone back to her ear, but the beeping continued.

"Well, I guess we'll just have to talk with the sound in the background."

She didn't doubt for a second her cousin would keep sending the request until one of them hung up...or got annoyed enough to press the green button.

"Fine." She huffed. As soon as Julie's face appeared, she regretted accepting the request.

In the top right corner, there was Sophia, looking like who

did it and why, while her cousin looked like a dewy-cheeked, doe-eyed, face-wash model. The kind with splashing water and eyebrows somehow remaining unrealistically tamed—the after picture with the added bonus of a fun-sized "before" image tucked in the corner. *Just peachy.*

Julie let her hair grow back out, but her mane looked voluminous and shiny, and her trademark bale of curls waterfalled over the top of the chair. Her skin was a warm bronze like she'd been basking out in the sun. And to top it all off, she was glistening with pre-wedding glow.

Not a stitch of makeup, naturally beautiful. But still, naturally, attitudy.

Sophia mimicked her pursed lips and pinched brow, failing to look as pensive and appealingly pouty since her lips weren't as full.

"Show me," Julie demanded.

The pale green walls of Aunt Marian's house filled the background behind her. She was sitting in her dad's recliner watching TV, too. The volume was low, but over the murder and mayhem on her own screen, Sophia could barely hear it... "Rory and Lorelai?" She ignored the bossy "show me" demand. Talk about calling the kettle black. "Are you freaking watching Gilmore Girls?"

"Yes."

Sophia shook her head, rolling her eyes. "Not even going to try to deny it. Gah, you're such a nerd."

"Takes one to know one." She stuck out her tongue. "And where are you?" She narrowed her eyes at the phone and leaned in closer. "What are you doing? Are you—"

"Under the covers. Yes. I'm still in my pajamas, eating ice cream under the covers, watching horror movies. Or at least I was when you rudely interrupted me."

"So, you look like shit, you probably stink to high hell, and you're moping, right?"

Before she could answer, Julie stopped and seemed to consider something. "Wait a minute. You said ice cream. What flavor?"

CHAPTER 17

"Strawberry Cheesecake," Sophia said, sinking deeper into the couch cushions. Strawberry Cheesecake was the dead giveaway. She could have gotten the movie marathon past Julie, but the ice cream? No. Not a chance with that flavor.

When the door rang earlier, Sophia made it through the messy living room obstacle course in record time, hurdling shoes and empty Chinese cartons and pizza boxes. Blessed be, she could have just hugged the GrubHub delivery guy, who, for the love of God, skipped the greetings and small talk and just gave her the ever-lovin' ice cream.

She hadn't seen another human being in days, apart from the army of delivery people from varying fast food restaurants. It was lazy and expensive, but the world was too people-y. Cats, dogs, anything with fur (other than rats) would have been fine, but she didn't have pets, and even they reminded her of Blue, who in turn reminded her of Everett. Just thinking of him reminded her of his thick, hard cock and her thighs clenched at the memory of him filling her so completely.

Wham! Dead-end road.

She simply could not go down that road, or, as a matter of self-preservation, any other roads.

Lord, I miss him.

Some body parts more than others, though. Just because Everett was gone didn't mean she wasn't horny as all get-out. She practically jumped the Amazon delivery guy's bones, and he wasn't even cute. The decision just made sense. It was best if she quarantined herself from anything with a penis, or anything remotely sunny and chipper.

Anything other than ice cream.

"Oh no. It's Strawberry Cheesecake bad? It's barely been a month."

Sophia nodded, feeling the lump—which she'd managed to keep at bay one jump-scare at a time—rising up in her throat again. With the exception of Mom via FaceTime, who insisted on checking on her every hour on the hour, she might as well have been on her own deserted island. Exactly where she wanted to be. Alone.

She'd already told Julie about everything. Everett, the house, Austin, her inevitable move back to Vegas if the hearing went the way she thought it would. Julie understood why this house meant so much to her, to Ainsley.

"Show me," Julie said again with much more urgency this time. "I want to see everything." Sophia fumbled out from under the blanket, pointing the phone toward her wasteland, she added, "Steady."

She suspected Julie's eyes widened with shock, though she was decent enough not to say what she clearly was thinking, based the stark silence. Her voice was level and measured, like she was dealing with a child. "Now pan the room."

The glow of the phone highlighted strewn clothes, piles of

shoes scattered where she toed them off, and dirty dishes and cups covering the gaps on the table not filled by the litter of half-eaten fast food trash.

Sophia's heart dropped.

When she brought the screen back to face her, she saw it in Julie's eyes. "I'm coming up there for the hearing tomorrow."

"No." Sophia's voice cracked. "I need to do this by myself. You shouldn't have to worry about me. You should be doing wedding stuff like revenge seating charts and Blacktalian (black and Italian) music playlists, last-minute emergency cake tastings. Not dealing with my—"

"Your what, your life? Everything else can wait. I'm not getting married tomorrow, Soph. Stop acting like you don't need anyone. Like you have to be so strong. What do you think I'm here for? What we're all here for." Julie dropped her chin and when she lifted it again, her teary eyes met Sophia's.

"You don't have to do this by yourself, you know? You have family, a whole army of us who care about you, so don't do this alone. Let us be there for you this time."

This time. That time. Next time?

The thought of there being another betrayal wrapped a vise grip around what was left of her heart. She wasn't sure she would even make it through this time. Losing Ainsley felt like a wildfire cleared away all signs of life, leaving her barren with nothing but ashen memories.

But then she went somewhere new and did something different. She met Everett, who made things bloom and flower again. He rained down on her roots and gave her the sun. She'd felt so alive and wild and full.

It wasn't like she could forget about her angel baby. This was just so much different. With Everett it was like she was reminded of the possibilities. Of maybe one day making a new life, this time rooted in love.

Losing him after everything she went through...this time Sophia knew she wouldn't recover. There was no coming back from the desolate truth.

TWENTY-SEVEN MINUTES AND THIRTY-FOUR SECONDS.

It took less than a half hour for the hearing to run its course.

You would think after all the weeks and months of man hours Everett spent on this one house, he would have felt an intense sense of relief to have it done and over with—the word "finally" loose on his tongue.

That maybe he'd feel on-top-of-the-world victorious to have reclaimed his family's property—the only house where it had ever felt like home. And perhaps he should thank Mike for helping him honor the last wishes of his beloved grandmother. Even then it would only be logical to think he'd be happy he got exactly what he asked for.

Of course you'd be wrong.

Even as the judge called for the next case, Everett didn't move. He sat in the hard wooden chair staring at the other end of the table where Sophia sat. She was long gone, her lawyer, Jacob Bornstein, his high school football adversary, in tow. But Everett was still numb, frozen in place.

"Come on, man. Let's go," Mike said. He just finished packing his files away in the weathered leather briefcase Everett gave him two Christmases ago.

Everett looked up at him from his seat as a smug grin twisted the lines of Mike's face into an annoying smirk. A nonverbal *I told you so*. But what did he tell him, really, that

Everett didn't already know? About Austin being an insidious bastard who left nothing but wreckage in his wake? According to Michael Kennedy-at-law, all the Harmans were. Or that Sophia was nothing but a pawn lost in the game?

He knew all of it, and none of it would bring Sophia back.

Almost two weeks had passed since he last saw her, but nothing could have prepared him for the way his heart plummeted into his stomach at the mere sight of her. The throbbing ache intensified everything and paralyzed him all at once. Seeing her again after such a long absence was jarring to his system to say the least, but she didn't look like herself. Her eyes were empty. She was still beautiful, but so serious, dressed in a navy skirt suit with her hair slicked back into a severe bun. It killed him a little on the inside to think he had any part in dimming her light, in helping her rebuild the walls around her heart, but stronger this time.

Mike's hand on his shoulder startled him back to the present and Everett stood abruptly. "I have to get out of here." He shook away the memory of Sophia's red-rimmed eyes. She didn't look at him once, but he couldn't take his eyes off her. "I'll catch up to you later. I'm not going back to the office today."

But as he turned away, Mike lurched forward and grabbed him by the arm. "Really, dude? You're going to go sulk somewhere?" His tone was sarcastic and cynical, like he meant to lighten the mood, but Everett couldn't downshift so fast.

In fact, with the move alone, Everett went from zero to sixty in no time flat. Tension curled into his fingers and his shoulders arched slightly back. His jaw squared under the clenching of his teeth. By the way Mike slowly retracted his hand, Everett suspected the acidic anger bubbling from his throat had made its way to his face.

He cut his eyes to the spot on his arm where his friend tightened his grip, then met Mike's eyes. "Don't ever grab me again."

This time, as Everett turned to walk away, Mike didn't stop him.

Everett wasn't sure where he was headed. He only knew he needed to be outdoors. The oak and marble walls seemed to be closing in on him, tighter and tighter, until he urgently needed to just breathe.

As he stumbled out on the sidewalk, a gust of August wind buffeted him, frantic and restless, sending chills down his spine. He was used to the air, full and damp with the promise of rain. Leaves rustled, noisy, clattering in fumbling swarms along the busy, tree-lined street. His senses had been numb, but suddenly he found himself taking note of every sound and scent and image. It was like a painting clashing with too much color. He wanted the noise and the movement to stop—if only for a moment—to give him time to think.

He ran his fingers through his hair and rested them behind his head, stretching. Right now he could go anywhere he wanted, but there was only one place he wanted to be. It just so happened it was also one of the only two places he couldn't go.

Getting out his cell, he found Sophia's name in his favorites. Everett knew she wouldn't talk to him, but it was dire—vital—for him to try. It rang one time before going to voicemail. As he expected, she ignored him, and the ache in his chest tightened.

Listen Sophia, I know you don't want to talk to me, and I don't blame you. But please give me a chance to explain. Please. I would never do anything to hurt you. I love you so much.

When he disconnected the call, he wasn't surprised to find Mike standing beside him. Not looking at him, but staring straight ahead.

"I figured when I didn't hear from you or see you in weeks, maybe you just needed some time," he said.

Everett lifted his chin, on edge as he listened.

"Got me thinking about life and how things work out sometimes. I could tell she loves you."

Everett turned and studied Mike's expressionless face. The hard lines of his jaw were locked in place.

"I just hope you really give it a chance," Mike continued. "It's not the same as with your pops. He was a self-serving asshole who didn't give a shit about his wife or his kids. He cared about money and appearances. You're not him. You wouldn't abandon Sophia. I know you. You wouldn't let your pride stand between you. Long as you and I have been friends, for you to square up on me the way you did back in the court-room..." Mike shook his head, like he couldn't have imagined the day would ever come. Not when it mattered. "I knew you loved her. Now I know just how much."

Mike's expression softened as he met Everett's gaze, and for a second they were boys again. Back on the playground, on the football field, at the funerals of Everett's mom and Mike's younger brother, in the club, in the office. They were kids with long, muddied pasts, who knew each other's dirt and loved hard despite them.

Emotion clogged Everett's throat. He shrugged and gave Mike a quick nod, smiling. "You up for a ride?"

He might not be able to be where he wanted to be, but there was still one place he needed to be.

CHAPTER 18

Laurie Strode, wearing nothing but a hospital gown and an ace bandage around her ankle, crept out of her hiding place just when Michael Myers gut-dropped the nurse.

Sophia was back on the couch again, binging on her horror movie marathon for the night. This time she went for the triple scoop of Rocky Road, Strawberry Cheesecake, and Mint and chips. Her emotions were all over the place, which meant only the classic horror movies would do, starting with the original *Halloween*.

"Don't just stand there, stupid! Ruuunnnn," Sophia yelled at the screen. "Or limp if you have to."

Michael was doing his supersonic slow-fast walk behind a limping Laurie, and the creepy music just hit high drive when Sophia's ears perked up at the distinct sound of jingling keys.

Only it wasn't coming from the TV.

Shit. At some point, I'm going to have to find a healthier way to lick my wounds.

Sophia froze and reached for the remote control to lower

the volume. Those damn movies were making her skittish. Her heart raced and she could feel her eyes widening while she listened for the sound again.

Immediately her mind went to Austin's last visit. How he popped up out of nowhere to make sure he'd thoroughly ruined her life. Her skin blazed at the memory of his smug smile. How he seemed to revel in being the bearer of hope-crushing bad news. For his sake, she prayed it better not be him—there were still a few jagged bones she intended to pick with him.

She waited and listened, every nerve ending in her body standing at attention. With the TV on mute, she heard nothing but the chirp of crickets and the hum of the refrigerator in the kitchen. It was practically killing her not to say *is anyone there?* If not for Laurie being chased by her crazed psycho lunatic brother right then, Sophia might have called aloud, *hello?* Only an idiot would do something so stupid. She watched enough movie murders to know the rules of stupidity and inevitable death by maniacal sociopaths.

Instead, she swiped her phone off the table and crept toward the formal dining room beside the front door. Ninja-like, she peeked out the window toward the driveway. A red sedan was parked right in front of her house.

At the static silence, the hairs on her arms stood up.

Sophia glared skyward, shaking her head. "Really? We're doing this?" she whisper-yelled. "You're adding home invasion to my list of shitty luck?" She didn't know anyone who owned a red car. The number of people she knew in Portland was limited. Other than anyone related to Everett, it was her lawyer, and Kara, who Sophia barely spoke to on account of the time she'd spent buried under Everett.

She let loose a spate of curse words as she turned away

from the window, searching the darkness for anything to use as a makeshift weapon. Her weekender tote was packed and sitting by the door with her purse. There was the broom she abandoned mid-sweep after spilling cereal, a metal lamp, and the dang black pump heel she'd been looking for since Monday.

The doorknob rattled and the keys jingled again.

Ducking down, she crept toward her purse, digging out the small Swiss Army knife clipped to her key chain—a gift from Mom during one of her super dramatic moments after Sophia told her about a guy following her in the grocery store. Rather than argue, she humored her mother by putting it on the chain.

Damn it, she hated when Mom was right.

As soon as she heard the sound of a key slide into the lock and turn, Sophia stilled herself on the other side of the half-wall facing the foyer. She held the sharpest edge of the knife upward and held her breath as the front door creaked open and muffled footsteps scuffed quietly along the tiled floor.

"Shit," she mumbled under her breath. There was more than one pair of footsteps.

"Where's the bedroom?" a hushed female voice asked.

"Upstairs. Should we—"

Of course her phone would vibrate at the worst possible moment, giving her no other choice but to charge at her intruders. She blasted around the corner with a vengeance, knife pointed straight ahead, crouched in a fighting stance.

By no more than a hair, she missed filleting her mother and Julie as they unleashed a hail of ear-piercing, blood-curdling shrieks and giving any B-movie scream queen a run for her money.

"What are you guys trying to *do* to me?" Sophia tossed the knife onto the entry table, holding her heart.

"Us? You almost stabbed us. I was like this close to dying before I make it down the aisle." Julie brought her thumb and forefinger within a millimeter of each other. "You're lucky, too, because Nico would have killed you."

"Both of you hush, now. I knew in my bones this thing would come in handy at some point. I just wish you knew how to use it." Mom put her large tote bag on the table and rolled her paisley suitcase next to her daughter's sensible black one by the door.

Sophia took one look at the two of them and burst out laughing. They were both wearing all black, from their expensive rain boots to their hooded coats and leggings. "You guys are a hot mess, you know? What were you doing, casing the place? Staking it out?" She shook her head, rolling her eyes as she bit back a grin. "And you rented a car?"

"Well, if you answered any of our calls, we would have told you we were coming. But since you shut us out the way you always do, we got worried and figured we would either rescue you or surprise you."

"By the looks of things, seems like we were successful with both," Julie chimed in as she peered into the living room, where Sophia's movie marathon was set.

"Whatever, Jules. You guys are so annoying."

"Aunt Helen, don't let her fool you. She's happy to see us. She's just moping right now." Julie pursed her lips and gave Sophia a telling look. It screamed *don't even try to deny it*. "Anyway, I would be willing to make a sizable wager that your predictable daughter has been stewing in her own filth on the couch watching axe-murderers and eating Strawberry Cheesecake ice cream. Am I right, Soph?" She gave her a condescending double pat on the shoulder as she waltzed into the living room toward the aforementioned scene of the crime.

Sophia loudly sucked her teeth and folded her arms, but she didn't deny it. "Whatever, Jules. You should try it. It works."

God, Sophia loved the way a good gut-wrenching, blood-racing flick could help put things into perspective. Mere heartbreak and eviction weren't even a blip on the radar compared to a murderer chasing you when it came to worries. Sure, she was going to have to uproot her life for the second time in less than two months, but she wasn't being hunted. She was alive and well.

Well, a shell of her old self, but alive with mostly regular vital signs.

"I know I'm right. And it's exactly why we're here. You're not going to shut down again." Her cousin was still talking from the other room. She could see her turning on lights and beginning to unravel the fluffy cloud of blankets Sophia was huddled in just a few minutes earlier.

"Oh, honey. Is this what you've been doing up here? Crying?"

"No." *Yes.*

From the living room, Julie cosigned, "Yes."

"Mind your own business, please." Sophia's perfunctory smile was there, etched in place. The only problem was, it only worked on people who'd never seen her in diapers or taken baths with her when they were toddlers.

Naturally Mom slapped on her mother mask, the one with the pointed stare and tilted head. The *you came out of my womb, so I know you better than anyone else on this earth* look. "Why don't we go sit down and talk about the hearing? You may not be ready now, but at some point"—she paused briefly for exaggerated emphasis, and to lift Sophia's chin so they were looking at each other eye-to-eye—"I'm going to need you to tell me about this fella who's got you all bent out of shape."

It was one thing to talk about Everett with Julie, but Mom?

Her mother tended to be cautious, to say the least. When it came down to it, she was worse than the CIA, the way she could scrounge up insignificant minutia and drag out a man's demons. Every man Sophia ever dated was, for some period, accused of having some strange affliction Mom felt it necessary to comment upon. Stuff out of left field, like a womanizing male chauvinist look, or serial killer eyes. And not once did Mom ever explain any specific criteria that led to her conclusions. She all but attacked Evan Landers in high school, practically strip-searching him because she was dead set on the idea that he was hiding a gun in his pants. Heaven forbid he admit he just dry-humped her daughter on the porch, resulting in a rather sizable stiffy.

Given her mom's tendency to jump the gun, Sophia was curious to see exactly which outlandish pigeonhole Everett would be shoved into. She almost laughed aloud at the idea, but then she remembered the reality of just how bad things were in the courtroom.

"There's really nothing left to tell." Sophia shrugged.

She didn't want to think about how it felt like a million miles and a lifetime were between her and Everett seated at opposite ends of the same table. How she felt the weight of his gaze crashing down on her the whole time. If they couldn't come to a meeting of the minds, she certainly couldn't meet his eyes.

"Oh, come on now, Strawberry Cheesecake and *Halloween*? He must really be something."

"He was. Past tense, meaning he isn't anymore, so can we drop it?"

Mom's chin fell to her chest, and when she looked up again a faint smile crinkled the corners of her eyes. "I know you didn't get this house. I can tell you're back there at the old house, and it feels like your father leaving all over again, but this is not the same. Your father was just selfish, but Julie says your guy did everything he could to do right by you in the courtroom."

Tears pricked at Sophia's eyes.

Everett *did* find every possible way to add in concessions, making sure the judge knew Austin willingly agreed on the divorce settlement with full knowledge his ownership was in question. Both with the move-out extension and his determination to point out the flaws in Austin's character, Everett brought everything to light. Together, he and Mike got the judge to amend the previous settlement and order Austin to pay Sophia the value of the property.

But the cherry on top of the rum raisin ice cream?

Based on the new documentation Mike presented regarding the Harman family's history of targeting elderly homeowners with financial difficulties, the judge reviewed the five other claims settled out of court, and the accusations of embezzlement in Austin's personal and business affairs, and he recommended initiating a new case against Austin.

It was good news.

Maybe even the best-case scenario.

"He did," Sophia whispered. "But how can I trust him now?"

Knowing her ex-husband was at the center of all this turmoil couldn't weld the rift ruptured between her and Everett. Every time Everett spoke, her throat closed in around the lump lodged there. Every time she felt her skin crawl with the undying need for him to touch her just once more, a shift traced the fault lines in her heart, and she knew it wouldn't be long before it caused irreparable damage.

He did what was right and maintained his loyalty to his family.

And although Sophia knew she shouldn't fault him for something he was fighting before she came along, she couldn't shake the fact he did exactly what she was afraid he would do. He let their good thing come to an end. Like her father, he took away everything with any meaning to her and left her to rely on herself.

So, in two days, she'd be on the first-thing flying back to Vegas, heading out with Mom's realtor in search of a cocoon where she could start anew. Again.

Sophia bit the inside of her cheeks to steady her nerves. She *was* bent out of shape, and she couldn't imagine in a thousand years how she was going to untie the knots twisting in her gut. It was all the flipping and flopping back and forth about running to Everett and shoving him away. It was seeing her mother here in the flesh, in the house she'd condemned before ever stepping foot inside.

Not even a couple of months ago Mom foretold this ending. And once again, Mom was right, and it pissed Sophia off—just a teensy bit.

She slowly blew out a small breath and looked into her mother's smiling eyes. "You should be happy. Looks like you're getting exactly what you want," Sophia said, her voice low and shaky.

"Honey, what on earth are you talking about?"

"The bet, or the pact. Whatever you want to call it, I know it's why you're here. Well, guess what? You win. I'm going back to Vegas, where you can keep tabs on me, and you didn't even have to wait six months."

OUT OF THE corner of his eye, Everett could see Mike sit up straighter as they parked next to the curb in front of Monroe

Manor, his father's showpiece of an estate. As they got out of the truck and stood shoulder to shoulder at the edge of the sprawling green lawn, there was something freeing about seeing the sold sign staked in the ground.

The smell of flowers and freshly cut grass whirled in the open air, natural and sweet. In all shades of pink, red, and yellow, they were blossoming, almost like they were finally free to bloom without Joseph haunting them.

Everett stood taller, his shoulders squared instinctively.

"Man, the pictures do nothing for this place." Mike cocked his head, and Everett recognized the mesmerized light in his eyes. Like a moth to a flame—you want to look away, but you can't. He felt the same way once.

When he first tried his hand at real estate, the cookie-cutter home designs of suburbia wouldn't do for Everett. Not the closely-packed garage-mahals with their curb appeal suffering at the expense of gigantic garages almost as big as the homes themselves. No, no bungalow, colonial, or Craftsman could measure up in his mind back then. Like Joseph Monroe, he needed his own namesake Antilia or Biltmore to carry on a yet-to-be-determined legacy. It needed to be the same red brick Southern or Georgian style, with shuttered windows and pearly white columns sectioning the home into quadrants. He wanted the clout of owning an impressive eight- to ten-thou-sand-square-foot home, even if he had no intention of filling its rooms.

Everett was dead set on becoming a man Joseph could see fit to call his son. Since Babs died, and now knowing what it felt like to go home to Sophia, it wasn't about the square footage or the showpiece any longer. He wanted more than beautiful surfaces. He wanted to decorate and fill every room of a simply stated, loving home. He wanted to share Patton Place with Sophia.

Everett inhaled and waved his hand in front of Mike's entranced face. "It's only an illusion. Don't fall for it."

"That's what you keep telling me." Mike's gaze was unblinking.

Everett watched him glide toward the glossy black door with the brass knocker centered below the peephole. He swallowed back the memories. "Go ahead and knock. I'm right behind you." But he hung back, thinking about how long it had taken him to get here.

By the year Everett turned eighteen, he was no longer the starry-eyed, scrawny kid waiting up for his dad to come back for him. A full-ride academic scholarship to State, a freshly-painted and rebuilt Mustang, and buzz about a promising football career later, he showed up at his father's house with his chin held considerably higher. He figured if everyone else bought into the hype, maybe Joseph Monroe wasn't exempt.

He went there with an inflated chest, finally believing he was enough. Like the stamp of approval he received every-where else would somehow translate to the acceptance and pride he so longed to see in his father's eyes when he looked at him instead of his new family.

So naive he believed he was finally the son a parent couldn't reject.

He bounded up the steps to the only glossy black door in a scarce sea of sensible slate grey and navy blue ones, feeling invincible. He stood on the porch, careful not to rouse the sleepy neighborhood, brimming with eager anticipation. But before he could lift his hand to the knocker, Joseph swung the door open and jumped down his throat, letting him know just how much thinner blood was than water. This man, who happened to share the same bloodline, heavy brow, square jaw, and dusky skin, saw fit to twist the angular lines of his face in loathsome anger. He was the same man, the mirror image. But they weren't family.

At least, Everett wasn't included in his.

Not even close.

Stupidly, after the door shut with him alone on the outside, he made his way to the line in the sidewalk facing the house, plotting and planning what it would take to cross over—to belong there. From then on, until Babs instilled the importance of family and loyalty in him, he navigated his life around the same coordinate on the map.

You're not him. You wouldn't do that to her, I know you.

"You coming, or what?" Mike asked.

Everett frowned down at his feet cemented on the pavement. There was the line drawn between the sidewalk and the first step to the house. It felt more like a gorge not so long ago. His shoes toed the edge of the line, almost as if he knew it was a point of no return. Like crossing it would have some undisclosed, significant meaning.

He balled and unballed his fists, cracking his knuckles as he shifted on his feet. Strangely, his heartbeat was steady at a comfortable rhythm. Everett couldn't get Mike's eye-rolling comment out of his mind.

He's been dead for two years. What's he going to do, call the cops? Babs?

The loud rap of metal on metal ripped him out of his thoughts. He lifted his chin to find his friend inspecting the structure up close and personal. Then Mike turned to look at him, his brows bobbing with excitement. "They don't even have a doorbell." He snickered. "Old school all the way."

Everett smiled back absently.

I knew you loved her. Now I know just how much.

He stifled a grin at Mike's amusement and remembered why he was there. He never replied to his half-brother, but assumed the invitation was still good. Along with taking all his own belongings, Joseph stole Everett's dreams. Or, at least the dreams Babs tucked away in a small wooden box for him. She said it wasn't fair for only girls to get hope chests. It was just how she was, fair and full of life and love. Babs called it the dream-catcher because she said boys needed a place to put their dreams too. He just hoped it would help him catch his new dream.

Right now he would give anything for some advice from his grandmother. She would know what he should do about Sophia. Babs would know how to unbreak Sophia's heart. How to show her how much she meant to him. Somehow let her know crossed lines didn't always have to be about the end—it could be a new start.

With the thought firmly rooted in his mind, Everett crossed the line on the sidewalk. When the door opened, he almost staggered back. His muscles tightened and the sound of his heavy heartbeat thudded in his ears.

Mike's eyes moved back and forth between Everett and the man at the door, who could only be Joseph Jr.

The similarity was uncanny, as if time ticked backward. As if history was rewritten and he was eighteen again, standing in the same spot, waiting for his father's welcome. The man stepped out into the setting sun, and the glare highlighted the warm, dark brown lines of his arched brow and square jaw. If Everett didn't have a certified copy of his father's death certificate filed in his cabinet at home, he wouldn't believe his own eyes.

"Everett?" Joseph Jr. asked, with the same husky rasp to his voice as their father.

When Everett said nothing, the man moved in closer. "I'm Joseph. Joe junior," he clarified with a shrug. "You got my message, then. I'm so glad you finally came. And I know you're here for your grandmother's box, but you're welcome to stay for a while."

Welcome.

The word hung in the air, buoyant and shocking, an unassuming olive branch. Everett took a deep breath and nodded his thanks for Joe's invitation before he walked into the house.

CHAPTER 19

"**Y**ou didn't hear the doorbell ringing? You have a guest," Mom roared, at the same time enunciating each word. "Now drag yourself up off the sofa and snap out of it, dammit."

She clapped her hands together right next to the one of Sophia's ears not glued to the sofa cushion. Her eyes fluttered in the direction of the door.

A guest?

Against her will, her heartbeat sped up. She tried not to let her excitement show, but already she could feel the heat crawling up her neck to her cheeks. "Who is it?"

"Well, if I knew, I would have said the name," her mom replied with a heated glare beneath a pair of expertly shaped raised eyebrows. "Why don't you go find out?"

Sophia eyed her mom suspiciously, as if this was some elaborate ruse to get her up off the couch. There was no way Everett would show up after the way she left things. He'd called too many times to keep count, and with what little dignity Sophia stashed away, she ignored and deleted each and every one of his messages without listening to them.

Horror-movies-and-ice-cream was one thing, but she wasn't a complete masochist.

Other than his declined calls, Kara called to check on her, but there hadn't been a peep out of Austin. She guessed he was either pleased with his handiwork—having effectively shoved a giant monkey wrench into her relationship with Everett—or gearing up to defend himself against the impending fraud and embezzlement charges.

A teensy giggle bubbled up inside her.

If she was going down, she would by God take everyone else involved in the farce down with her. She came all the way to Portland to start over, and somehow, in record time, she managed to lose her house, leave her new restaurant plans in limbo, and get her heart broken again. As if the job wasn't done right the first time around, she enlisted the first guy she met to really get in there good and crush it all the way.

Now Mom snapped her fingers a couple of times, signaling for Sophia to hop to it.

"I'm going. Good lord," Sophia said, rolling her eyes as she levered herself up off the couch.

As she stood, sliding her feet into her slippers, she was suddenly aware of the fact she was basically stewing in her own filth. She hadn't showered in two days. Frantically, she combed her fingers through her hair, smoothing the flyaways as she moved slowly down the hallway to the door. A messy ponytail wasn't so bad, but she was pretty sure her mean case of raccoon eyes nicely accented a pair of chapped lips and stained hot pink fleece pajamas.

Seriously? The timing can't be worse. If it is Everett at the door, it would just be typical.

Going back to square one with a vengeance.

By the time she reached the cracked-open door, Sophia's heart was basically doing speed cycle on crack. Her breathing swished and swashed and thwacked in her ears until she was at the entry. But her heart plummeted fast and hard into the pit of her stomach, and from the way her shoulders slumped almost instantly, she couldn't deny the weight of the letdown.

It wasn't him.

A breath she was holding leaked slowly out of her chest. "Hi."

"Hey." Zora beamed a genuine, if tentative, smile. Sympathetic as it might have been, it wasn't hard to see Zo recognized how Sophia deflated at the sight of her.

Her heart was set on someone else.

Here Sophia was, standing in the doorway with the sister of the man she was in love with, her would-be sister-in-law, and all she could think about was...what?

Zora had been a genuine friend to her from the get-go. Heaven forbid Sophia be thankful to have someone sane to talk to—someone who wasn't trying to rush her back to Vegas for their own selfish reasons. Like a grade-A ingrate, Sophia met Zora with a giant *Fuck Off* sign stamped on her forehead.

Unsure what else to do, she offered a conciliatory shrug and a weak smile. Basically an awkward *I'm sorry for being a douchebag to you.* Zora stepped backward, the way people do when they feel like they're imposing, and Sophia immediately felt like a complete asshole. It would be a swift blow to anyone's ego.

"I'm so sorry. I don't know where my manners are. Would you like to come on in?" Awkwardly, she went in for a forced hug, then grabbing Zora's hand and leading her into the house.

"No. You were expecting—"

"No. Well, yes, but...I promise. Don't worry about it." Sophia waved the idea away before Zora could verbalize all the knots tangled up inside her. She nodded her head in the direction of the living room. "You must think I'm so rude. Please come in. I insist."

"I can't." The words came out on a low breath. Traces of fear and pain stained the words like there was undoubtedly more behind them. It wasn't like an *I hate to impose, but ask me again and I'll concede* type of response. The firmness in those two simple words felt more like a physical incapability.

What's more, there was an unmistakable tinge of remorse Sophia couldn't overlook.

She glanced over her shoulder into the living room, and paused for the slightest moment, hoping to get a glimpse from another perspective. Her study lingered on the clean lines of the white built-ins balanced by the soft curves of the off-white sofa and Mediterranean blue accents.

There was nothing.

When Sophia returned to Zora, she remained cemented on the steps, unwavering, frozen in place. Her lips were pressed in a thin, polite smile, but there was pain behind her gaze.

It was then it hit Sophia.

What was Sophia really losing in this house? An unsteady home built on lopsided promises and lies? The memories of Ainsley? She would never be without those memories. There was nothing left for her here. She couldn't say the same for the woman standing before her, the quiet fire and peacemaker. Zora was her brother's keeper. She was the woman who befriended Sophia.

No, she couldn't say the same for Zora, or for Everett.

There was still a chance for them to hold onto the good.

"Zora, when's the last time you were here?" she asked tentatively and pressed her hand to her heart. She studied her friend for the briefest time, and in that moment, the way Zora's eyes turned up innocently, open, Sophia could almost see an endearing, childlike expression. The same mesmerized, melancholy stare she saw in Everett's eyes.

"He told me how your grandmother raised the two of you in this house. I know what it's like to lose someone you've centered all your hopes around." Sophia leaned against the doorjamb and let her chin graze her collarbone. "For what it's worth, I'm glad you're getting her house back."

They stood there on two sides of the same line drawn in the sand. But it wasn't the least bit awkward. Somehow, it was like they both said everything that needed to be said. Still, neither one of them moved to turn and close the door, or walk down the steps and drive away.

Sophia watched a bird perch right down on one of the potted topiaries framing the door. Its grayish-blue feathers contrasted in a ray of sunlight, only more vibrant in the backdrop of the red-bricked pavement. A faint breeze ruffled them slightly, but the tiny little thing continued pecking away, somehow unfazed by its surroundings and the presence of humans.

The corners of Sophia's mouth tugged upward.

This too shall pass.

Zora cleared her throat, interrupting Sophia's musings. When she looked up and followed Zora's line of sight into the house, she felt the tension come flooding back. Sophia ran her fingers over the length of her tousled ponytail.

"Does he know?"

Sophia shook her head hesitantly, still focused on her suitcases lined up by the entry table.

"Are you going to tell him you're leaving?" All traces of

empathy drained from Zora's tone, replaced by the unmistakable smear of judgment. She was protecting her brother.

On a half-squint, half-wince, Sophia shrugged. "It's better this way. Trust me, we were headed for the exit anyway."

"Better for who?" Zora jerked her head back, a smirk quivered at the left corner of her mouth. "I've seen you two together. You don't have to convince me. I know love when I see it, and you guys have it. I saw the way he looked at you."

Now Sophia did look at Zora, square in the face. She said, "have it," not "had it." She hadn't used the past tense. She believed it was still there, still strong, despite everything.

When she met the pointed stare aimed at her, she knew there was no sense denying the truth. Tears stung her eyes. Before she could say a word, Zora yanked her into a tight, urgent hug. Her lean, taut arms roped around her and knotted in place.

"What time's your flight?" she asked. Her voice was thick with the tornado of emotions they shared.

On a stuttered breath, Sophia whispered she was leaving early in the afternoon the following day.

"WHAT ARE you going to tell her?" Mike asked as they arrived back at Everett's house. "I mean, where should I say we were?"

Most of the drive home, Everett was in a daze and, frankly, unwilling to talk. What in the hell was there to say, anyway, when he couldn't really work out the magnitude of what just happened?

"Don't say anything," Everett muttered as he climbed the stairs and dug the key out of his coat pocket. He pivoted to Mike before turning the key, straight-faced and even-toned. "I got what I went there for. Nothing happened, so just chill.

My sister will get over it. Plus, she's the one who called all wired up. This is probably just another one of her little fire drills."

Mike entered first, looking guilty as all hell. Damn, what a mistake it had been to take him along. Everett always knew the guy couldn't hold water, but he always seemed to have the best of intentions. Lately, though, his inability to keep his pie-hole shut appeared to be directly related to his proximity to Zora.

When is he going to finally just admit it so we can skip to the good times?

Everett let the door shut behind him and shot Loose Lips a *play it cool* look. Hopefully, a few-decades-long friendship would override his friend's played-out efforts to get in good with Zo. He'd barely set the wooden box on the entry table when Zora started yelling for him to come into the living room.

"What took you so long?" By her tone and perma-raised brows, he could tell she was annoyed.

Long? With everything Joe told Everett weighing on his mind and his lead foot, it only took twenty minutes to get back. She was wrong, but it seemed fruitless to argue the point. "Had some things to take care of. What's so damn important? What can't wait this time?"

"We have to talk, like now. We don't have much time." She patted the couch cushion beside her and shifted, so she was facing him when he sat.

"Okay. And? I'm here. So talk."

Zo scooted closer. Their knees were practically touching as she sat up straight with a sharp intake of air, as if readying herself. How did she know Everett had gone to Joseph's house? As if on some cellular level she could feel his betrayal—his broken promise.

We don't go where we're not wanted. He's dead to us. We're all we need now.

Everett taped off the boundaries for the two of them years ago, and as far as he knew Zora upheld their agreement. Joseph was no more than a sperm donor as far as Everett was concerned.

She lifted her arms now and firmly gripped his shoulders. "Ev..."

"What the fuck is going on? Do I need to be worried here? Because I getting there. Fast."

With the seriousness he hadn't seen on his sister's face since the day Babs died, Zora pressed her lips together before letting out three words. "She's leaving tomorrow."

He couldn't figure where his mind went, but he searched through what felt like a million faces before he understood Zora meant Sophia.

Mike had steered clear of the room up until this point, up until the direction of the conversation took a turn out into left field, but he just materialized in the doorway out of nowhere.

The second Zo dropped the bomb about Sophia, Everett felt Mike's attention riveted on him.

"Bro, if you want to go, it's cool. We've got this." Heat crawled up to Everett's cheeks. His heart raced, and he swallowed hard, unwilling to meet Mike's gaze. He didn't know why, but he felt guarded all of a sudden. Defensive.

As if to echo his inner turmoil, both Zo and Mike barked the same thing at him at the same time: "You can't keep running."

The hollow thud of Mike's footsteps on the tile growing nearer to them sucked Everett back into Babs's house. He was nine and Zora was four. It wasn't even six months after they found their mother unconscious on the bathroom floor surrounded by empty pill bottles, when they heard the hard cracks of Joseph's boots searching Babs's house. Then he paused and loomed over the two of them, curled in the corner beneath the kitchen table, and said the words Everett had been trying to unhear ever since: *She was the only one who wanted you.*

If his mother loved him, how could she leave? How could they both have left?

As Everett swallowed the memory, he studied his sister protectively, then looked at Mike, blinking away the sting of tears. He asked himself the same question now about Sophia. She didn't even give him a chance to fight, to be there, to explain, or let her explain.

"It's time to do something. Now." Zora's words blasted a hole in his conflicting thoughts, and he gave her a shaky smile.

"What can I do? She doesn't want me." He straightened his back before he could collapse against the cushion. "Plus, I made a promise to Babs, and I'm keeping it."

"Fuck the house, Ev. Babs isn't here, but Sophia is. At least until tomorrow." Zo's hands went flying in the air, and the low rumble beneath her shrieking tone made her frustration almost palpable. She paused briefly, seemingly to let her nerves settle before starting in on him again. "Patton Place is a piece of property. This is the rest of your life we're talking about here."

Everett ran his hands over his hair. "I know. I know."

"I don't think you do. Are you honestly telling me you're going to sit here and do nothing when it's all in your hands this time?" Zora asked. "This isn't about Mom, or Joseph."

Just the mention of his father's name made his skin prickle and pulse with a mixture of anger and anxiety. He'd never held out on his sister until now. Knowing what he was keeping from her only added to his mounting worries. Sooner or later he was going to have to figure out a way to tell her what he learned today. And, judging from what happened with Sophia, it better be sooner.

For now, he let his head fall back and closed his eyes. Beside him, he could hear Mike plop down on the stuffed leather armchair. A second later, he felt both their hands wrapped over his—a mixture of hot and cold blending together, leaving him warmer on the inside. Even though his eyes were still closed, their proximity surrounded him with warmth, and the soft, even rhythm of their breathing soothed him.

They were rooting for him.

Their combined wills were so strong their effect was more like a single, powerful prayer uplifting him.

As much as Everett wanted to take the prayer and use it to rationalize what he needed to do—what his heart wouldn't allow him not to do—nothing could excuse his behavior. His lies. How much he'd behaved like his father.

"You have what you need to get her back, so go to her," Mike whispered. "I didn't trust her at first, but if you love her, I'm sure I will, too."

Taking her cue, Zora leaned in close to add her own two cents. "She expected it to be you when she opened the door, Ev. It's not too late to turn this around. Do you love her or not?"

She was challenging him the way she always had since she was born. Keeping him on his toes, meeting him measure for measure. But something in what she said didn't quite make sense. He heard her clearly, but what was she talking about?

What door?

What's more, there was Zora's question. *Do I love Sophia?*

Deep down, though, it wasn't his love he was worried

about. If she asked him a million times, his answer would be a million times yes. Yes, he loved Sophia.

Admitting it wasn't the hard part, either.

There wasn't a doubt in his mind how much he loved her, or where he could see this crazy, mixed-up match between them going. Everett knew himself. But there was still the elephant sprawled out in the middle of the room. The one thing he couldn't get around. As much as he was aware that he made his own bed, he'd given her no reason to trust him, let alone love him.

It was *her* love Everett doubted. *What if she doesn't love me back?*

"Does it even matter?" he asked. "If she loved me, how could she leave?"

"I could ask you the same question. If you love her the way I know you do...because you wouldn't be sitting here beating yourself up about it otherwise...then how can you even fathom letting her go? You have to fight when it matters." Zora was pleading now, the strain in her voice begging and all but shoving him to move forward, to do *something*.

To not give up.

It was annoying as hell, but it was exactly what Everett needed. Of all the things that could motivate him to act, goad him into action, what always worked was the terrifying thought that he could be anything like the man who gave up on him and Zo. Joseph chose not to raise them, not to be a part of their lives. Abandonment was the worst thing you could do to a person you claimed to love. Essentially, it was saying, *you're not worthy.*

And Sophia was worthy of love.

With a renewed sense of urgency and his heart thumping erratically against his rib cage, he sat up, a mixture of adrenaline and defeat leaving him breathless and hopeless all at once.

"So what do I do?" he asked, unfamiliar with being on this side of right and wrong. His posture was bone-straight as he scooted to the edge of the couch.

He was ready for...for whatever would work.

Zora and Mike flanked him, seeming as anxious as he was. She nodded at him, as if agreeing to whatever thought zapped through his wired mind. Mike all but gave him a fist pump and an attaboy. This was the high school locker room all over again, but with two coaches instead of one, hyping him up until he was ready to take on an ironclad defensive line.

But then, Everett's brows knitted together. "Wait...what did you mean, 'she thought it was me at the door?' Whose door? Where was she?"

Only then did Zo's pep rally come to a halt. Her unwavering gaze dropped as she raked her fingers through her hair. "I went to see her at Babs's house."

"You—"

"I couldn't go in," she blurted out before her brother could get a word in edgewise. This was his consolation. She still couldn't set foot in the house, but she made it there finally. Not to visit Babs's grave or funeral, but to the house where Babs raised them, and without her big brother holding her hand.

He should have been hurt to learn Zora was holding out on him, but he was doing the same thing. The disappointment weighed down on him. Secrets.

When did they let the distance between them grow so wide?

She swallowed hard, her big brown eyes round and innocent and remorseful.

"It's okay. I'm glad," he said, forcing a closed-lips smile.

"Wait." Zora shook her head and held up her palms, as if to halt all conversation while she rewound the back-and-forth and sorted through her thoughts. "What did Mike mean when he said you have what you need? And you still didn't tell me where you guys were all day."

If the timing wasn't all wrong, Everett might have entertained his sister's questions, but the clock was ticking, and fast, if Sophia was leaving tomorrow.

So he didn't utter a word. He simply got up from the couch and strode to the entry table, where he retrieved Babs's wooden box. When he returned to the couch and set it on Zo's lap, her mouth fell open, her eyes welled with tears, her lips began to quiver, and the dam broke.

With his hands over hers, he quieted her sobs.

"How did you—?"

Before she could finish her question, Everett responded. "It's with us now. And I think I know a way to make everything right," he said.

Babs gave him the tools to see things through. Now he had a plan for how to achieve his goal.

CHAPTER 20

After Zora's visit, Sophia decided not to delay leaving Portland. With a call to the airline, she was able to get on the redeye that same night, and the second she landed the weight of everything she'd been through crashed down on her. She was back home in Las Vegas, but nothing about it felt like her home.

She was lost in space, floating, waiting to feel something solid—needing something real.

With Julie's wedding creeping closer every day, Sophia threw herself into the plans and last-minute details, content to let the spotlight remain firmly on her cousin. She attended the prim and pearls bridal shower, and the wild, raunchy bachelorette party, all while wearing a toothy Vaseline smile...but deep down, the hollow ache in her heart gnawed at her from the inside out.

She was still existing somehow, but she missed Everett like mad.

Weeks had gone by since she spoke to him or Zora, and he'd stopped calling and texting. He was moving on. Her only

Portland tie left was Kara. Just last week Sophia called and gave her an update on the house and the move. She told Kara she wished they'd hung out more and promised to hire her the second she figured out how she was going to get her restaurant up and running. But then she hurried off the phone because the restaurant made her think of Everett, the way everything did.

Don't think about him.

"Snap out of it," Mom yipped in Sophia's ear, unscrewing her from her downward-spiral thinking. "The lady is talking to us."

"Oh. Sorry." She could feel her face burning. "What did you say?"

"No problem. I was just saying, please have a seat. And would you care for any tea or macaroons?" The woman at the bridal salon where Julie was having her final dress fitting looked like she was doing her best to plaster on a carefree smile, but her coastal blue eyes were impossibly wide and her woodsy brown locks were frazzled around the edges—like she, too, was having a day.

Along with Mom and Aunt Marian, Sophia followed her instructions and shuffled into the sitting area sans the tea and crumpets. The place was small, a tight space with a petite, dusty pink velvet settee where Sophia was sandwiched between her mother and aunt, suddenly finding it hard to breathe.

"I'll let you guys sit," Sophia said as she worked to get to her feet, but in classic Mom form, she was not having it. She jerked her daughter back down. Apparently the sandwich was by design.

She squished back into the teensy hybrid sofa/loveseat, chair, deflating with a loud sigh. "What?" Her legs, crossed at the ankle, ticked impatiently. She could just throw her hands up at this point. This was supposed to be about Julie, but somehow she knew Mom and Aunt Marian would find a way to make it about her.

"Now wait a minute, honey. While we've got a few minutes, I want to show you something." Seriously, her mom could be like gravy. A filling, spicy mix of warm and smothering.

Mostly out of necessity as opposed to choice, Sophia crossed her arms too, and shifted in the seat. She clenched her teeth and pasted on a tight smile. "Yes, Mother. What would you like to show me?"

Finally, with the spotlight, Mom whipped out a single, razor-sharp business card. As nonthreatening as it should have been, Sophia could feel in her bones that the glittery rectangular card was yet another one of Mom's boxes—ones to be checked off methodically. Find Sophia a house within a one-mile radius. Box. A budget-breaking retail pad able to meet Mom's high standards for a restaurant. Box. A new, handsome, wealthy man worthy of being her son-in-law, located no farther than Summerlin (because anywhere in the northwest or the southwest was acceptable, but the northeast and southeast were both beneath her and beyond her city limits).

Box.

Box.

Box.

Box.

"Is this really what we should be discussing while Jules is in there slipping into the dress she's going to be married in?" Fumes threatened to leak out of her ears. "Today is not about me. It doesn't always have to be about me on other days, either."

Given her usual expedited timeline and the peppy-looking realtor's card, Mom was already hard at work. It wouldn't be long until the plots for marriage and grandbabies were back in full force.

"Aw, honey. I'm just trying to help you."

Lord have mercy, woman, listen to reason.

"Any minute now Jules will emerge from that dressing room to show us this gorgeous gown. She's going to tell us she's never felt more beautiful, and we're not even going to notice because you insist on talking about how your friend has property listings for me. I have a house, and I found a place to open up my restaurant, but it's a little far from here, wouldn't you say?"

"And him? Do you still have him?" *Ouch!*

With a sharp intake of air, Sophia opened her mouth to unleash her fury. "Are you kiddi—?"

Aunt Marian pressed her hand down on Sophia's knee, silencing her. "It's just because you look so down, sweetheart. Like you're lost," she said, in her velvety voice. The woman hardly ever said anything, but when she did, you knew you better listen, and listen good. It was going to be something sage, something Maya Angelou-like, filled with depth and wisdom and inspiration.

Tears sprang to her eyes as she met her aunt's warm look.

"Now I know he's a nice young man. A good one, too, if you gave him your heart after everything you've been through. It's unfair, I know. We just want to remind you you're not alone. We can help you put down new roots here with us."

She laced her fingers with Aunt Marian's and squeezed, leaning against her.

"Do you remember when you were about seven and you played with this little tin baking set? Might have been six or seven. Anyway, it might not have seemed like it then, but you were running a bakery right from your mother's kitchen."

"Oh, shit, Marian. What's any of this got to do with the listings?" Mom chimed in. "Yolanda found one only three blocks away from us. She should be thinking about getting her life back in order. You know they have an app you can use for that kind of thing now." She waved her phone over Sophia's shoulder, apparently on the off chance that Sophia wasn't aware of what an app was or how to use one. "It's short for application. Like little websites on your phone, computer, or tablet."

"Thanks. I know what an app is, Mom."

Satisfied with her daughter's digital knowledge, Mom stuffed her phone back in her purse and picked up a bridal magazine. Just past her, a girl holding a long veil and a bedazzled sash in her hand slipped into Julie's room down the hall.

Sophia imagined stepping into a sheer lace and tulle ball gown with a sweetheart bodice and a modest engagement ring on her finger. Nothing elaborate or too fancy, just family and a few friends coming together to celebrate two needles who found each other in a haystack. Even if Everett hadn't loved her enough to tell her the truth, Sophia still loved him. She didn't know if she ever could get past it, but her heart still hoped they could share their love for the only home able to tie the good from both their pasts and futures together.

And somewhere deep down she knew it was all Mom wanted for her, too.

Sophia looked away from Julie's dressing room back to her mother with her golden heart and iron will. Softly, she brushed a kiss across her cheek.

"I want you to be happy. Whatever it means for you," Mom said.

"Thank you for everything, Mom." She kissed her one more time before turning back to Aunt Marian.

"Anyway, it wasn't a restaurant you wanted back then, but you were selling cookies for fifty cents, and milk or lemonade for another fifty. You were a pint-sized businesswoman. But it was never about the money then. Your father's the one who put all the importance on material things. Do you remember what you told me?"

Sophia shook her head.

"I about fell out of my chair laughing when I told your mother what you said, but somehow I didn't doubt you. It wasn't the way you were built. You told me you wanted to be the owner, because then you could be in charge of your own life. I want you to remember your dreams. You're still in charge of your own life, so if you want something...and now your mom is going to be mad at me for saying this...go for it. But it may or may not be here in Las Vegas."

"Goddammit, Marian. Now, don't you start. Why can't you look at the pretty dresses and mind your own business?" Mom pursed her lips. She was fuming mad.

Aunt Marian and Sophia doubled over with laughter, but her aunt, sweet as she was, continued advising her niece despite Mom's agitation.

"It may or may not be a house around the corner from your family, or a family restaurant. It might be following your heart or starting a family of your own. You have to decide, sweetheart. It's your decision to make. Not mine. I'm sure she'll disagree with me, but it's not your mother's either."

On such an amazing note, Sophia reeled her aunt in for a breathless, giggling bear hug. The embrace itself was like clarity. She wasn't sure how she didn't notice it before, but she must have been waiting for this. For permission. For her mother's blessing, although she'd take her aunt's in lieu of her mom's.

She wasn't walking out on her family.

Sophia would have done anything to avoid being like her father—and she wasn't about to walk out on her family. She didn't want to be the one to leave. Even the move to Portland was tethered by time. It was never about leaving forever. Six months was stuck in the back of her mind. Boxes still lined the wall in the garage because it only ever felt temporary.

Is this why I didn't fight harder for him?

Once the laughter died down, Aunt Marian sat up straighter and squared her shoulders, dipping her chin to look Sophia in the eyes. "Now. Do you love him?"

"Yes, she does." Julie glided down the hall toward them looking like some kind of ethereal goddess in an ivory cloud of ruffled organza and tulle with a diamond-encrusted sash cinched at the waist and a flowing, lace-lined veil. With the pure white and glitter of her dress against her golden bronze skin, she was a glowing watercolor dream of bliss.

"Oh, my god." The three women on the settee oohed and ahhed in unison.

Mom tossed the magazine on the end table. "Stop looking, right now."

Sophia and Marian spun toward her, both gaping, both ready to pounce on Helen if one negative thing came out of her mouth.

"This is the one," her mom continued. "It's gorgeous. Divine." Her hands were held up, framing the vision before her. "Nothing else will compare."

Typical Julie, she wasn't trying to hear anything Mom said. Apparently, the walls in the dressing room were about as thin as her tulle veil because she began to weigh in on the whole *get Sophia's life back on track* discussion.

"This is the fitting, so I sure as hell hope this is the one. And as far as this Sophia situation goes, she loves Everett. I knew she was putty the second I met him when I went up there to Portland. Then, when I saw this fool balled up on the couch watching Michael Myers and eating Rocky Road...confirmed."

The mothers hummed in agreement.

"It was Strawberry Cheesecake." Sophia corrected her, laughing. "If you're going to throw me under the bus, at least get it right."

"Potato, potahto."

"Oranges and apples."

Mom snapped her fingers to break up the bickering. The whole salon stood at attention. "Then why are you running?"

Floating on the carpeted riser in front of the full-length mirror, Julie rolled her neck at her reflection. "Don't be trying to send her back already. She may not need to go back yet."

"Why?" Sophia asked, confused. "Why 'yet?' If it works, I can bring him to your wedding." Just the idea of him standing beside her while they witnessed Julie and Nico take vows of love and loyalty made her heart swell.

"Just...because." Julie's eyes were glued to the floor as she leaned back and teetered on her sparkly heels, looking guilty as all heck. But Sophia still wasn't sure yet what she was hiding.

Sophia cocked her head to the side and glared to capitalize on Julie's discomfort. "Hmm. 'Because,' huh? Well, in this case, with such a strong argument..." A wide smile tweaked the corners of her mouth as she shook her head. "You do know you're a horrible liar, right? The dress is incredible on you, but you're still a liar."

The woman was definitely up to no good. Sophia didn't know how, or what, or why, but Sophia was on to her.

"Mm-hmm." Julie hummed, closemouthed.

Somehow Sophia was going to find out what Julie had up her sleeve.

"Let him wallow for a minute to figure out what he lost. Dang. Let him sweat for two weeks. If you need something to do, look at me and how hot I am in this Monique Lhuillier."

Seriously, the woman could give a master class on deflection.

THE SUNDAY of the wedding was pure chaos.

A rainbow of families and friends on both sides of the couple filled the pews of the picturesque church, now turned into an ivory and blush menagerie.

The colors and theme were elegant and romantic, and at the same time classically traditional. Think lots of silk, low, shimmery lights, and flowers galore. Not a single surface, from the altar to the paved road in under the Alfa Romeo parked out front avoided being peppered with frilly, flowery garb and congratulatory best wishes. Everything was primed and set to launch Julie and Nico into *la dolce vita*.

Talk about living the sweet life.

Sophia leaned on the door to Julie's dressing room, her heart and mind full, in the best way, with all the festivities and people. On one end of the craziness there were his loud, boisterous, hugging, Italian family members, who were downright aggressive about trying to feed Julie's skin and bones. And then there was Julie's blended spectrum of black and white family with nonstop "advice." Mostly about never going to bed mad and learning the give and take both of dirty sex and clean fights.

With his steely bicep wrapped around Nico's neck, Uncle Antoine could never be accused of being subtle. *This is my little cousin you're about to marry. As long as she's safe and happy, so are you.*

It was no wonder Julie locked herself in the bride's room.

"Open up," Sophia whisper-yelled through the wooden door.

After a few seconds she heard her cousin's muffled voice disguised as a deep baritone. "Who is it?"

Julie has been hiding for going on half an hour now. Well, not hiding, because everyone knew where she was, but she wasn't letting anyone in. Sophia was denied once, but this time she came armed with incentives.

"I have chocolate and alll-co-hol," she singsonged, knowing they were the two things her cousin was hard-pressed to say no to.

Just like I thought. Click.

The door cracked slightly, then she was yanked inside by a Wedding Barbie version of Julie, complete with sparkly tiara, lace-edged veil, and a sweeping ball gown even Cinderella couldn't resist. She replaced the latch behind Sophia with a swipe of her hand. Using her French-manicured fingernails, Julie pried the chocolate out of Sophia's hands and stuffed it into her mouth. And, with closed eyes and a satisfied moan, she finally relaxed.

Here was this stunning, golden-bronze bride, draped in the most beautiful dress, going through chocolate withdrawals she was so stressed out.

"Who else do I need to add to my hit list? Was it his Nona again?"

Seemingly in recovery mode after scarfing down the entire chocolate bar, Julie lightly fingered her hair out of her face. She took a deep, calming breath...and then unraveled again.

"I'm going to kill them. If one more person tells me about these damned Italian traditions, I'm going to scream."

The woman was practically sniveling and snarling.

"Ooh, you said damn in a church. I'm tell-ing!" Sophia was teasing, but she still felt their Sunday school superstitions clawing at her. She pressed her palms together and lifted her eyes heavenward. "I'm sorry, God, for me and this blasphemous child. But please give her a break. She *is* getting married today."

But her attempt to get Julie to laugh, to break the ice, didn't appear to have worked.

"Saturday would have been way more fun, but they said Sundays were luckier for prosperity and fertility. Like, we haven't even exchanged vows yet and they're already hinting at babies." Her eyes were wide, and a pink flush crawled up from her neck to her cheeks. All the while, she rolled her eyes and neck, lips pursed in annoyance.

"Do you know the woman actually told me it was bad luck to look in a mirror unless I removed a glove or a shoe? They're talking about cutting the tie I bought him, too. Who's going to pay money for half a damn tie? Ooh, ooh," she fumed, and swish-stomped around the room for good measure.

Patting the counter to make sure it was clean first, Sophia propped herself up against the beveled edge, careful not to wrinkle the requisite fitted satin bridesmaid gown. With a nod, she signaled for Julie to continue with her rant.

"Don't even get me started on throwing rice. How many birds do we have to kill in the name of luck?" Julie twisted the top off of the mini bribery tequila and took a long swig. "And do you see this?" She held up a frayed end of her delicate veil with a noticeable tear. "I have a fucking rip in my veil. Some fucking luck, all right."

A knock sounded at the door. "Sophia, someone is looking for you, but it's time. We seated him on the bride's side," said a skittish older female voice. The voice was familiar. It sounded like one of Aunt Marian's church friends, but before she could ask for more details, they heard the click-clack of heels scurrying away.

A giggle bubbled up inside Sophia. Julie really instilled the fear of God in these women.

That's my girl.

She chewed her lip and stared off into space.

Who could be looking for me?

"Probably just Nico's cousin, Gianni," Julie blurted before Sophia could put too much thought into it. "Apparently he's got it bad for you. I don't think he's ever been turned down before."

"Good lord, this guy." He'd been a freaking stage-five clinger ever since Nico introduced them the week before. He was all hands and slimy kisses on the cheek, and no concept whatsoever about personal space. And of course, leave it to her mother to sneak him her phone number. The woman was such an off-kilter Sour Patch Kid—most times sour, sometimes sweet.

"Mom is going to pay for that one." She playfully rolled her eyes, but then she caught sight of panic streaking through her cousin's wide eyes.

Julie jolted up, ramrod straight, like she was arming herself for battle. Teeth clenched. Her shaky feet causing the skirt of her dress to billow and vibrate.

"Just breathe, Jules. I'm here. I'll kick their asses if you want me to...or, maybe I'll get Gianni to do my dirty work." Sophia winked and wrapped an arm around her cousin's shoulders. When they were eye to eye, she let her smile dissolve for a split second. "All kidding aside, though, I want you to know you're beautiful and strong, and I'm so happy for you. You deserve all this, and so much more. I know your dad is looking down on you, smiling and celebrating with you because this is just the beginning of the blessings in store. And if you ask me, Jules, Nico is the lucky one, because he gets to have you."

Julie's eyes welled and reddened. She seemed to sniff and swallow back emotion as she flashed a quivering smile. Sophia squeezed her hand while she struggled to get the words out.

"Thank you. I love you," she mouthed.

"Don't mess up your makeup."

Sophia dragged her into a tight embrace.

Today Sophia believed in happy endings, even if hers was still up in the air.

Almost twenty minutes later the hypnotically soothing sound of *Ave Maria* swept through the church.

Sophia stood beside Julie's best friend and maid of honor, Liz, on one side, and two more of her friends and Nico's sister on the other. They were all staggered on the steps and holding lush, bejeweled pink peony bouquets.

Facing them on the other side of the altar were Nico and five pretty decent-looking groomsmen, four of whom were his brothers. And then there was the last one, Casanova, none other than Nico's hyper-sexy, NC-17, greasy, lip-licking cousin Gianni.

Just as Julie began her march and locked gazes with Nico, Sophia remembered what the woman outside the dressing room said. *The bride's side.* She glanced over at Gianni, staring at him for probably too long.

Wait. He wasn't on the bride's side. And while he was looking *at* her, there was no sign that he was the one looking *for* her.

If it isn't Gianni, then who is it?

While she should have plastered on her best over-the-top bridal attendant grin to watch her cousin take on the white mile, Sophia couldn't deny the sudden frantic beat of her heart. Her eyes darted to the pews on the left side of the church—her right, facing the door—where her family and Julie's guests were seated.

With a tentative smile she panned past Mom and Aunt Marian, who were sitting with Stan and Otis. They really were adorably cute couples. Not far back, she saw Liz's boyfriend Derrick with a few tatted, muscular gym-type guys, all of whom looked incredibly uncomfortable in bicep-choking suits. Beyond them, she didn't recognize many more faces aside from Aunt Marian's church friend, Mrs. Hill, who was hard to miss in a rather large purple sunhat blocking the back corner near the door.

Still, she couldn't discount the niggling feeling that whoever it was might still be here. She'd been feeling antsy all day, like she was the one jumping the broom. Or rather, breaking the glass.

The pastor began to read from his Bible, and Julie and Nico looked completely calm, as if their fate were decided by the stars and the moon above—for all the goo-goo eyes they were giving each other.

From where she was standing, she couldn't see her cousin's face. But Nico's expression? Her heart overflowed to see what love could look like on a man in love's face. His glowing eyes spoke volumes. There was this sort of urgency about his expression. Like he wanted the pastor to hurry up and marry them before Julie could get away. Like he gave someone a ten and got back change for a hundred.

In that one moment Sophia could understand the Italian traditions around luck. Julie was his fortunate surprise. Somehow just being able to witness it made her feel lucky, too.

Until she took one more look around the bride's side of the church.

Mrs. Hill leaned forward, and now Sophia knew what all Julie's deflection was about.

She did have something up her sleeve—or rather, someone. A couple of rows from the back, off in the corner, there, in her city, under the same roof, was her Everett.

He's here.

CHAPTER 21

For a few seconds they locked eyes.

A fresh wave of longing and desire slammed into Everett like he'd been away from home too long. He was overwhelmed by the urge to run to Sophia and beg for her forgiveness.

"Isn't she lovely?" The older black woman seated on his right leaned over and whispered to him. She was talking about the bride, but he still couldn't tear his eyes away from Sophia.

"Beautiful," he replied, his tone even and matter-of-fact.

The most beautiful he'd ever seen. She must have seen him. But she only looked in his direction once, and now she just stood there, expressionless. Not a flash of anything in her eyes. Determination and adrenaline pumped through him back at home with Zo and Mike, but now they had evaporated. He didn't know exactly what he hoped she'd do when she saw him.

For God's sake, they were at a wedding ceremony where two people were vowing to spend the rest of their natural lives together.

Did he really expect her to drop the flowers and run to him?

It was unreasonable, and he knew it. Still, everything notwithstanding, the rationale didn't settle the sinking feeling in his stomach. It sure as hell did little to patch up the gaping hole in his heart.

Her unblinking, deer-in-the-headlights look wasn't much to go by, but it was enough to make him pay attention.

When the elder woman's warm hand covered his, he turned to her, for the first time really looking at her. She was full-figured, with soft skin and kind eyes. There was a small beauty mark on her left cheekbone, and her complexion was a lighter shade of brown, but she reminded him of Babs. The impulse to hug her gripped his heart and squeezed.

"I hear she's back from Portland. Getting over some fella she met up there." She winked and smiled. "Why don't you go on and talk to her at the reception?" She patted his hand and turned her attention back to the altar.

Everett's mouth fell open and he couldn't stop staring. Not because the woman knew who he was watching. It was what she said. Sophia was getting over him. It explained her earlier look. She saw him, but she was moving on.

As the guests stood in preparation to exit the church behind the newly wedded couple, Everett gripped the wooden box, ducked out of the main door, and rounded the corner. He could just as easily hop back on a plane to Portland and she'd be none the wiser. Maybe she'd believe he was an apparition. Maybe she'd know he was a coward. But his pride would still be intact.

His heart though, would not recover.

She's getting over me.

"I hope you're not thinking about punking out on me."

Halfway down the steps, Everett turned to find Julie standing behind him. Her tiny, diamond-clad fingers were still twined with Nico's under a confetti storm of rice and roaring cheers of congratulations.

"Auguri!" The crowd chanted between claps. Best wishes to the couple.

All at once his senses were overloaded. He was dizzy as his glances flitted back and forth between the growing swarm of people celebrating the new marriage and the serious deadpan Julie gave him. The thunder of a thousand claps made it impossible for him to concentrate on any one thing. His skin buzzed with anticipation, and the taste of bile rose in his throat. He was giving up on all this—his only chance to have all of this with Sophia.

"She needs *you*," Julie said, simply. She and Nico were both looking at him as she planted an encouraging peck on his cheek, somehow jumpstarting his heart. "I don't know what's in the box, but whatever it is, it's not what she needs. It's just you. To *her, you* are enough."

At her words, a flurry of emotions swept through his heart, and he could feel small pieces of it, some newly cracked and others he'd believed to be irreparably broken, falling back into place.

He leaned in to embrace the couple. "Congratulations. Thank you," he whispered.

Whether he admitted it to himself or not, he wanted what his grandparents enjoyed for years—endless love, somehow winning against the odds. Against every hurdle and obstacle. Even against a small lie somehow blooming into so much more than he could have imagined.

❧

"LADIES AND GENTLEMEN, Mr. and Mrs. Nico Farfalla, " the DJ announced into the mic as they finished their first dance as a married couple. "Let's give them a round of applause before we get this party started."

Cheers erupted while an upbeat song blasted out of the speakers. Bass throbbed throughout the room and galvanized everyone into getting out there and dancing. From his post just off the entrance to the casino floor of the hotel, Everett watched Julie make her way over to the DJ. She leaned in, shielding her mouth near his ear. *This is it.* She promised him fifteen minutes, and he promised she wouldn't regret giving them to him on her wedding day.

As the DJ handed the mic to Julie, Everett steadied himself.

He stood taller and picked up the wooden box he'd set on the ground. Every nerve ending in his body pulsed. His heart pounded in hard thuds, as if time were slowing. With a deep breath, he took two steps forward before coming to a stop.

The music faded into the background and Julie's voice flooded the mic.

"My husband and I...my *husband.*" Julie repeated to herself, seeming to test the word on her tongue before letting a giggle slip out. "I can't get over it. It still sounds so weird, but I love it. We love you guys, and we just wanted to take some time to thank everyone for coming out to share our special day with us." She was glowing and giddy as she dragged Nico to the center of the dance floor. "Get over here with me."

Laughter rolled over the tables at Nico's bashful reluctance to take the spotlight.

"We are so happy and so in love. I can't even tell you how thankful we are to have you guys. And the gifts you've given us... I can't even tell you how much—"

"Okay, okay. They get it. Get to the point," Nico interrupted her to the tune of a fresh wave of giggles.

Julie playfully rolled her eyes and began again. "Anyway, before we start the Electric Slide and La Tarantella and all that good stuff, we thought, what better way to show our thanks than to give a gift of our own?" The guests immediately went wild with speculation. Oohs and ahhs buzzed among the wide-eyed, open-mouthed family and friends. By the way Julie said it, *a gift of our own,* there was plenty of room for conclusions to be drawn about further extending the family.

"Um, no. We're not pregnant." She pursed her lips and cocked her head in a sassy, reprimanding way. It said, *you know me better than that.* "The gift we want to give is for my cousin Sophia." Nico and Julie turned to face her and a spotlight followed.

Sophia was talking to a curly-haired Latina bridesmaid seated beside her, but at the mention of her name, her head shot up just in time for the light. She shielded her eyes with her hand, but judging by her unblinking stare, the surprise worked.

Everett slowly put one foot in front of the other and moved down the sloped walkway toward the courtyard.

She continued to scan the tables, appearing to find a couple of hundred pairs of eyes trained on her. The way she ran her hand over the nape of her neck was innocent and sexy all at the same time. Immediately, he felt a tightening low in his belly. Still, she didn't look in his direction.

"Can we get a little help?" Julie said into the mic. She was looking right at Everett as he reached the tables surrounding the dance floor. "All the way from Portland to help us deliver this gift... Zora? Mike? Can you help me?"

Uh, come again?

For a split second, Everett thought he misheard. But then, from the right of the dance floor, near a gazebo tucked in between the trees emerged his sister and his best friend.

Everett's brows twisted in knots. This was not part of the plan. Julie gave him the time. He was going to beg for her forgiveness, atone with his grandmother's box. He was going to give her everything, no strings attached. And if she didn't want him, she would have to push him away, because he wasn't going anywhere.

He needed to do this by himself.

It was what love meant. Everett was going to give her every opportunity to try again. He wasn't going to be the one walking away this time.

"Come on up, guys." Julie squealed and bounced, while the hem of her dress rose and fell like a graceful, slow-rhythm bird's wings.

His sister took the mic and, just as she was about to speak, movement behind her caught Everett's eye. Sophia was standing. Disbelief and shock smoothed the fine lines of her face, and she was staring right at him.

Somewhere far off he could hear Zora talking, but he couldn't tear his eyes away from Sophia. Her warm brown eyes were clear as glass and unblinking. Soft waves framed the curves of her face, and she was even more beautiful than he remembered. They were too far apart to say anything to each other, but he could feel the weight of her gaze skimming over every inch of his body, searching him. Without saying a word, he was telling her he was here. He showed up when it mattered.

He was begging her not to get over him.

"Congratulations, Nico and Julie, and thank you for helping us do what my brother should have done in the first place. Oh, and by the way, we see you, Ev." Zora pointed out into the crowd.

Out of nowhere, another spotlight weaved through the tables and found him.

"That guy, right there? He's my brother and Mike's best friend. He's older, but he's stubborn, hardheaded, and childish. If he had listened to me in the first place, we could all be dancing together and getting way too drunk by now, but here we are."

Heat crawled up Everett's neck to his cheeks as he smiled through clenched teeth. *I'm going to put you in a headlock, Zo and give you the most excruciating noogie I can manage.*

"Look, I know you're going to kill me later for this anyway, so you might as well let me enjoy it." She smirked and stuck her tongue out at him.

Luckily, Mike yanked the microphone out of her hands. "In the interest of time, I'm going to sum this up. Take a look at these two people in the spotlights." He paused for an excruciatingly long time while an endless sea of faces got a good look at Everett and Sophia. Mike's expression was both endearing and serious, like what he was about to say was of the utmost importance.

And long.

Everett's ears perked up and he straightened. If anyone could recognize the changes in him, it was Mike.

"They have a love—"

Before he could finish his sentence, Zo, who appeared as clued in about Mike's tendency to be long-winded as her brother, grabbed the mic back. In her typical, impulsive way, she blurted out, "Sophia, please marry my brother and be my sister. We love you, and he's a miserable mess without you."

The roar of the place going wild seemed to be perfectly

timed with the first teardrop tracing the curve of Sophia's cheek. As soon as she covered her face with her hands, Everett set the box on a tabletop and frantically pushed his way through the crowd.

He was being drawn to her.

As soon as he reached Sophia's side, he pried her fingers away, and her eyes snapped open. The same longing he felt every second they were apart brightened her brown irises, and he knew, deep down, that if he hadn't shown up for her, he would have regretted it for the rest of his life.

"I'm here." He was breathless. "Please don't be over me." Even to his own ears, he sounded strained and desperate. He didn't let go of her hand. He twined their fingers together.

She blinked back a fresh wave of tears and, in a whisper, said, "It *was* you." The raw emotion in her voice hit him right in the heart.

She did see him in the church.

Everett nodded and folded her into his arms. She was warm and comfortable, like coming back home after a long time away. "She's right," he said. "I do love you, and I am a complete mess without you, Sophia."

The tightness in her shoulders loosened against his arms, and the natural ease of their embrace lifted and expanded something inside him, as if he was weightless and floating. Her sweet, tangy scent teased his senses, and his stomach flipped. Heat seared through him, nudging the carnal need inside him, and he stiffened.

Every part of him hardened.

Sophia peeked up at him with a glint of amusement. "I can tell you've missed me."

"Every inch of me missed you. Every. Inch." A crooked smile lifted the corner of his mouth. She felt so good. Touching her was life. Electricity coursed through him. "I love you." With a press of his palms over the small of her back, he lowered his mouth and softly brushed his lips against her full pout. It started out gentle and tender until Everett deepened the kiss. His breath turned shallow and labored, and he couldn't let go. His hands roamed over the smooth silk dress, gripping the fabric tight. How he wanted to feel her skin against his again.

For a moment they weren't surrounded by hundreds of people, waiting and watching. They all fell away, and it was just the two of them, with Sophia skimming her fingertips over the back of his neck, holding him tight against her body, the need between them growing more urgent.

She kissed him again. "I love you too. I was trying, but I'm not over you." She snickered, her shoulders shaking gently in his arms. "Are they all still watching?"

"Uh-huh."

It didn't take long for Zora, who still refused to unhand the mic, to clear her throat in surround sound. "Ahem. You do know we're still here. Wedding. Marriage. Is any of this ringing any bells for you two perverts? There are children here."

This time, Sophia and Everett doubled over in stitches. The agony and hopelessness he felt moments before melted in laughter, and it felt so good. For the first time since he arrived at the wedding, he finally felt like celebrating.

When they came up for air, he raised their clasped hands to the sky victoriously and announced, "She's not over me!"

Champagne flutes raised and clinked. "Aguri!" someone shouted in the distance.

"Okay, so can we wrap this up?" Zora asked.

"Wait." Everett held up his index finger, begging his sister and Julie for a few more minutes. He kissed Sophia's hand before releasing it to walk over to the table where he left the box. When he retrieved it, he hurried back to her and went down on one knee.

Sophia gasped and covered her mouth, which was apparently contagious, because a wave of gasps circulated through the tables.

Everett clutched the wooden box in his left hand and tenderly held hers in his right. "Sophia Kent, I love you."

The din of the crowd fell away, and Zora rushed the microphone over to him. "We can't hear you."

"I said, I love you, Sophia Kent," he repeated for the sake of his audience, which normally would have rendered him speechless, but something about the way she was looking at him now, mesmerized and hopeful, gave him the push he needed.

"For so long, all I thought about was getting my grandmother's house back, putting it back in the family name. But it didn't bring her back. It didn't change what family means to me. It took me almost losing you to realize my family's house won't be a home without you in it."

He sat the mic on his lap for a second and opened Babs's box.

"This box belonged to my grandmother, Barbara Monroe. She raised me and my sister, and loved us the way our parents couldn't. She gave me this box when I was a kid, telling me it was for capturing all my dreams. When she passed away it was taken from me, and I just this week got it back." He reached in and lifted out a yellowing paper folded in half.

"Almost every wish she made for me has come true," he continued. "I'm giving this box to you now, Sophia, hoping you'll make her last wish and my dreams come true. Inside, along with her list, you'll find her wedding ring, my grandparents' love letters, a rattle, and a silver spoon from my childhood, and the keys to *our* family home, where I hope we'll live happily ever after together. And I've already added a few other things for you too."

She was crying freely now, but Everett remained steadfast in his mission. lifting out a neatly folded stack of papers while smiling at her. "This is the lease for the retail pad for your restaurant, and a love letter for every day we were apart. Sophia, if you'll make my dream come true and be my wife, I'll spend the rest of my life working to make your dreams come true, too."

The sting of overwhelming joy pricked at his eyes as she nodded. "Yes," she cried through a million kisses.

It was really happening.

He placed the papers back inside the dream catcher, retrieving the sparkling diamond ring from its small velvet box before setting everything else on the ground. "I can't wait to marry you."

As he slid the ring on her finger, Sophia beamed, glowing with joy. "I love you so much."

She grabbed the mic, laugh-crying, and said, "And I'll be your sister, Zo. I'll be Blue's fur mom, too. And I'll even be your sister, Mike. Now let's celebrate."

CHAPTER 22

Sophia ripped the strip of duct tape off the seam of the last box, feeling awesome and mighty. She bounced up and down releasing a few air punches and cracking her neck like a lightweight champ.

"It's done! We're officially unpacked," she announced to her big, loud, annoying, amazing family.

"Whew, what a relief," her mother yelled from the living room, where she'd parked herself hours ago beside the fire-place with a glass of Pinot Grigio.

Finally, she did feel like a badass, knife-wielding chef, complete with her big girl panties. From the box she removed a few dozen movies and set them on the dining room table. "It's fucking amazing."

She cursed like one, too. She hoped Julie noticed and approved of her gratuitous profanity.

A roar of laughter pinballed off the walls in the other room. Awash in the smorgasbord of chortles and giggles, she was both validated by and enamored with her family. She could make out each one just as easily as their familiar faces.

This was home.

"Hallelujah, we found my cousin!" Julie shouted. She lifted her hands in praise from the kitchen, where she was stuffing her face. The leftover chocolate ganache truffles Sophia was considering for her new restaurant, *Bite-Sized,* got at least six or seven votes of approval from Julie alone. "That's more like it. You curse like a badass boss, Soph. I can't tell you how fucking tired I was of all those peachy-something or the sugar-honey iced teas. Ugh." She giggled.

She and Nico flew into Portland after their honeymoon in Italy, and the next thing Sophia and Everett knew, unloading and moving into Patton Place turned into a full-fledged unpacking party.

Full house was right. Not only were Julie and Nico there, but Aunt Marian and Stan decided to take a coastal drive up. Not to be outdone, Mom opted to invite Otis, who just so happened to have a pilot license...and a private jet.

The house was almost as noisy as Julie and Nico's reception at its height. So loud Sophia could barely hear herself think, but she loved it, every nit-picky bit of her mother making a big to-do about nothing. Every room filled with life and laughter, all the love in the world under one roof.

For the first time in a long time, this was not a one-woman job.

"Soph, pause the movie. What flavor do you want?" Everett asked from the kitchen. "I'm feeling brave. Going to try the pickle ice cream. We have antacids upstairs, right?"

"Shh, shh. The ghost killer is about to get him." From the couch, Sophia squirmed and hugged her knees to her chest. Her eyes were covered, but she could see slivers of the horror movie on the screen through her splayed fingers. The senator was hidden from the demon, but she knew the jump-scare was coming.

"Last call," he said, rinsing the scoop under the faucet. "You've seen this one a million times. I don't know why you act like you don't know what's going to happen."

No sooner did he clank the bowl on the counter did Sophia let out a gut-wrenching yelp followed by an ear-piercing shriek, which seemed to set off the rest of the women in the house.

"Goddammit. I don't know why you can't pick something normal to watch. There are plenty of good movies out," Mom said. "I've been dying to see the new one with Meryl Streep. You know it got an Oscar nod. Blood and guts are just not my thing, honey."

Sophia ignored her mother. "I'll take the Rainbow Berry, babe."

"See? This is how I know you love this movie. You would never pair fruity with a horror movie unless it got a good scare out you."

After filling a bowl for her, Everett plopped down on the couch beside Sophia. "Here you go." He tilted his head and leaned in for a quick kiss.

She came up for air just as Julie gave Nico a look.

"Wait a second, Jules. What was that about?" She watched as a mischievous grin curved like parentheses around Julie's mouth, then she turned to Nico. "Well? What did the look mean?"

"My name is Bennett, and I'm not it." He held up his hands and turned his attention back to the screen. "I'm just enjoying the movie."

"Don't even. Tell me, Nico."

The scratch of a nasally snort jerked Sophia's attention

back to Julie who was glaring at her with a smirk. But then her eyes got wide and her brows lifted as she cocked her head to the right. Her eyes kept flitting to the side. Sophia was still no closer to unscrambling what she was hinting at, but it was definitely a bumbling attempt at discreet communication.

Julie cleared her throat and put her hand over her heart, pointing a finger toward their mothers.

Sophia, who was about as good at reading lips as she was at hiding her ice cream moods, fumbled. "Wow, let me check my cellular device. I think I have a text message," she said, way too loud and way too B-movie actress.

With a roll of the eyes, Julie shook her head and slipped her phone out of her pocket, adjusting back into her comfortable spot on the couch.

Sophia: WTF???

Julie: You can't read lips for shit. LOOK at the mothers.

Sophia raised her eyes. The mothers. What was wrong with them? Their own daughters weren't good enough for them? Now they're plotting on someone else?

Sophia: Oh for fuck's sake. What are we going to do with them?

Julie: Everyone is coupled up. They're getting antsy. We have to do something before Zora and Mike get here. Nightmare ahead.

Sophia: Straight-up shit show.

Julie: They're already arguing about how they're going to do it. What did we really expect? The score is tied. Mom picked Otis and Aunt Helen picked Stan. I have Nico and you have Everett. Mike and Zora are the tiebreaker.

Julie tilted her head and gave Sophia a knowing grin. *Why don't we do nothing and watch this train wreck unfold,* it said.

She couldn't deny it. It would be kind of nice to sit back and take it all in from the sidelines. Zora was tough, and even though Mike had fully redeemed himself with Sophia, he still had it coming in a big way.

"Mom?" Sophia called.

"Yes?" Both mothers answered in unison.

Sophia twined her fingers in Everett's, thinking about the mothers and their matchmaking. Mom seemed genuinely happy with Otis. Maybe she was on to something with her time limits and wagers. Maybe being on the outside looking in wasn't without it's advantages.

"What are we talking, three months?" she asked. "Six like you gave me? It might take a year to help them see each other in a new light."

Everett put his empty bowl on the table and shifted toward Sophia. "What exactly are you guys talking about? And who?"

As if on cue, the doorbell rang.

"Nothing important, just my meddlesome family," Sophia said, standing. She narrowed her eyes and shot them a knowing glance. A reprimanding, *behave yourself* look. "Go easy on them." She warned, amusement in her tone.

Guilty as ever, they threw up their hands in synchronized, feigned innocence.

"I don't want to tell you young ladies again, you hear?"

Sophia eyed them one more time before she opened the door to greet Zora and Mike. "Come on in. Ice cream is in the freezer. Truffles are on the counter. We're just about to put on the next movie."

They were in the living room for all of five seconds before Mom started to rub her forefinger over her top lip while she nibbled the bottom lip.

"Hey, everyone," Zora said to the group as she made her rounds, giving hugs, as Mike followed suit behind her.

Stanley took one look at Aunt Marian and Mom, who were both champing at the bit for the opportunity to seal off another couple. "Uh-oh."

"It's so nice to see you two again." Aunt Marian cooed.

Always a flare for the dramatics, Mom chimed in. "Yes, it is. You guys were an unstoppable pair at the wedding, the way you pulled off the surprise. What a match." She winked at Sophia.

Everett raised a brow at Sophia, flashing his disarming, cocky little smile.

"If I tell you, promise not to overreact?" She watched as suspicion twisted the lines of his handsome face. She pressed. "Well, do we have a deal, or not?"

He nodded.

"Love is love, right?"

"Yeah," he said tentatively.

As Everett drew Sophia closer for a kiss, she couldn't help thinking how much her life changed.

She stepped out on faith and a prayer, and somehow ended up surrounded by love on all sides. Her family was together and growing, she was smitten with a man she couldn't imagine living without, her restaurant dreams were turning into reality, and apparently she did have a (non-depressing) horror-movies-and-ice-cream phase.

"I'm so glad you feel that way."

It really was funny how sometimes things *did* work out.

Thank you for spending your time with Sophia and Everett. If you enjoyed Mixed Match, please consider leaving a review.

Keep reading for an excerpt from Mixed Emotions.
See what happens when Zora needs to crash at her brother's best friend's house...

Join me in my reader group. I'd love to chat! That's where I connect with readers most.
Mia Heintzelman Reader Group

AN EXCERPT FROM MIXED EMOTIONS

ZORA

Zora Monroe rubbed her arms as she looked up at the old building wishing she had taken one more shot of tequila before she left the house. "Brr. I'm freakin' freezing." Her top lip curled as she sighed. "Tell me again why we couldn't meet somewhere else...indoors, brighter, maybe less sketchy-looking."

She and her best friend, Olivia, were at some place a few blocks off Burnside Street near the concert hall, but she'd never been to this particular spot. From the outside, it looked like any other ancient gray, unmarked hole in the wall— nothing fancy that would have caught her attention otherwise. If not for the glare of the neon lights from the Portland sign, Zora's guard might have been raised higher than it already was.

The skimpy blue dress Oli had forced her into certainly wasn't keeping her warm, but just the look of the building had the hairs on the back of her bare neck standing taller than the spikes of her pixie cut.

"Try to remember this is a night for celebration and not

some deranged plot to get you out the house," Oli said with a straight face. Her eyes twinkled the tiniest bit, though.

"That's what you keep telling me." Zora peeked at her phone. Three little irritating dots were still sitting there baiting her.

"We're going to toast to you getting the best agent out there for your cookbook, and then we're all going to dance and drink way too much, and, hopefully, we won't remember any of it in the morning."

Ah, yes. The foolproof plan.

Though she was still feigning irritation, a smile crept across Zora's face because all of it did sound amazing. Well, except for the whole "drink way too much" part of it. She and alcohol were a slightly less greasy version of oil and vinegar: they did not mix.

"Wait a minute. Who is 'we all?'" she asked.

To this, Oli grinned and moved forward in the line before she turned her gaze back.

"Well, Sophia's scared about her little baby bump, and Everett goes where she goes, so they won't make it, but..." She dragged the word out. "Kara, Steph, Remi, and Lexi said they should make it..." Her brows danced and she bit back a shit-eating grin like she was going to burst if she held in the rest too long.

"And?" Zora slowly lowered her chin to her chest, waiting for the other shoe to drop. The crisp air shimmied up her arms, causing a shiver to vibrate through her, but she maintained her focus on Oli.

"And...you'll finally get to meet Andre."

Zora sighed, and her arms slumped at her sides. Disappointment hummed through her body.

Andre. The dude Oli met at a concert a few months back,

smashed, friend-zoned, and was apparently the perfect leftover to regift to her best friend.

Yay, me!

"Yeah, no thanks. I'm good. Who else?"

"Oh, do you mean Mike?" She pursed her lips and lightly tugged her earlobe—a surefire sign she was lying. "No. I didn't invite him."

Zora squinted her eyes at Oli, reading her.

"So, Mike *is* coming? I saw that little lippy earlobe thing you always do."

"No. He…was not invited." She shrugged and pivoted back toward the front of the line.

Zora stared for a few more seconds hoping to break her. Her friend was hell-bent on keeping whatever scheme she was up to under wraps.

The only problem was, when Zora allowed herself to be talked into this skanky dress, she imagined Mike's tongue falling to the floor when he saw her in it. If he wasn't going to be at the club…well, that just sucked. She was going to be stuck in a skimpy getup that highlighted every one of her physical insecurities. The skintight blue dress, the clear five-inch heels, and the pancake makeup were all part of a costume, hand-picked by her best friend, to supposedly boost her confidence and make her look fierce. As it turned out, it was all a big charade so she could meet a hand-me-down guy.

Perfect.

The thing was, Mike wasn't just any guy. He was her brother's best friend. Or, rather, her brother's older, disarmingly scrumptious best friend who'd been her "pedestal guy" for years. Over those years, no one had measured up because her fun-sized kid crush had developed into an insanely good-looking, green-eyed stunner with a lean build and broad shoulders.

"So, who else, then?" Zora snapped then immediately bit her tongue because the irritation in her voice was too telling and needed to be stopped. She tried not to let her shoulders slump.

"I've got a few surprises up my sleeves." Oli tossed a mischievous look over her shoulder before looking away. She knew Zora could read her better than anyone.

Again, why on earth did I let Oli talk me out of staying in?

"I'll have you know I'm missing an eighties movie marathon for this. You know, they're starting with *Weird Science.*"

"Oh 'you know, your basic high school orgy type of thing.' 'It's a mindscrambler.' 'Hurts so good,'" Oli said in her best British accent. She was mocking Kelly LeBrock. Her thick brows dropped into a deep V, and beneath them, her brown eyes skewed into beady lasers. Everything about Oli fit the bill of sex goddess—her blunt-cut black bob, her olive-toned skin, and her full pout.

Blush pink bandage dresses worked for Oli because she had a banging body with normal-sized breasts and killer calves. She was perfection science couldn't manufacture, but a terrible actress, nevertheless.

A sex goddess, Zora was not.

Even with her best friend's fashion advice and styling, aside from the shimmery blue nails, none of her getup made her feel like herself. She'd tried to help Oli see that playing someone else's cards would only leave her lost in the shuffle.

She wanted no part of losing herself for a man.

She hugged her arms to her chest and bit back the chattering of her teeth.

"Whatever, Buttwad. The fact that you quoted the movie proves my point."

"Oh, you might miss it!" Oli put the back of her hand to her forehead in distress. "It's been out for like thirty-five years. I'm sure you already own it, along with every other movie released that decade, so just be present and enjoy yourself, for once."

In the midst of all the shivering and merriment, Zora's phone pinged, and now she really was excited.

It was her turn.

After a couple of minutes, she bit her bottom lip and thought for a second before tapping out a message rapid-fire on her phone. Her thumb hovered over the small green vertical arrow while she considered whether to send it.

Zora:
1. *Haggis burgers are going to be the secret weapon for my cookbook.*
2. *I'm home with Oli on the couch binge-watching the second season of* Stranger Things.
3. *I've been forced to listen to Ev and Soph have sex for the fifth time today.*

Ugh, this is too easy.

Zora could feel a serious case of side-eye coming from Oli's general direction. Together they inched forward along the black velvet ropes. Before she could second-guess it, she pressed send. Almost instantly, the phone pinged again.

Her smile was too wide to suppress.

"You're about to meet a fine-ass man, and while you should be practicing your stale flirting skills, you're seriously playing two truths and a lie with Mike?"

"Relax. I'm just—"

"Keeping tabs on him? Whipped? In denial that you're in love with him and have been since forever?"

Zora ignored Oli and read Mike's message as a second one popped up on the screen.

Mike: #2 You suck at lying. lol

Mike: First off, if you ever plan on beating me at this
game, the two truths should not be glaringly obvious.
lol. Your life and your career are food, so I already
knew number one was true. But, for the record,
haggis is disgusting. No clue how you're going to mix
Scottish and Creole food into one book. Second, if Ev
and Soph weren't screwing like rabbits, I'd be worried
they were calling off the engagement. Where are you?

Oli grabbed for the phone, but Zora yanked it back. "What did he say?"

"Mind your own business. Go back to sending *your* little mysterious texts." Zora giggled and attempted to unscrew the lines of her face to give Oli a pointed look, but it did not deter the woman with balls of steel.

"Seriously, what did he say?"

Zora bit the inside of her cheek because she was dying to show Oli, but she liked to see her sweat, too. After a few seconds, Zora flashed the screen to her and Oli burst out laughing. "I love you Zo, but he's right. You really can't lie for shit."

"What?"

"Dummmmb," she dragged out the word. "Even if he did think the haggis thing was a lie, why did you include me in it? Literally, my motto...my mission...my *mantra* is to never be home on a Friday night. The day I cuddle up on your couch on a Friday night fantasizing about the Upside Down is the day I'm officially old."

Dammit, I knew that was too easy.

Zora yanked the phone back.

"And don't tell him where you are. Why does he care?" Oli asked.

As if to underscore Oli's rant and rub it in, the phone pinged yet again. Almost word for word, Mike reiterated the point about Oli's Friday night motto then listed his own three truth-lie options before sending another message.

> **Mike:** *BTW, congrats on the lit agent. I'll buy you a round when I see you.*

> **Zora:** *Thanks!!! I still can't even believe it.*

Beaming, Zora went back to check out his latest three truth-lie options. She could feel the heat of Oli's eyes blazing down on the screen as she tried to read.

"Shhh." She waved her away. "I can't hear myself think with you hovering like that."

"When you make your choice, will you please put the phone away before you ruin the whole night?" Oli folded her arms. Now, her tone was more serious than playfully pissed.

Why is she being so touchy about the phone?

Zora had no clue, but just when she was about to delve deeper into it, the corner of Oli's mouth lifted. "I want you to have some bubbly, get loose, and maybe try Andre on for size...pun intended."

"Gross."

"You have a book agent and a hot guy chilling on ice

waiting for you to uncork him." A squeal escaped her lips as she held up her hand for a high five.

Reluctantly, Zora slapped her hand, but Oli held onto it for a second.

"Besides, I swear you and Mike act like freaking two-year-olds—truth, lies. It's all the same thing. I just wish you guys would go ahead and smash again. Then you can decide whether he's worth all this torment and angst you've been putting yourself through. Or, *maybe* give someone else a chance. You're adults now. It's safe to stop playing games."

"I'm not listening to you." A giggle spilled out, but Zora only shook her head.

"Fine. Don't admit it, but Andre does kind of remind me of Mike. He's also a light skinned, baby faced, full-lipped brother, but less cerebral and brooding and more swaggalicious. He's a little bit taller...and a *doctor*," she said as if she was waiting for applause.

Zora peeked up over her brows. "Not following..."

"Think of the role playing you could do!" She swooned. "Plus, you are so fierce tonight. You're like a sleek, tall, Amazon bombshell dipped in bronze. Seriously, that dress never looked as good on me."

Zora snickered. "'Fierce' isn't exactly the word I'd use. Between this tight dress and these heels, I don't even know what to say." She shook her head in disbelief through a fit of giggles. "If Andre is so fine, why aren't *you* still with him?"

Come on, tequila, kick in.

Before Oli could answer, Zora dropped her gaze back to her phone and typed the number three followed by a long-nosed liar emoji.

"You know he's way more your type than mine." Oli grunted. "Anyway, you can't stop texting Mike for a night? The only lie is the one you guys keep telling yourselves. You've been holding each other at arms' length for I don't know how long. Why can't you just tell him how you feel and see what happens? It can't be that bad."

"Because I don't know if that's how I feel." They'd been over this. Innocent flirting and hanging out was one thing. Going after him, being vulnerable... That was another thing completely.

Anxiety and irritation were affecting her words.

"I just...I like what we have. It's fun and comfortable and uncomplicated." *And perfect. He's perfect.* "I don't want to mess it up, and I don't want all that awkward insecurity and second-guessing. We're friends...practically family." The inflection in her voice rose to a high-pitched squeak when she said "family."

Oli covered her mouth with a fist and pointed at her. "Ooh, now there's a lie—a bold-faced lie."

Zora sighed and shrugged, but Oli's gaze narrowed.

"Yeah. Uh-huh. Keep telling yourself that. I have an eye for this sort of thing. The way you act around each other? I should snap a picture to let you both in on it."

Shit.

The thing about falling for a guy before hitting puberty is it has a way of ruining it for everyone else down the line. Oli knew it. Whether Zora wanted to admit it or not, she knew it, too. It certainly didn't make matters any better he was her brother's best friend.

"Look, let us be. We're good the way we are. We're just... having fun together. I don't want or need a man."

"Is that the story you're sticking with?"

"Yes, and anyway, I don't need any distractions. My agent —" Zora giggled at the way it sounded so surreal on her tongue. "She gave me twelve weeks to get this book ready. She wants me to find my niche and come up with a new title to go along with the pictures, recipes, and personal stories. I *really* don't need a man right now."

Well, maybe for a few things that didn't require her to buy batteries in bulk at Costco, but, no, really, she didn't want a man at the moment. *Especially, if it isn't Mike.*

Oli turned and grabbed Zora's hands, squeezing as she deepened her gaze. "Fine. Whatever, but just for tonight, let's *lose* ourselves."

Oh, just...lose ourselves. No big deal. Nothing to write home about.

Except that it was for Zora.

Ever since she was four, her singular goal in life had been to *avoid* losing herself and to stay true to the woman her grandmother raised her to be—strong against the odds. It was exhausting but worth it when she knew what being weak did to a woman. *Mom.* Every day that she looked in the mirror, she was reminded.

For one night and for the friends who were coming to celebrate with her, though, she could afford to let loose. Heck, she was already dressed the part.

Zora put on her game face. "Fine."

Oli did a bouncy, happy dance and stepped forward as they reached the door. She opened her purse for the beefy doorman, then stopped to give him a sultry, batted lash look before she turned back and waggled her eyebrows at Zora.

"Work and play don't have to be mutually exclusive," she purred.

Zora was pretty sure that last bit wasn't meant solely for her benefit, considering the fine specimen of man her friend was flirting with.

Zora opened her small clutch, smiling awkwardly at the

bouncer. "Thanks. *Anyway,*" she said to Oli. "Mike and I are friends. That's it. I'm fine by myself. Plus, he's with Kate, and, he's not here."

Oli snickered. "I'm just going to mind my own business, sit back, and watch what happens."

Get MIXED EMOTIONS Now!

ABOUT MIA HEINTZELMAN

Mia Heintzelman is a graduate of the University of California, Berkeley and the University of Nevada, Las Vegas. She is a Chicago native who always has a book in her purse, loves to pair sweet and spicy tea with fluffy socks, and can't go wrong with polka dots and pearls. She lives in Las Vegas with her husband and two children.